Jubal

Jubal

Gary Penley

PELICAN PUBLISHING COMPANY
Gretna 2003

The word "Pelican" and the depiction of a pelican are trademarks
of Pelican Publishing Company, Inc., and are registered
in the U.S. Patent and Trademark Office.

Library of Congress Cataloging-in-Publication Data

Penley, Gary, 1941-
  Jubal / Gary Penley.
      p. cm.
  ISBN 1-58980-129-6 (hardcover : alk. paper)
  1. Boys—Fiction. 2. Race relations—Fiction. 3. Southern
States—Fiction. 4. African American men—Fiction. 5.
Brothers and sisters—Fiction. I. Title
  PS3616.E55 J83 2003
  813'.6—dc21
                                    2002154258

Printed in the United States of America

Published by Pelican Publishing Company, Inc.
1000 Burmaster Street, Gretna, Louisiana 70053

to
George Michael
in loving memory

Acknowledgments

I want to thank the following good people for sharing their time, knowledge, and life experiences:

Mr. Thomas Jefferson Huddleston III, for entertaining me in his home, sharing pictures of his family, relating the history of his amazing grandfather, T. J. Huddleston, and describing the interior of his grandfather's hospital in Yazoo City.

Dr. Fred Birch, physician and lifelong friend, for consultation on the historical treatment of burn victims and early twentieth-century surgery.

Richard Barron, instructor, Lafayette, Louisiana, Fire Department, for patiently answering many questions on the ignition and spreading of house fires.

Johnny Broussard, a man who ran through an inferno and lived to tell the tale, for sharing painful memories of the ordeal of healing.

Stanley Kolodzie, writer and forever friend, for honest critiques and unfailing encouragement.

Jennie Shortridge, whose editorial suggestions enliven every story she touches.

Jody Rein, my agent, for handling the messy details and allowing me time for the fun stuff, writing.

Others, who related personal experiences, read the manuscript, and shared their feelings: Donny Hughes, Neal

Coats, Neville Crowson, Brian Houlihan, Pat Hughes, George Penley, Melanie Crowson, Phil Reed, Jocelyn McCormack, Bob Kuykendall, and George Armistead.

And Karen, for helping me find the end of the rainbow.

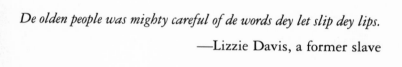

De olden people was mighty careful of de words dey let slip dey lips.

—Lizzie Davis, a former slave

Prologue

The house was ablaze by the time the truck arrived. The porch hadn't totally caught fire when the men rushed the door, but the flames spread across the front as they ran. The chief stopped at the bottom step, covered his face with a gloved arm, shook his head, and motioned them back.

I would hear the story dozens of times over the years. People ran from everywhere, stopping in the dark street to watch the sweating firemen sweep their tiny streams of water across the tall flames. Sheriff Turnbull ran into the yard and halted abruptly. "Who's in the house?" he hollered.

"Jessica, Lucas, Sarah—I think they're all in there, Sheriff," the chief said. "We tried to get to the door but the heat was like a blast furnace; we couldn't do it."

Suddenly the sheriff yelled, "No! No!"

A large figure loomed out of the darkness and charged across the yard. Heedless of the sheriff's words, the searing heat, or the roaring orange flames, the man leaped onto the porch, turned his shoulder, and drove his body through the blazing front door.

The porch roof was burning now, flames licking their way down the tall posts supporting it. Spectators held their breath and watched the doorway—a dark hole in a wall of flame that engulfed the front of the house.

Time stopped. Even the fire seemed to stand still as they waited. Then someone hollered, "There he is!"

His massive outline filled the flaming doorway.

"He's got something in his arms!" a man shouted.

"My God," the sheriff muttered. "He's on fire."

Jubal

Part I
Chapter One

I can still see him as he looked when I was a kid, moving slowly down a hot, dusty street, big as a mule and black as a man can be, lumbering along in faded overalls on wide bare feet, his thick body leaning to one side as he rounded a corner with his wagon, three or four dogs following along behind him.

Not only was he considered simpleminded, he lived much of his life with a disfigurement that caused people to stare, and because we humans can manage to be so unkind to each other at times, he gained a rude nickname that threatened to replace his own.

I knew Jubal nearly all of my seventy-five years, ever since I was a boy growing up in the Mississippi Delta, and I've missed him every day since he passed on. I'm the only one who knows the entire story, and now that I can sense my own sunset drawing near, I feel it's time to tell it.

I owe my existence to Jubal—an unlikely turn of events to say the least, that in that time and that place a simple black man would make my life possible.

It was the 1930s, and for awhile it seemed we were the two luckiest kids in the world, Sarah and I. And, compared to most children in that little Mississippi town, we probably were. The Depression dominated the economy, and most people's lives, but we were fortunate. Although our family didn't have any of that "old money" as Mama called it, our father, Reid Dunaway, was top salesman at Hardiman's Mercantile, the biggest store in town.

Daddy could sell anything, and everybody in Linville and all of Crowden County loved him. He's the one who named me Lucas.

Daddy grew up in the cotton fields, a "hayseed kid" as he liked to put it, though he'd hardly ever seen a bale of hay. He delighted in referring to himself as a "ridge runner" too, which was also ridiculous, because not many people in that flat Delta country had ever even seen a ridge. He thought it was funny, though, and he grinned every time he said it. I can hardly remember him when he wasn't grinning.

However Daddy chose to describe himself, he was a country boy all the way, and he surely looked the part. He stood six-foot-two, and though he filled out some after he became an adult he never did lose that gangly, boyish look.

He had a wealth of freckles and a shock of sandy hair that went wherever it wanted—flying around his head and settling first one way and then the other according to the direction the wind was blowing and which way he happened to be pointed at the time. And ears—Daddy had those ears that only country folk seem to get, the kind that look like somebody left the doors standing open on a car.

Daddy walked with a long, loose-legged stride, stretching out as far as his legs could reach with every step—a gawky gait that one could recognize a quarter of a mile away. He ran the same way, and whenever someone kidded him about it he just laughed and said it got him where he wanted to go, and saved him a few steps in the process.

As a boy Daddy had been an accomplished athlete. Although Sarah and I could hardly imagine him as a baseball player, he was better coordinated than he appeared, and that long-legged run of his was deceptive; it carried him faster than it looked like he was going. Folks said when he ran the bases in high school he looked like a bounding ostrich, but the team of frustrated guys trying to take him out failed to see the humor in the spectacle.

Daddy may have been a poor country boy, but he was a winner. Being a baseball star who happened to possess an irresistible personality, he managed to land one of the prettiest girls in town: Jessica Tolliver, our mother.

When it came to looks, Mama was Daddy's opposite. She was tall herself, about five-foot-ten, with a striking figure that never lost its youth. And my mother's face was something to behold—skin light and silky smooth, cheekbones high and sculptured, eyes the palest blue with long dark lashes, and shoulder-length auburn hair that glistened in the sunlight. She sat and brushed it every day.

No one ever failed to treat Mama with respect—she being a mannered southern lady and beautiful besides—but no matter what front they put on I always knew they loved Daddy more. Daddy was smart enough to know that too, but it didn't matter to him; he loved Mama enough for everybody.

Most black people—men, women, young, and old—worked on cotton plantations when we were growing up, but Jubal never did. At an anxious age when young Negro men worked the cotton fields like feverish colts from daylight to dusk and chased black girls when the sun went down, Jubal spent his days helping his mama and his nights sitting at home with her in their little shack on the far side of the railroad tracks.

My first memory of him goes back to when I was about five years old, which would have made Sarah just two or three. Sometimes we question the accuracy of our earliest memories, but I have no doubts about the first time I saw Jubal. He was a young man at the time, around eighteen, and his stature was not something a kid my size would easily forget.

He stood six-foot-one, not really as tall as he appeared to me at the time, but he had a bulky frame and a thick waist—one of those big-bodied people who appear obese at first glance but prove to be strong, and sometimes surprisingly agile.

Mama, Sarah, and I were in Stern's Department Store, which happened to be one of the few downtown shops that catered to black people as well as white. Even though the blacks had to stand back and wait their turn until all the whites had been waited on, Mama avoided such stores as much as possible.

Mama was waiting in line at the cash register with Sarah and me standing on either side of her. Sarah, being little and naturally shy, had a fistful of Mama's dress and a thumb in her mouth. I, feeling smug about being several inches taller than my little sister and therefore quite independent, had backed away and was standing a few feet behind Mama and Sarah.

I don't know if I brushed against him or just sensed something large behind me, but when I turned around I found myself staring at a thigh thicker than my waist. My eyes followed his body upward until I found myself looking straight up the side of a blue denim mountain.

He looked as wide as I was tall. His fencepost arms hung loosely at his sides, and way up above the bib of his overalls his broad face turned down toward mine. Any fear I might have felt faded when our eyes met. His eyes were deep pools of softness, and he smiled the faintest smile I'd ever seen. Sarah stared up at him too, but he avoided looking in her face, and he kept his eyes totally averted from Mama.

Mama grabbed me by the collar, spun me around, and pulled me to her side. Then she jerked Sarah around so that she faced away from him too. Jubal kept a proper distance behind us until we checked out. Sarah tried to turn around and look at him a couple of times before we left, but Mama wouldn't allow it.

"Who was that big man, Mama?" I asked as we left the store. "He looked like a giant."

"That wasn't a man, Lucas," Mama said. "That was a nigger, and you stay away from him. People call him Dummy,
and most folks think he's crazy."

Then Mama jerked Sarah by the arm again and said
harshly, "You listen to what I'm saying too, little girl."

That night I told Daddy about seeing a black man called
Dummy and described how big he had looked to me. He
grinned and nodded. "Yeah, he's a pretty big fella. And
something else you ought to know; his real name is Jubal,
Jubal Jefferson."

"Mama says folks call him Dummy."

"Yes, some people do," Daddy said. "They have ever
since he was a kid, but I never thought it was a very nice
name to call anybody."

I began to notice Jubal more after we saw him in the
department store. His mama took in washing and ironing
from white people, as many Negro women did. Her customers paid her a dollar a week, and Jubal made pickups
and deliveries for her all over town. He hauled the clothes
in a faded red wagon he pulled behind him, a rusty relic he
had altered specifically to suit his purpose.

Because the original wagon bed was too short and narrow to hold many clothes, Jubal built a wooden platform
on top of it about three feet wide by four feet long. To this
flat surface he fastened sideboards three feet high. With the
old wagon bed and narrow wheels barely visible beneath
the large rectangular basket, the carriage looked top-heavy,

and unusual to say the least, but Jubal could stack a great load of clothes in it.

He also lengthened the tongue of the child's wagon to allow someone as tall as him to pull it. This he accomplished by sawing the tongue in two and inserting a three-foot length of hoe handle, which he wired solidly in place.

Jubal made quite a sight pulling that wagon. Leaning forward with both hands behind him holding onto the handle, he'd stare at the ground in front of him and trudge down the street as if he were pulling a thousand pounds. And though the wagon might be heaped four or five feet high with clothes, his big, slow-moving body dwarfed the load.

He worked all year round, and dressed according to the season. In spring and summer he wore a light chambray shirt under his overalls and went barefooted. In fall and winter he wore a long-sleeved shirt, a faded black coat, and heavy Brogan shoes that looked like they'd been chipped from a solid block of leather.

Because Jubal picked up and delivered clothes to a different set of customers each day, he took circuitous routes that carried him all over town. I was sure he couldn't read street signs or the numbers on the houses, so I decided he must have all of Linville mapped out by heart.

Knowing that black people were not allowed to walk through white neighborhoods except for work-related purposes, I was curious to see how he conducted his business. My curiosity got the best of me one day, and I followed him around town so I could spy on him. I probably wasn't as stealthy as I thought, but if he was aware of my presence he never let me know.

Jubal would pull his wagon just through the front gate of a customer's house so as to leave the sidewalk clear, then walk around to the back door and knock, softly. Normally a Negro maid came to the door, and normally Jubal said nothing as he handed her an armload of finished clothes or picked up a stack to be washed and ironed. A few of the black women were friendlier, though; at the sight of one of them a smile would light up his face and he'd nod his head and say, "Sure is a pretty day, ain't it, Ma'am?"

And the black maid would answer with something like: "Yes, Jubal. It is a pretty day. I hope you's enjoyin' it." After such an exchange he'd turn and strut back to his wagon as if he had just spoken with royalty.

If the lady of the house—the white lady—happened to come to the door, Jubal would turn his eyes away and say nothing while they exchanged the clothes. Once, as I watched from behind a tree, a haughty white woman dropped a number of coins into his hand and abruptly shut the door in his face. Walking back to his wagon, Jubal opened his hand, glanced at the coins, and stopped. He picked out one of them, returned to the back door, and knocked again.

"Yes?" the woman said impatiently.

Looking steadily at his feet, Jubal held out the coin and said, "You gived me a nickel too much, Ma'am."

Every dog in town knew him, and according to which

neighborhood he happened to be passing through as many as five or six could be seen following along behind him. Whenever he stopped and sat down to rest, one of the dogs would lay his head on Jubal's knee while he patted it and whispered something that only he and the dog could hear.

We happened to see Jubal downtown one afternoon when Sarah was five, and she made a big mistake. Mama, Sarah, and I were standing on the sidewalk when he came down the street toward us with his head down, pulling his wagon behind him as usual. Just before he passed, Sarah waved at him. It was just a little wave—she didn't even raise her arm—but Jubal saw it and smiled at her, a smile as small as her wave.

Mama noticed the slight exchange. She grabbed Sarah by the arm and practically jerked her off her feet.

"What do you think you're doing, girl, waving at him?"

Holding her bruised arm with the opposite hand, Sarah tried to explain. "He smiled at me, Mama. He likes me."

The fury in Mama's face scared Sarah, and it scared me. She bent over at the waist and scolded Sarah in a voice that turned heads half a block away.

"Of course he likes you!" Mama said. "You're white, and he's a blue-gum nigger, the blackest kind there is. No telling what he might do to a little white girl like you if he could. No white girl waves at the likes of him, Sarah—no white girl. You understand me?"

Sarah nodded, but I knew she didn't understand a thing Mama said.

Linville was an old town even when we were kids. Spreading oaks draped the sidewalks and streets while tall cottonwoods, elms, locusts, and magnolias shaded a variety of homes that reflected a great disparity between the haves and have nots—a condition that had persisted since the land was settled forty years before the Civil War.

Several mansions on Robert E. Lee Street boasted tall columns and second- and third-story verandas reminiscent of the antebellum period, proud symbols of an Old South that refused to die. Along the same street stood stately Victorians with sculptured turrets rounding their corners, thin spires reaching for the sky, and wide porches draped in gingerbread trim—trophies of high-living planters who had cleared an impenetrable swamp and sown a million acres of cotton in its place.

The trees were just as tall on other streets such as Stonewall Jackson and Nathan Bedford Forrest (they had all been named after Confederate generals), but many of those streets weren't paved and some neighborhoods lacked sidewalks. There the trees dwarfed modest cottages, frame houses, and an occasional Victorian of lesser size and majesty than those on Robert E. Lee.

The Tollivers lived on Jeb Stuart Street. It wasn't Robert E. Lee, but when Mama was growing up their two-story Victorian with its white picket fence and neatly trimmed hedges dominated every house in sight.

Grandpa Tolliver had descended from overseers, a coarse,

hard-driving class of whites who worked the slaves in the fields and sometimes ran entire plantations for absentee owners. He owned two businesses, both strategically located near the edge of town: a small grocery store that attracted both townspeople and farmers and a machinery and harness repair shop that sat next door.

Burris Tolliver was one of those men who had so much mechanical ability that normal folk just stood back and watched in awe as he performed his magic. His shop was too small for his business, but that didn't matter; most of the repair work took place in the yard anyway. A high mesh fence enclosed the yard, and he always had more wagons, plows, buggies, and automobiles waiting to be repaired than he had hours in the day.

Although Burris Tolliver seldom drank, his father had been an alcoholic, and his father's father before him. He was a short, stocky man, balding when I knew him, and conspicuously missing several teeth. His wide forehead and narrow eyes seemed to reflect his uncompromising views on nearly everything. A rough, ambitious man who lived life in a hurry, Grandpa Tolliver charged around his shop with a mouth full of chewing tobacco, a rag in his hand, and grease streaks covering his overalls and chambray shirt, shouting orders and voicing his opinion on every political issue of the day, particularly anything concerning race.

A middle-aged white man tended Tolliver's Grocery, and although black repairmen were common in those days, all who worked in Grandpa's shop were white.

"I'd never work a colored in my place, Lucas," I remember him telling me when I was too young to be concerned about such things or even attempt to understand them. "Niggers is lazy, and some of them are beginnin' to get uppity, which I damn sure won't stand for. And even them that knows how to keep their place and act like they're supposed to can't be trusted. Niggers is just niggers, Lucas— always was, always will be."

Mama grew up an only child, a pampered girl known as Jessie when she was little—a name that became history as soon as she reached her teens. At the insistence of both Mama and her mother, she became Jessica. Even her daddy, the one who had first begun calling his little girl Jessie, succumbed to their wishes.

Grandma Tolliver, an attractive woman with a perpetually anxious look, had been christened Teresa, a name she felt befitted her proper station. At an early age, however, Grandma became Tessie, and to her silent chagrin she remained Tessie forever.

A kind person by nature and more down to earth than she cared to admit, Tessie Tolliver might have spent her life helping people in some way had she not been possessed by the trappings of society. Endlessly involved in church socials, afternoon teas, and the like, she looked for any excuse to invite ladies to her home, especially those she considered members of Linville's upper class.

Although Grandma had several regular members of her little "club," as she called it, and every now and then succeeded in snaring Mayor Hasting's wife and the wives of

other civic leaders as well, her ultimate dream was to hob-
nob with the wealthy.

Every Sunday after church Grandma did something that
should have embarrassed her, but it never seemed to. She
would accost Kathleen Hardiman, an aloof woman whose
husband's family owned not only the Mercantile but four
plantations that encompassed more than ten thousand acres
of cotton land. They lived in the biggest house on Robert
E. Lee Street.

"Some of the ladies are planning to get together at my
home this afternoon, Kathleen," Grandma would say.
"Jessica is going to do a piano recital, and we'll be playing
bridge afterwards. You're more than welcome to join us."

Mrs. Hardiman spoke with the finest Southern accent
imaginable, and every Sunday she would answer Grandma
as if it were the first time the exchange had ever occurred.

"Why, thank you, Tessie," she'd say with practiced sincerity. "I can't promise anything, but I'll surely try to make
it. It's terribly nice of you to think of including us."

Kathleen Hardiman never once set foot in Grandma
Tolliver's house.

Tessie Tolliver remained as tireless in her quest for
acceptance as the rich were in rebuffing her, and when
Mama was growing up her mother strove to finagle invita-
tions for her to every social event in town.

Every upper class family and most middle class as well
employed black maids, or "domestics," in their homes.
Every morning by 6 a.m. a great number of black women

could be seen walking to work from the far side of the railroad tracks, a rundown section of town that consisted of rows of tarpaper shacks, dilapidated shotgun houses with swaybacked roofs, and narrow streets where scraggy dogs lay and Negro children played in the dirt—a sprawling place of poverty known by a nondescript name that seemed to deny it very existence: across the tracks.

Many white men in Linville knew their way across the tracks well. Some of the town's leading and wealthiest citizens could easily navigate its dark streets at night, the only time they went. Black prostitutes were readily available across the tracks, and some white men even kept mistresses there. No one, white or black, ever mentioned this practice—a holdover from the days of slavery—but everyone in town was aware of it.

While the wealthy often employed several black maids in their homes, most middle class families could afford only one. Grandma and Grandpa Tolliver had two.

The Tolliver's older maid, Pernella, did the cooking, served the meals, and scrubbed the kitchen. Grandma Tolliver had known and trusted Pernella for years, and treated her with obvious affection. The younger maid, Estella, a slender mulatto whose ivory skin revealed an excess of white blood, cleaned the rest of the house, changed the beds, and waited at night in her own bed across the tracks for Burris Tolliver's visits.

Grandma Tolliver seldom found occasion to talk to Estella; Mama grew up hating the sight of her.

Chapter Two

It has been called the most Southern place on earth. As a kid I knew little about the history or geology of the Mississippi Delta, and after I went away to college I learned it's not really a delta at all.

The three million acres known as the Delta is actually a floodplain of the great river—a sprawling expanse of bottom land stretching from Memphis on the north to Vicksburg on the south, a distance of two hundred miles. Bordered on the west by the river and the east by abruptly rising hills, the Delta bulges seventy miles wide at the center and narrows to a blunt point at each end.

Before white planters began clearing it in the early 1800s, a monumental task that took more than a century to complete, the Delta was nothing short of a jungle—a steamy, swampy mass of cypress, sycamore, oak, pecan, cottonwood, and sweetgum laced together with tangled vines and impenetrable canebrakes—an endless thicket infested with bears, wolves, panthers, rattlesnakes, water moccasins, and even alligators. In places a man needed a machete to make his way through the spongy mess.

This dark, mysterious wilderness where only wild animals dared enter lay flat as a board as far as one could see, and due to the Mississippi overflowing its banks annually for thousands of years—each flood depositing a fresh veneer of material over the preceding layers—the Delta consisted of hundreds of feet of some of the richest soil on earth.

Planters in older, more settled parts of the South knew what rich soil lay hidden beneath the tangled jungle of western Mississippi, and they also knew it was no place for the small farmer dreaming of a little piece of land on which to raise his family. Clearing and planting the Delta required a large work force from the beginning, a force that would face endemic diseases such as malaria, typhoid, and yellow fever while working like beasts of burden twelve hours a day.

Established planters, men who owned large plantations further east but desired to expand their operations, ferried great loads up the river on flatboats, bringing tools and materials with which to build homes for their families along with supplies needed to attack the wilderness and survive in it: cattle, horses, mules, hogs, chickens, and slaves—thousands of them.

The planters—high-living, risk-taking men who gambled by night, tended their vast holdings by day, threw great parties on the weekends, and controlled the politics to their own ends—built opulent homes and set about establishing a genteel way of life, the romanticized memory of which their descendants would cling to for generations and forever revere as the epitome of the Old South.

The slaves, driven by white overseers, cleared the Delta.

After clearing, the rich land made for prolific cotton fields, but the crops ran the risk of yearly floods. A little flooding each season was natural and expected, but every five or six years a heavy flood would wipe out the crops completely, and historically every fifteen or twenty years the entire Delta would be inundated with several feet of water that might remain standing for weeks.

By the early 1900s the Army Corps of Engineers had lined the river with levees. Enormous earthen dams set a mile or more back from the natural river banks, the levees stretched from Cairo, Illinois, to New Orleans, a distance of eleven hundred miles. At flood crest the levees could contain a roaring Mississippi several miles wide and prevent its flooding the crops of the planters who lived within its shadows.

Built with horses and wheelbarrows, the triangular-shaped levees were a wonder of engineering and a monument to hand labor—two hundred feet wide at the base and sloping upward to a crown four stories high. This made the crown, a flat top only eight feet wide, the highest elevation in the Delta.

Daddy's family was poor when he was growing up—much poorer than Mama's. The Dunaways had only four children, two boys and two girls, which was a small family for country folk. Daddy was the youngest, and because we knew Grandma Dunaway had at least one miscarriage after he was born, I suspect she couldn't have any more.

Grandma and Grandpa migrated to the Delta from the hills of eastern Mississippi where they had grown up in sharecropping families. And though the Delta had its share of white trash croppers—shiftless folk who cared no more for tomorrow than yesterday—it offered slightly more opportunity for those with ambition.

Much of the Delta remained virgin when Grandma and Grandpa started sharecropping, and the land they farmed butted right up to the uncleared forest. Marauding bears still roamed the countryside at night and wolves carried off livestock.

Besides raising crops and sharing the take with the landowner, the Dunaways' contract required that they clear several acres of additional land each year. Grandpa was a tall, stout man who didn't have a lazy bone in his body, and neither did Grandma. She was a short, solidly built woman who, besides tending a garden and raising chickens and pigs, worked in the fields alongside Grandpa and the kids.

The house Daddy grew up in was little more than a shack, and their standard of living was no better than most of the black sharecroppers who were their closest neighbors. John Dunaway didn't dwell on such things, however. Grandpa had more important things on his mind than the color of his neighbors' skin, and when the countryside

exploded over some unproven crime supposedly committed by a Negro and the night came alive with the glow of
running torches, baying hounds, and gunshots, he refused
to participate.

Because the endless cotton fields required the same labor
force as they had in the days of slavery, blacks still outnum-
bered whites eight to one. Except for slight modifications,
the economic system also dated back to slavery. Whites controlled everything—the towns, the plantations, and the lives
of all black people who lived in either. And within this
strange, dual world of white and black there existed an
unspoken paranoia; despite their overwhelming control of
the blacks, the whites feared them. They may have considered themselves superior to Negroes in every way, but the
sheer numbers of blacks in their midst fostered an underly-
ing fear among whites that bordered on the pathological.

In order to perpetuate the cheap labor required to raise
cotton, the white minority felt a great need to keep their
Negroes intimidated. Within this slow-talking, agrarian
society known for its politeness and hospitality there existed a paradox: a violent undercurrent that served to maintain the status quo between the races.

Lynching black people became common practice in those
days, even a cherished tradition in the minds of some, but
John Dunaway kept to himself and held to his own beliefs.
He wasn't naive enough to try to buck the system, however. Although he chose not to take part in the violent racial
practices, he also knew better than to speak out against

them. To be branded a nigger lover might get you lynched yourself, or covered with tar and run out of the country in the middle of the night. Grandpa worked the land, raised his family, and kept his head down.

The landowners marketed the cotton and kept the books, and since most black sharecroppers were incapable of reading or doing simple math, their share seldom came out even at the end of the season. When the landlord divided it up the croppers usually found themselves faced with various extra charges, most of which they had not anticipated. And being disenfranchised citizens who had no rights that would stand up in court against the word of a white man, if a black did think he'd been cheated he had no recourse.

During particularly bad years the Dunaways didn't break even either, and ended up owing the landlord money at the end of the season. But the landlord trusted Grandpa enough to tide him over until they hit a few good years in a row and managed to make the next move up the ladder; they rented the land on which they had been sharecropping.

Grandpa bought his own mule and started making his own crops. By the time Sarah and I came along, Grandma and Grandpa Dunaway owned their farm, more than a hundred acres of prime cotton land, and had several families, both black and white, working for them.

Daddy's older brother and his two sisters attended a small country school for five or six years, after which they went to work full time on the farm. His brother Robert wasn't especially bright, and while neither he nor the girls seemed very interested in learning, Daddy studied incessantly and absorbed everything he read. And though it was a stretch for small farmers trying to make it in the Delta, when Daddy finished elementary school Grandma and Grandpa managed to send him to high school in town. Somehow they even made time for him to play baseball.

Since they lived only three miles from town, Daddy walked, or ran, to school and back. He spoke fondly of those days, and I can picture him carrying his books in a tow sack and loping down that little dirt road, eating up the miles with his long-legged stride. He waved at everyone working in the fields, white or black, and they would all straighten from their labor a moment, grin, and wave back.

Large portions of the Delta—deep forests where famous folk such as William Faulkner and Theodore Roosevelt came to hunt—remained uncleared when Sarah and I were kids. In the portions where it had been cleared, the tree-lined creek beds could be seen snaking their way across the fields for miles. One of those creeks held Daddy's favorite swimming hole.

Sorghum Creek wound close to Linville at one point, its line of tall cottonwoods, oak, and sweetgum running within a quarter mile of the black section of town across the tracks. A lazy stream not six feet wide through most of its length, the creek trickled along less than a foot deep. At a spot a mile or so from town, however, it took a sharp bend against the roots of several large oaks.

Here, floodwaters had carved a wide pool; still, green, and deep. One could either swim in the cool water or sit in the shade of tall trees dangling bare feet over the bank and fish. Using a cane pole and worms or crickets for bait, a kid could catch a stringer full of bream and maybe a catfish or two.

Daddy had spent some of his finest childhood days at the swimming hole, and it was his favorite place for family outings. He'd rouse us all on a Saturday morning when he didn't have to work, tell Mama to fix a picnic lunch, and run around gathering up the fishing equipment for Sarah and me. He had a floppy straw hat that just looked ridiculous, a huge thing which he'd put on his head before he woke us up. When we saw the hat, we knew where we were going.

"Come on, y'all," Daddy would say loudly as we sat up and wiped the sleep from our eyes. "Those fish'll be filling up on something besides our bait!"

Along with his funny hat he wore cutoff pants that reached to his knobby knees, and he went barefooted the same as he had done as a kid. His feet were big too, of course. When Mama saw him decked out for the swimming hole she just shook her head and began preparing lunch.

Sarah wore a tiny pink swimsuit, her blond curls framing a demur smile and bright blue eyes that danced at Daddy's silliness. I wore a wide-brimmed hat like Huck Finn's and cutoffs like Daddy's. With the picnic basket perched in the back seat between Sarah and me and the cane poles fastened on top, Daddy would open the car door for Mama and grandly usher her into the passenger seat as if we might be going to visit the White House. Daddy didn't exactly look like someone going to the White House, of course.

Mama wore a sun dress, sandals, and a wide white hat to shade her face—a pretty hat, not vaguely in the same league with Daddy's. I don't think she enjoyed the outings as much as he, but Daddy loved them so much that she went along to please him. They knew each other well, and usually managed to keep their differences in check as they went about life. A few of their differences lay shallow within them, however, and refused to become dormant.

Sorghum Creek paralleled the main road for several miles, and we could see the line of trees that marked it as we drove along. About a mile from town Daddy would turn off onto a little dirt road that wound through the cotton fields toward the creek half a mile away. He'd stop, step out of the car, swing open a creaky wooden gate, drive through, and get back out to close it before we headed through the fields.

Within a few minutes we'd drive under the shade of the big trees and be there. The land actually rose up a few feet near the creek bank, a result of its natural levees and the slow buildup of soil beneath the trees. The air at the creek felt ten degrees cooler than the hot fields we had just crossed.

Mama would spread an oilcloth under a tree and set the picnic basket out while Daddy got down our fishing poles, adjusted the cork bobbers on our lines, and baited Sarah's hook. Being a boy, I baited my own. Then while Sarah and

I perched on the edge of the bank and watched our bobbers for any slight motion that might indicate a bite, Daddy and Mama sat under the tree and talked.

After a while, if the fish didn't bite or if they quit biting, we'd hear Daddy coming.

"Yahoo!" he'd holler, his bare feet pounding up behind us. "Duck!" he'd shout, leaping high over our heads and winging his way out over the creek, arms flailing the air like some giant ridiculous bird. Just before he hit the water, he'd fold his body into a perfect cannonball and drench us both. At that point Sarah and I would laugh, drop our fishing poles, jump in, and try to get even by splashing him. Mama would sit under the tree reading a magazine, shaking her head as the three of us cavorted in the water.

When we tired of swimming and splashing each other, we'd all climb out, dry off, and join Mama under the tree. She'd open the basket and set out plates of sandwiches, fried chicken, pickles, potato salad, and cookies, then pour us each a glass of sweet tea.

One day as we were enjoying our lunch Sarah jumped like someone had poked her in the ribs.

"There's somebody behind that tree!" she said, pointing a trembling finger at the trunk of a large cottonwood near the end of the swimming hole. "Over there! Somebody peeked around that big tree."

Daddy's eyes grew wary. "Y'all sit still," he said. He laid his hat on the ground, stood up, and walked cautiously toward the tree, circling widely around it as he approached.

"Jubal!" he said. "What are you doing here?!"

Slowly, shyly, he emerged from behind the tree.

"It's Dummy!" Sarah said, then clamped her hands over her mouth as if trying to catch her own words before they got away.

"I comes here ever now and then, Mistuh Reid," Jubal explained in a low voice. "It's a good place."

"It's one of my favorite places too, Jubal," Daddy said. "Come over and meet my family."

Jubal followed Daddy toward us, but stopped several feet away and stood looking at the ground. "These are my children, Lucas and Sarah," Daddy told him, "and this is my wife, Jessica."

Looking up at him, I remembered the first time I'd seen him in Stern's Department Store. The same incredibly soft eyes met mine for a moment, and the same fleeting smile passed over his face. Jubal glanced at Sarah as well, but he avoided looking at Mama altogether.

"Would you like a piece of chicken, Jubal?" Daddy asked him.

He stood silent, arms hanging at his sides, and said nothing. Daddy picked up the plate of chicken and held it out to him. "Go ahead," he urged. "We've got plenty."

Jubal reached out and took a drumstick, carefully avoiding touching any of the other pieces. "Thank ya, Mistuh Reid," he said softly. Then he smiled. "Sure is a pretty day, ain't it, suh?"

"Yes, it is a pretty day, Jubal," Daddy replied. "Sit down

and eat with us, please." Mama hadn't said a word nor looked at Jubal since he appeared; now she cast a perilous frown at Daddy. If Daddy noticed, he ignored it.

Jubal sat down on the ground ten feet from us and began eating the drumstick carefully, almost delicately. We all went back to eating in silence; nobody seemed to know what to say. Daddy spoke a few polite words to him that I don't remember, and Sarah and I kept stealing glances in his direction until Daddy's frown warned us not to be impolite.

When he finished the drumstick, Jubal eased to his feet. It was the first time I noticed how deftly he could move his big body.

"I thanks y'all for the chicken, Mistuh Reid," he said without looking at us. "I gots to be goin' now."

"All right, Jubal," said Daddy. "You take care."

With that he turned and walked to the big tree where Sarah had first seen him, disappeared behind it, and was gone.

"How'd he get here?" I asked.

"There's a path that runs alongside the creek," Daddy said. "Black folks across the tracks used to use it a lot, walking to and from work in the fields before they had any other way to get there. Now most of them ride in wagons or trucks.

"Jubal and his mother live in a shack a little ways outside the Negro settlement. The shack sits in a grove of trees next to the creek. He can walk from his house to here without leaving the creek bed or the shade of the trees."

Mama had fought to control her anger; now she let go.

"The *Negro settlement*," she said sarcastically. "He could

see all over the countryside from that creek bed, including the road we came in on. He must have known we were here before he showed up."

"Maybe so," Daddy replied with a shrug.

"How could you do that, Reid?" Mama said, her eyes seething. "Ask him to sit down and join us in a meal! What would folks think if they knew?"

"Aw, Jessica," Daddy said. "We're out here on a picnic. It's not like I invited him to come into our house and sit down at the table."

"That's what it felt like to me," she said. "That's exactly what it felt like."

"He's a good fella," Daddy said. "He just stays to himself and minds his own business. Hardly anybody in town is nice to him."

"A good fella!" Mama said, throwing her napkin to the ground. "I don't wonder that folks aren't nice to him. He's the blackest thing I ever saw, and big.

"He didn't even talk when he was little," she continued. "People thought he didn't know how; that's why they called him Dummy. And everybody knows about him throwing that man off the levee."

"That happened during a tough time for the whole Delta," Daddy said. "From what I heard, the guy just pushed him too hard."

We sat in silence for a strained moment, then Daddy tried again to plead Jubal's case. "Come on, Jessica, you know what happened to his daddy and all."

Mama shook her head in disgust. "Yes, I've heard that story," she said, "and others like it. I don't believe that kind of stuff goes on as much as people say it does.

"And I don't necessarily care, either," she said, grabbing up dishes and tossing them loudly into the picnic basket. "His Daddy was a big buck nigger just like him, and an uppity one at that. Always making sure everybody knew he could read and write. I've even heard it said he looked at white women, and looked white men in the eye."

Sitting silent between them, Sarah and I grew increasingly uncomfortable with their arguing. I knew better than to speak at such a time, but Sarah naively asked a question: "You called him Jubal?"

"Yes, I did, Sweetheart," Daddy replied. "Jubal is his name."

"Dummy sounds better to me," Mama said.

Bathrooms were a scarce commodity in those days; hardly anyone who lived in the country had one and many in town didn't either. Wooden outhouses stood in the backyards of more than half the homes in Linville. Our home, however, a comfortable single-story frame house built around 1910, had its own bathroom. Mama insisted on modern conveniences, and Daddy would have broken his back to see that she got them.

Our house sat in the middle of a shaded block on George Pickett Street, or Pickett as it was commonly known. (In normal conversation street names were shortened to Jackson,

Stuart, Pickett, etc., with the exception of one; no one ever abbreviated Robert E. Lee.)

Pickett Street wasn't paved, but a concrete sidewalk did run in front of our house. Except for an excess of greenery surrounding it, our house resembled many others on the block. Even so, I thought it quite special, and Sarah did too. Its overhanging roof sloped upward on all sides to a peak in the center, and with the exception of gray shingles the house was totally white. A covered porch extended all the way across the front, under which hung a swing that Mama and Daddy often shared in the late evening.

Great oaks and magnolias shaded the house while lilacs, azaleas, and the reddest roses in town adorned every side and filled the back yard, a brilliant array that Mama spent many of her daylight hours tending. Neat, trim, and enclosed within a white picket fence, our home was very white and very Southern.

With six rooms including the bathroom, the house seemed huge to me as a kid. It wasn't, of course. The front door opened into the living room, or front room, as we called them then, and a wide archway separated the front room from the dining room. A swinging door led from the dining room to the kitchen at the back of the house. The bathroom, also at the back, adjoined the kitchen on the right.

The door to the room Sarah and I shared opened to the right off the front room, while Mama and Daddy's bedroom adjoined the dining room on the same side.

While flowered curtains adorned the kitchen windows, white ones hung throughout the rest of the house—not the long, expensive kind, but attractive and tasteful. A great oak table and matching chairs that Daddy borrowed money to purchase sat in the dining room; other than that the furnishings were modest, with the exception of two pieces: a piano and a rug that Mama and Daddy received as wedding gifts from their parents.

The dark mahogany piano, an upright, dominated the left wall of the front room; it had been a gift from the Tollivers. And covering the front room floor was a thick Persian rug that Grandma and Grandpa Dunaway had given them, it's golds, blues, and touches of red adding warmth to the room. The piano and the rug were Mama's proudest possessions.

Emiline, our black maid, was a stout, middle-aged woman with light copper skin that seemed to contrast with her distinct Negroid features. A tall, engaging woman with intelligent eyes that took in everything, Emiline did not suffer fools. She kept our house spotless, washed our clothes, changed our beds, and cooked meals that permeated the kitchen and dining room with aromas that hung in the air day and night.

We knew almost nothing about Emiline's life or even where she lived across the tracks—a typical situation, as white people generally knew very little about blacks, even the ones they might see and talk with on a daily basis. Also typical was Emiline's extensive knowledge of us; in ways, she probably knew more about our family than we knew about ourselves. From the days of slavery, blacks had learned to keep their personal lives to themselves, a rather simple thing to do since white people considered their ways childish and irrelevant anyway. And the blacks kept their eyes and ears open and absorbed everything there was to know of the whites who controlled their destiny.

Emiline would bake a tray of oatmeal cookies, our favorite, while Sarah and I hung around the dining room trying to act like we didn't know what she was doing. Finally she'd poke her head out the kitchen door and eye us narrowly.

"All right, you two spies," she'd say, "run in and get your hands washed and sit down in here like the little lady and gentleman you knows how to be."

We'd run through the kitchen to the bathroom, wash our hands too quickly, then sit down at the table and wait for Emiline to set out the cookies and pour us each a glass of milk.

"Here, child, this one's for you," she'd say, handing Sarah the biggest cookie on the tray. I figured she must like girls better than boys, but that didn't stop me from loving her more than I loved my own aunts.

After we finished our treats and were headed out the door to play, Emiline would shake a finger in my direction and caution me: "Watch out for your little sister, Lucas. She needs you."

Chapter Three

Around five thousand people lived in Linville, a small town by modern standards but sizable when we were kids. This figure included the blacks who lived across the tracks, an area considerably smaller than the rest of Linville but which held the majority of the population.

By the time I turned eight and Sarah was five, we were allowed to walk nearly anywhere in town by ourselves. Everyone in Linville knew us, and as long as we stayed together, didn't cross the tracks, and avoided the tramps and hobos that came through on the trains, Mama didn't worry.

Some days we made it all the way to Tolliver's Repair Shop near the edge of town. Sarah didn't particularly like going there because Grandpa Tolliver kept a vicious dog chained to a corner of the building near the front door. The dog lunged at everyone who entered the yard, the chain serving as its only restraint. At night when the gate was closed the dog ran loose in the yard to keep intruders away.

The men who hung around Grandpa's shop didn't seem to mind the dog's barking, drooling, and lunging at the chain, but it scared Sarah. She didn't care for the grease, dirt, and smell of chewing tobacco and cigars that pervaded the place either, but she'd hold tightly to my hand and follow me in. Then she'd stand close by my side and watch Grandpa Tolliver with a wary eye.

The only thing that did impress Sarah was the inevitable trip next door to Tolliver's Grocery where Grandpa would show us off to customers, fill our pockets with candy, and caution us not to tell Mama where we got it.

The shop fascinated me, and so did Burris Tolliver. How could one man learn all the things he had to know to run such a place? Everyone there, employees and customers alike, kowtowed to him as he went about repairing something himself or loudly explaining to one of his mechanics how to fix it, seeming more sure of himself than anyone I knew.

Grandpa Tolliver was the boss, and I was impressed.

We stopped by Hardiman's Mercantile to see Daddy more often than we should have, but he never said a word about it. If he happened to be busy with a customer when we came in, he'd grin, wave, and tell us to look around. The Mercantile, housed in a rustic wooden building that had begun its life as a cotton barn, was a two-story wonderland of horseshoes, harnesses, wagon wheels, plow parts, oil cans, overalls, straw hats, work boots, gloves, and a thousand things I couldn't name.

Graydon Hardiman, a tall man with steel gray hair and

eyes that told you he was in charge, ran the Mercantile. He and his brothers controlled an empire begun by their grandfather, expanded by their father, and solidified by them. And although Mr. Hardiman lived in the biggest house in town, he never failed to acknowledge Sarah and me when we visited his store. Bending down to shake my hand and squatting to give Sarah a kiss on the forehead, he was the first rich and powerful person I ever knew, and one of the first true gentlemen as well.

Others we met in the Mercantile were not so grand. Nap Canfield, a wiry wretch who lived in a pigsty of a shack on the same side of the tracks as the black people, approached us one day.

"So y'all are Reid Dunaway's kids, huh?" Nap said, stopping directly in front of Sarah and me and blocking the aisle. "Your daddy's a good friend of mine. Always treats a fella with respect."

Sarah pressed against me as I looked Canfield up and down warily. A grimy felt hat cast a shadow over his ferret-like face and his scraggy body hung in a perpetual lurch; one loose suspender dangled from his threadbare overalls, exposing a cotton shirt ragged beyond belief. His eyes, at once fiery, defensive, and ignorant, frightened me. I reeled from his breath as he leered down at us with a near toothless grin. He didn't extend his dirty hand for me to shake, thank God.

I didn't hear Daddy walk up behind us.

"Say hello to Mister Canfield," he said, startling me from my curious fascination and relieving my fear.

"I'm real proud to meet you kids," said Nap. "I always get your Daddy here to wait on me in the store. He's the finest gentleman in this here town."

"I'm glad to meet you too, Mister Canfield," I managed, as Sarah abandoned me and clung to Daddy's waist.

With a crooked nod at Daddy and a final leering grin at Sarah and me, Nap turned and left. The smell of his body lingered long after he departed.

Yankee soldiers burned and looted many of the older Mississippi towns during the war, but Linville hadn't yet come into existence by then. Founded in 1886, it grew and prospered as the South struggled to regain its footing and King Cotton reigned in the Delta once more.

Many of the older, more picturesque homes and municipal buildings remained standing when we were kids— most notably the courthouse. An early structure that towered three stories high in the middle of town, the courthouse formed the focal point of Linville. Its gleaming white dome rested on arched pediments supported by half a dozen columns on every side while its steep marble steps provided an impromptu meeting place for bankers, businessmen, lawyers, and judges who stopped and stood on them to talk business and politics. Those with a more leisurely agenda might sit down, lean back against the next higher step, and spit tobacco juice out onto the lawn.

Sidewalks and tree-shaded areas ringed the courthouse, bordering the brick streets that surrounded it, streets that turned to dirt just half a block away. Across the streets from the courthouse stood most of the prominent businesses: Stern's Department Store, Monck's Drug, Woolworth's Five and Dime, Dinkin's Bakery and Candy Shop, Eudora's Dresses, Samuel's Barbershop, Hankin's Hardware, and the Planters Bank with its big clock high on the corner of the building.

Sidewalks ran in front of all the stores, the shaded areas separating them from the streets the same as those around the courthouse. Retractable canvas awnings were cranked out over the sidewalks to provide shade for window shoppers. Many of the storefronts retained high-water marks left by the great Mississippi flood of 1927.

The courthouse, the storefronts, the shaded areas, and the brick streets formed the town square, a place where whites and blacks alike could bring a sandwich, a bottle of pop, or a picnic lunch. Resting on benches, curbs, or the cool grass, they fanned their faces and watched the slow life of the Delta pass by.

Sarah and I visited the town square often in our wanderings. The heart of everything we knew seemed to beat there. Sweating horses and mules, creaking wagons, smoking cars, and every interesting character imaginable passed by as we sat on a bench under the trees or walked along looking in store windows.

We occasionally saw Nap Canfield on the square—a strutting scarecrow who talked loudly and derisively to anyone who would listen, mostly about black people and what a scourge on society they were. A longtime crony of Nap's, Herman Slocum, was often with him. Herman was shorter and stockier than Nap, and just as dirty—a slovenly creature with a weak chin, cruel eyes, and a horribly bent nose. During a teenage dispute one of Herman's drinking buddies had slammed him in the face with a baseball bat, fracturing the bridge of his nose and flattening it across his face.

Herman smirked most of the time, and his eyes, which never quite met anyone else's, seemed to hide some dark secret that kept him amused. Besides being one of the ugliest humans I ever saw, he had a well-earned reputation for not being very smart. Nap and Herman had run together since they were kids—a pair of mean, devious boys who had been known as Pigpen Canfield and Slow Slocum back in those days.

Sarah and I always turned and walked the other way and hoped that Nap and Herman wouldn't see us.

An ancient black woman known as Mama Jingles was a common sight on the square. Wizened and bent with a face deeply lined and toothless, Mama Jingles wore the same tattered black dress every day, and bells. Dangling on a leather thong around her neck were two little bells that chimed her presence wherever she went. We never knew her real name, why she wore the bells, why she muttered to herself and rolled her head as she walked along bent over at the waist, or why she stopped and talked to trees, walls, dogs, cats, horses, and mules. I don't suppose Mama Jingles knew why she did those things either.

Few people paid any attention to Mama Jingles, but Jubal did. He passed by the courthouse several times a day pulling his wagon heaped with clothes, and he'd often stop and speak to the old lady and smile and listen to her babbling. Sometimes late in the evening we'd see him walking her back to her shanty across the tracks.

When Jubal stopped to rest on a curb in the middle of town, one or more stray dogs would nuzzle him and demand his attention. One day as he sat petting a little white cat two of the dogs came along and chased it up a tree. Jubal frowned at the dogs and shook a finger in their faces, an admonishment that only caused them to wag their tails and rub their noses on his legs. He stood up, shook his head, and led the dogs away, apologizing to the cat as he left.

"I's sorry little kitty," he said, looking up into the tree. "These old dogs just ain't got no manners."

Nap Canfield's boys, a ragamuffin bunch that ran the streets like a pack of feral animals, delighted in jeering at Mama Jingles.

"Crazy old nigger woman!" the boys would holler, bending over and mimicking her addled walk. "Whatcha wearin' them bells for, old black witch?"

But the old woman was oblivious to their insults. Lost in her hallucinatory world, Mama Jingles would go on talking to whatever animal or inanimate object that currently held her attention and not even look their direction.

Jubal didn't escape the Canfield boys' torment either. Though he never looked up when they spotted him pulling his wagon down the street toward the courthouse, the boys would run out, fall in behind him, and begin a mocking chant: "Jubal is a dummy! Nothin' but a dummy!" Butch, the oldest Canfield and the one who resembled his sleazy father the most, was the leader. Hollering things such as "Bigger'n a mule and twice as dumb!" Butch would swagger down the street behind Jubal while his younger brothers doubled over with laughter at his cruel wit.

After the jeering boys had followed Jubal a block or two, they'd return to the square grinning at their accomplishment. But one day they took it too far. Butch scooped up a fist-sized rock, threw it, and hit Jubal in the middle of his back. Without so much as flinching, Jubal dropped the handle of his wagon and turned on them. The boys stopped short, their voices trailing off into silence, and looked warily at the towering object of their taunts.

I could see Jubal's eyes darken and his body stiffen even from where Sarah and I sat. He took two steps, bent down, and deftly swept up the rock that had bounced off his back. Then straightening to full height, he scanned the gang of boys in front of him, extended his right arm, and pointed down the street behind them.

Butch broke first, then they all turned and tore back down the street like scalded dogs—cussing, tripping, and falling over each other as they ran. Men and women all over the square tried to hide their grins as Jubal dropped the rock and continued on his way.

The incident didn't stop the Canfield boys altogether.

They still hollered at Jubal from a distance, but it marked the one and only time they ever threw a rock at him.

Sheriff Anson Turnbull could often be seen on the square, talking with a businessman here, a farmer there, waving at someone, or simply observing. He knew the square reflected the pulse of Crowden County, and so kept a watchful eye on it and everyone there. A big, square-jawed, clean-shaven man, Sheriff Turnbull wore pressed khaki pants, a starched khaki shirt, polished black boots, and a gleaming Colt .45 strapped to his side. A gray, narrow-brimmed hat pulled low on his forehead and cocked to the right shaded heavy eyebrows and dark eyes that missed nothing.

We once saw a fight break out on the square. Two strapping farmers who were neighbors began arguing over a longtime boundary dispute between their properties. Sheriff Turnbull watched from half a block away as the volume of the men's voices grew, but he didn't move until one of them threw a punch. Then he ran like a racehorse and placed himself between them.

"Now, boys," the sheriff said, "the square is no place to settle this kind of thing. You two have got a whole countryside out there to quarrel in if that's what you've a mind to do."

One of the men wasn't smart enough to listen.

"Get out of my way, Anson!" he hollered, charging at the other with upraised fists. "I aim to . . . ."

And that was all the poor fellow got out. The sheriff swung from the waist with his right hand, smoothly extracting a lead-filled blackjack from his hip pocket as he swung. The blackjack caught the man squarely on the side of the head with a loud smack, knocking him out cold on his feet. His mouth dropped open in stunned surprise and he simply stopped moving. He stood stock still for a moment, then fell like a stone.

When the man's face hit the dirt, Sheriff Turnbull turned to his opponent, the blackjack still gripped in his fist. The man raised his open hands in front of him.

"No, Sheriff. I don't want none of that," he said.

Sheriff Turnbull's father had been a foreman on a cotton plantation, working black people in the fields all his life. Because Anson had practically grown up with blacks— working beside them, eating noon meals with them in the fields, and playing with black children as a child—he knew their ways better than any other white man in the county.

Anson Turnbull knew the law too, and whether dealing with whites or blacks he lived to enforce it. He also knew about lynching, the unspoken law that existed outside the written law—night-riding mayhem that was not only accepted by the white populace but tacitly condoned by those in power. Many newspaper editors, though dancing around the subject and refraining from stating their position precisely, actually encouraged the practice.

Harlan Johnson, editor of the *Linville Examiner,* was no exception. In one instance after vigilante groups had spent several days searching for two Negro men accused of murder, his newspaper printed the following:

Although we know from past history that the guilty are not always caught, we feel certain that these boys will be found. We do not feel there is room in the county jail for criminals such as these, and when they are found we are confident that the men who capture them will act in the best interests of the citizens of Crowden County.

Sheriff Turnbull knew that only a handful of people had ever been prosecuted for participating in a lynching, and because the law stated that only whites could serve on juries, virtually all had been acquitted. He also knew that the sheriff in charge of the prisoner was not always over-powered by a mob; in fact, some lawmen gave up their charges willingly and at times joined in the festivities themselves. A few had even acted as hangmen.

Lynchings had occurred in outlying parts of Crowden County before Sheriff Turnbull could stop them, but never within the bounds of Linville itself. He did keep unpopular prisoners locked in his jail at times, and public rumblings had threatened lynchings, but no one had ever dared challenge him. He intended to keep it that way.

As a kid I was even more bookish than Daddy had been, and since I was never good at sports like him he didn't try to force me in that direction. If I wasn't walking around town with Sarah I'd either be curled up somewhere with a book or at the library looking for another one.

The library, a square building made of gray stone, stood

a block from the courthouse. Its wide front steps led to a pair of high wooden doors with arched tops that seemed to defy the rest of its stern architecture. To me the tall doors appeared majestic, a fitting entrance to the world of books.

Miss Hawkins, a snappily efficient woman born to be a librarian, would stand behind the high desk and peer imperiously over her wire-rimmed glasses.

"Well, Lucas, what are we exploring today?" she'd inquire. "Twain, Dickens, or another of those wild Tarzan tales set in an Africa that Edgar Rice Burroughs invented? He never actually traveled there, you know, so his stories can't possibly be authentic."

On a good day I'd check out something that would gain Miss Hawkins' nod of approval, but until I finished reading everything Burroughs wrote I had to endure the clucks and frowns that assured me I was wasting a perfectly good mind.

Sarah didn't care for books or anything associated with them, including school. She just loved dolls. When we went to the library Sarah would sit and play with one of her dolls while I looked through the books. She had several expensive dolls that Mama had bought her—composition, papier mache, wax, and two with porcelain heads and shimmering silk dresses. Her favorites, though, were the rag dolls that Emiline made for her. She had five or six of them. Her nicer dolls mostly gathered dust on a shelf over her bed while she carried at least one rag doll everywhere she went.

Although Sarah's blue eyes could laugh by themselves, at times they reflected a great uncertainty within her, changing from merriment to worry in an instant. She inherited Mama's stunning looks, and a smattering of freckles about her nose and cheeks added a cute little-girl touch. Sarah was unaware of her beauty, however, and despite Mama's constant reminders of ways in which she could use it to her own advantage, she really didn't seem to care about it. She only cared about her dolls, and Emiline.

Many Southern children, especially those who grew up with any semblance of affluence, were practically raised by black people. Although Mama sometimes played the piano for us and read to us in the evenings, she spent her days making herself beautiful, working in her flower beds, and attending meetings of the garden club and church groups with Grandma Tolliver. We had more day-to-day contact with Emiline than we ever did with Mama.

Daddy saw Emiline only once a day, in the morning when she served breakfast to him and Sarah and me. He and Emiline had known each other for years, and he never failed to kid her about something. She always grinned when she first saw him in the morning, and within minutes he'd have her laughing at a joke of some kind. He often asked her to sit and eat with us, something a maid would never think of doing unless invited.

Emiline was gone by the time Daddy returned in the evening, but before she left in the afternoon she cooked our supper and set it in the oven. After supper the leftovers were saved for Emiline to take home to her family the following day—an accepted practice for all domestics.

Mama and Emiline had a strange relationship—strained and impersonal. Although Emiline followed Mama's every instruction perfectly and served her breakfast each day and lunch when she was home, Mama treated her with an aloofness that was unusual between the lady of the house and a maid who had been with her for years.

Because Mama didn't make an appearance in the morning until after we left for school, Sarah and I saw her only in the evening. After she served the supper that Emiline left, we'd all sit at the table and talk for awhile or retire to the front room where Mama would play the piano. Occasionally she and Daddy went out to sit in the porch swing and enjoy the cool of the evening before she kissed us goodnight and tucked us into bed.

Emiline was an integral part of our lives, and Sarah and I had the distinct feeling that she was there just for us. She packed our lunches, made last-minute adjustments to our clothes, wetted and patted down errant cowlicks, and admonished us to be good as she ushered us out the door to school each morning. In the afternoon she met us at the door as if we were the most important things in her life; she asked about our day, sat us down in the kitchen—after the obligatory hand washing—and gave us some sort of mouth-watering treat.

I remained curious about Jubal, and one day when Emiline was dusting the front room I approached her.

"Emiline," I said, then I stopped, uncertain as to whether or not I should be asking.

"Yes, Lucas," she said impatiently. "What you got on your mind, young man? Spit it out."

"Do you know Jubal," I asked.

"Jubal?" she said.

"That big Negro man, the one they call Dummy."

"Oh, Dummy," Emiline said with a little laugh. "I've been callin' him Dummy for so long I near forgot his actual name. Yes, I know who he is, same as everybody in town does."

"I mean do you really know him?"

Blacks normally avoided discussing members of their own race with white people, but since I was just a kid I guess Emiline felt more comfortable.

"I don't know Dummy, or Jubal, that is, very well," she said. "I stay away from him, and his mama too. They's both kind of standoffish. They don't talk much and nobody talks much to them."

"Do you think he's crazy?"

"Do I think he's crazy? Well, he stays out there in that shack with his mama and don't never go nowhere except to pull that wagon around town with all them clothes in it. He went to school for awhile when he was little, but he wouldn't try to read nor write nor do anything. Shied away from everybody, and he wouldn't say nary a word. That's why they called him Dummy. Then, when he got bigger, he begun to speak to a few folks, mostly just about what a pretty day it was. That's still about all he says to this day."

"What happened to his daddy?" I asked.

"Oh, you too little for that," Emiline said abruptly.

"You'll find out about such things all too soon."

"Did he throw somebody off of a levee?" I asked.

"Yes, I heard tell that during the big flood he throwed a man off the Mississippi levee and killed him."

"Killed him?! Why'd he do that?"

"During the flood they forced black men to work on the levee for weeks at a time, whether they wanted to or not. This other man—he was black too—kept ridin' Jubal every day; at least that's how I heard it. The man kept callin' him Dummy, and since Jubal wouldn't answer when he taunted him, he allowed that Jubal didn't have brains enough to talk. Well, he just kept on Jubal day after day, laughin' and carryin' on at his expense, and Jubal went on workin' and not sayin' a word. Then one day Jubal just reached over and grabbed the man, picked him up over his head, and threw him in the river. They say his body never even come to the surface again."

Emiline stopped dusting, shook her head, and looked thoughtful.

"Is Jubal crazy?" she said. "I don't rightly know; I just stay away from him."

Sarah kept a constant watch for Jubal on our walks around town, and would grow uneasy when we didn't see him.

"Where is he?" she'd say. "Do you think he's okay, Lucas?"

"Of course he's okay," I'd tell her, but nothing I said seemed to calm her anxiety.

"There he is!" she'd say, and I'd look up and see him coming down the street with his wagon. Then, as he passed by, Sarah would give him the same little wave that had got her into trouble with Mama. If Jubal thought nobody was watching, he'd grin shyly in our direction then continue on his way.

Shortly after Sarah and I left the house one morning she looked up at me and said, "Let's go to the swimming hole, Lucas."

"The swimming hole?" I repeated. "We can't go to the swimming hole. Mama would skin us alive if she found out."

"If we went now we could get back before she found out."

Although her suggestion had taken me by surprise, I knew she was right; the walk would take less than an hour. It was a nice day, and against my better judgment I let her talk me into it.

We walked on the edge of the fields in order to stay off the road, and ducked down behind the tall cotton whenever somebody passed by. When we arrived at the swimming hole, Sarah stood under the trees and looked around expectantly.

I asked her what she was looking for, but she said nothing. Suddenly her face broke into a happy smile and she pointed at the large cottonwood near the end of the swimming hole. Jubal peered out from behind the big tree, a shy grin creasing his face. I felt uneasy in his presence, even somewhat alarmed, but not Sarah.

"Come out," she said, and bounded toward him. Five feet from where he stood half hidden behind the tree, she stopped and held out her hand. They stood motionless for the longest time, a timid giant and a beckoning waif. Slowly, with his eyes lowered to the ground, Jubal stepped into the open. He reached out, took Sarah's small hand, and wrapped it in his.

"My name's Sarah," she said, leading him to where I stood. "And this is Lucas."

"I know," said Jubal. "I knows who you is. Sure is a pretty day, ain't it?"

At last I found my tongue, but only for an uncomfortable moment.

"Yes, it is a pretty day, Dum . . . Dum . . ." Red-faced, I stammered to a stop.

"It's okay, Mistuh Lucas," he said, his eyes dancing. "It's okay."

To my own surprise I thrust out my hand. "I'm pleased to meet you, Jubal."

"I'm pleased to meet you too, Mistuh Lucas," he said, engulfing my hand in a gentle shake.

"We see you walking around town with your wagon," said Sarah, "sometimes on our street."

"I knows where you live," Jubal said.

"You ought to come visit us at our house sometime," she said.

Her suggestion horrified me, but Jubal knew how to handle it.

"No, Sae-rah," he said, pronouncing her name with a long drawl. "I can't go to your house."

"Okay," she said with disappointment, "but I wish you could."

"And don't tell your mama about today neither," Jubal cautioned.

"We won't," Sarah said.

"Y'all better get on back now," he said, "before you get in trouble," and before Sarah could protest he stepped around the trunk of the big tree and was gone.

I looked at her inquisitively. "You seemed to know he was going to be here," I said.

"I did," she answered.

On the way back to town we squatted behind the cotton and watched the slow passing of an old black man on a creaky wagon pulled by a gaunt mule. I leaned close to Sarah and whispered: "Jubal sure is big. Don't he scare you?"

"No," she replied. "What's there to be scared of?"

Part II
Chapter Four

Although I was just a kid and perhaps poorly qualified to judge such things, it appeared to me that Mama had a pretty easy life. She didn't seem to view it that way herself, however. Like her own mother she was a frustrated social climber who found it impossible to gain acceptance into the wealthier circles which she envied so much. And being a beautiful woman who had ended up marrying a hometown guy and never experiencing anything beyond the limits of her cloistered world only added to her frustration.

When Mama wasn't working in her flower beds she'd be off attending meetings of the garden club or some of the same church and social events that she and her mother had frequented since she was a girl. Grandma Tolliver continued to accompany her to these gatherings and still sat and beamed when Mama played the piano to entertain the women.

I remember the first time Mama took Sarah with her to one of the ladies' clubs. She bought her a new pink dress just for the occasion, and matching pink bows to adorn her blond curls. The little dress billowed out prettily from her tiny waist, and when Mama stood her out in the middle of the room and turned her around and around I had to admit to myself that she was beautiful even if she was my sister.

"Look at my little beauty queen!" Mama said as she finished arranging the bright bows in her hair.

Grandma Tolliver, who was present for the occasion, echoed the praise.

"Why, Sarah Ann Dunaway, I declare you're as stunning as your mama was at your age, and I know you're going to knock the boys dead just like she did."

Sarah held tightly to her rag doll and said nothing.

"Okay, pretty girl, it's time to go," said Mama. "And let's leave this old doll at home." She pulled the doll from Sarah's reluctant grasp and tossed it on the sofa.

"But Mama, I want to take my dolly," Sarah said, a hint of panic in her voice. "She always goes with me."

"No," Mama said firmly. "You're going to be my little lady today, and you won't need a doll for that."

The doll lay askew against the back of the sofa, its head flopped to one side as if its neck was broken. Sarah looked at it longingly as she followed Mama and Grandma out the door, but she knew better than to protest any more.

When they returned from the party late that afternoon, Sarah retrieved her doll before going to change back into her play dress.

"Did you have fun?" I asked her.

"No," she said.

"Were there any other girls there to play with?"

"Yes, there were two other girls, but we all had to sit on

chairs and be still. I didn't care, though; they didn't want to play with me anyway."

"What makes you say that?" I asked.

"Because they were older than me, and all they wanted to do was sit and look prissy like their mamas." Then she hugged her doll and said, "I don't want to talk about it anymore."

Shortly after that, Mama decided it was time for Sarah to start playing the piano.

How would you like to learn to play the piano, Sarah?" Mama asked her one evening.

"I don't want to," Sarah said.

"No?" Mama exclaimed. "Why not?"

"Because I won't be able to do it like you."

"Oh yes you will," Mama said. "I know it sounds hard now, but you'll be playing like me in no time."

"No I won't," Sarah said.

Despite Sarah's protests, Mama hired a lady to come to the house and give her lessons. Mrs. Quitman, a prim, portly woman who wore plain black dresses and her hair in a tight bun, had taught Mama to play twenty years before. She would tutor Sarah once a week.

"This is Sarah, Mrs. Quitman," said Mama. "She doesn't think she can learn to play."

"My, aren't you a pretty little thing!" exclaimed Mrs. Quitman. "Why, you're just as pretty as your mama, Sarah, and we're going to teach you to play the piano like her too. What do you think of that?"

Sarah clung to her doll.

I seldom stayed in the house when Sarah was taking her lessons. Not only did it sound awful, it was a painful thing to watch. She and Mrs. Quitman sat side by side on the piano bench, Sarah's tiny frame dwarfed by the woman's bulk, her rag doll lying lonely on the floor behind them. There they would struggle through forty-five minutes of frustration for the woman and absolute hell for Sarah. Sometimes Mama sat and listened for awhile, trying but failing to overcome an ever growing frown, then finally she'd shake her head and get up and leave.

Sarah had to practice in the evening after supper, with Mama sitting close by and correcting every wrong note she hit, which was nearly every one. I couldn't escape the torture, nor could Daddy. Mama wouldn't let me retreat to my room where I could close the door, so I'd sit at the dining room table and read, trying inconspicuously to cover my ears.

That way I could at least separate myself from the horrific sounds by one room. Daddy wasn't so lucky, and I have to give him credit; when Sarah played, he sat in the front room and took the punishment head on. For awhile I worried that I was the only one who considered the incessant plinking offensive, but one evening I caught Daddy's eye from the front room and he winked at me. I felt some solace knowing that he shared my misery.

One afternoon as I walked into the yard I heard the piano playing in the front room. Who could it be? I knew Mama wasn't home, and it sounded far too good to be Sarah. I opened the front door and gasped in surprise. Sarah sat at the piano playing while Emiline stood behind her, humming and swaying to the music.

"Oh, play it, girl!" Emiline said. "Listen to your sister, Lucas. Ain't she good! When I heard she was takin' piano lessons I knew she'd be good at it."

Sarah turned her head toward me and grinned shyly.

"Keep it up, Sarah," Emiline said. "You gonna be knockin' folks dead all over town playin' like that."

Sarah basked in Emiline's praise and played the piano as I'd never dreamed she could. I sat and listened for half an hour, shaking my head in disbelief. Later that evening, when it came time for her to practice, I waited for Sarah to take the rest of the family by surprise as she had me. It wasn't to be, however. When Sarah began playing, with Mama standing over her shoulder and ridiculing her every move, she went back to plinking out the same ragged, broken lines as before. I felt bad for Sarah, and I never told anyone how she had played that afternoon.

The holiday season had begun, and one day a couple of weeks before Christmas Emiline mentioned Sarah's playing to Mama. On several occasions when Mama had been gone, Emiline told her, Sarah played every piece in her practice book without opening it. Since Emiline knew how to play the piano herself, Mama listened closely when she described how talented Sarah was for a child of six.

"That girl must take after you, Miss Jessica," Emiline said, "playin' all them songs by heart like that."

Mama didn't answer, nor did she smile.

Graydon Hardiman knew the value of an employee as talented and conscientious as Daddy, and every year he and his wife invited us to a holiday dinner on the weekend before Christmas. Visiting the Hardiman house was the highlight of Mama's year. She began talking about it sometime in November, her daily allusions to the event arousing the interest of those who envied her and the chagrin of those who tired of listening to it.

Whether she happened to be talking with the members of one of her clubs, a group of ladies at church, or a clerk in a downtown store, Mama would manage to bring up the subject. "Oh yes, we enjoy our regular holiday visits to the Hardimans," she'd say, quite matter-of-factly, of course. A lady never bubbled over such things.

Grandma Tolliver talked about our Hardiman visits as much as Mama, maybe more, vicariously living a few grand hours she could never experience herself.

The Hardiman mansion stood at the end of Robert E. Lee Street—not on the side of the street like its large neighbors, but across the end where it dominated the scene. A wrought-iron gate flanked by tall spires opened onto an oak-lined lane that stretched a hundred yards through the grounds, the commanding entrance to the house looming at the far end.

Although the house had been built after the turn of the century, the Hardimans faithfully reproduced an antebellum-style structure of light brick with white trim fronted by majestic columns—a bold mansion reminiscent of the grandeur of the Old South. A second-story veranda spacious enough for ballroom dancing overlooked the expansive grounds. Half a dozen varieties of oak towered as tall as the peaks of the slate roof while the brilliant greens of sculptured magnolias interspersed among the oaks served to brighten the grounds even in winter.

Daddy and I wore suits and ties, which we both hated, and Sarah wore the pink dress that Mama had bought her for club meetings. She hated that too. Mama wore a long white gown with a bright red sash that Daddy allowed had cost more than our car.

"Try not to swoon in the entryway, Jessica," Daddy said as we drove through the front gate.

"Now don't try to make light of this, Reid," Mama said. "Not everything in the world is a joke, you know. The Hardimans are one of the wealthiest families in Mississippi, and it's our good fortune to get to visit their home once a year."

"It just might have something to do with my hard work too," said Daddy, with a wry grin and a sidewise glance at Mama. She ignored him.

"Sarah, you leave that old doll in the car," Mama said. "You're going to be a little lady this evening."

Mama could have swooned in the Hardiman's entryway and been justified; it was surely the most stunning in the Delta, perhaps in all of Mississippi. A handsome black butler, tall and formally dressed, showed us in with a bow and took our wraps. He hung them on an elegant hall tree that probably had cost as much as our car.

Sarah and I turned our heads slowly, taking in the burgundy draperies that fell in great folds on either side of the massive front doors and the standing portraits of ancestors that reached nearly from the floor to the lofty ceiling. A grand chandelier of glass and polished brass sparkled in the reflections of a thousand tiny prisms dancing among its lights.

Graydon and Kathleen Hardiman appeared from a side door.

"Good evening, Reid, Jessica," said Graydon. "And hello, Lucas and Sarah. Merry Christmas to you all!"

Then just as he did when we visited the Mercantile, he bent down grandly to kiss Sarah on the forehead and shake my hand.

"Merry Christmas, Graydon," said Daddy, shaking the man's hand heartily. And though Kathleen Hardiman was standing stiff and aloof beside her husband, Daddy reached out and gave her the same warm hug he might have given Emiline.

"Good evening, Mister Hardiman," Mama said, tentatively holding out her hand to him. Then turning to his wife, she swept her eyes up and down the hallway and exclaimed, "Kathleen, I am forever awed by the grandeur of your home."

"Why, thank you, Jessica," the woman said with a counterfeit smile. "We enjoy it, and we do so enjoy having guests for the holidays."

With that she turned and led us down the hall to another door which the dark butler hurried to open before us. "Please, come join us in the parlor," Mrs. Hardiman said.

The parlor was larger than our front room and dining room combined, and the high ceiling gave it a grand feel. Antique furnishings of flowing Empire design shone in the reddish glow of satin-shaded lamps while holiday candles flickered in various spots throughout the room. The ceiling was twelve feet high, and the perfectly sculptured Christmas tree adorning one corner nearly touched it. The tree was decorated in two striking colors only: red and white.

A large bay extended out from one side of the parlor, a grand piano gleaming in the light that fell through its tall windows. I remembered the piano's fine, clear tone from Mama's playing it on previous visits.

Mama and Daddy shared a sofa of mahogany and velvet while the Hardimans sat facing them in a pair of great wingback chairs. Daddy laughed easily as he discussed family and business with Mr. Hardiman, but Mama appeared ill at ease conversing with Kathleen. I wondered what made coming here so important to her.

Sarah and I sat on a second sofa of dark horsehair, saying nothing. I looked around the room and remembered the first time I had discovered that the walls were not papered, but covered in canvas and painted by an artist. Initially the walls didn't catch one's attention, but after a moment's concentration the subdued browns, yellows, ochres, and greens came alive in a panorama of rambling fields, wooded glens, and wildlife—landscapes that seemed to appear out of the imagination.

I don't think Sarah noticed anything. She sat holding her hands in her lap and stared at them intently.

When a black maid opened a door from the next room and nodded at Mrs. Hardiman, she smiled and said: "Dinner is served."

"Sounds good to me, Kathleen," said Daddy, standing up and patting his belly as if he might be preparing to eat in a downtown cafe. Mama nodded sternly at Sarah and me as we filed into the dining room, a silent warning to remember our table manners.

The dining room had the same painted walls as the parlor, only in slightly lighter shades. Mr. Hardiman sat at one end of the long table and his wife at the other; two glistening candelabras flanked a golden turkey that rested between them. Mama and Daddy took seats on one side and motioned Sarah and me to sit on the other.

As Sarah struggled to pull the heavy chair up underneath her, she managed to bump the table, causing the candle flames to wave back and forth and the water glasses to rock. A few drops of water sloshed from the glasses onto the linen tablecloth.

"Sarah!" Mama said with a grimace. "Do be careful, girl."

"Oh, don't worry about it," Graydon said, smiling at Sarah. "When our kids were growing up they've been known to knock things completely off the table and onto the floor."

Sarah looked mortified when it happened, but she relaxed when Mr. Hardiman passed it off.

We bowed our heads while Mrs. Hardiman said the blessing, then Graydon stood up and carved the steaming bird. After he served each of us a portion of turkey, two black maids appeared; one poured wine for the grownups and milk for the children while the other ladled food onto our plates.

The low seat in Sarah's chair forced her to reach higher than she was accustomed. Halfway through the meal she misjudged while reaching for her glass of milk and knocked it over. As the milk soaked through a great patch of tablecloth, ran under the turkey, the serving dishes, and onto the floor, the maids hurried in and began cleaning it up. Mama covered her mouth and stared at the table in horror; Sarah dropped her hands in her lap and closed her eyes, trying to hold back tears.

"I'm sorry," she said, her words barely audible.

Daddy stood up and walked around the table.

"It's all right, Sweetheart," he said, leaning over and wrapping his arms around Sarah's neck. "It's Christmas, and everything is kind of overwhelming, isn't it? It's not the end of the world, though. We'll just wait 'til they get the milk cleaned up, then we'll go on and finish eating."

Mr. Hardiman smiled at Sarah and nodded his agreement. His wife tried to smile but did a poor job of it. Mama picked up her wine glass and drained it.

After we resumed eating, one of the maids refilled Mama's glass. She offered to refill Daddy's too, but he declined.

Sarah had stopped crying, but now seemed afraid to move.

"Go ahead and eat some more, Darlin'," Mama said with a forced smile. "Everything's okay now."

Sarah picked up her fork and began eating, but didn't touch her milk again.

Mama began talking more toward the end of the meal, and I noticed that her wine glass was empty again. The maid refilled it. When everyone finished eating, Mr. Hardiman sat up straight in his chair, dashed his napkin to the table, and announced, "Shall we retire to the parlor and let this big meal settle? Bring your drinks with you if you'd like."

"I believe I will," Mama said. She was the only one who did.

I put my hand on Sarah's shoulder as we left the dining room. She looked at me and smiled "thank you." After everyone had taken seats in the parlor, Mr. Hardiman turned to Mama and said, "Well, Jessica, are you going to honor us by playing the piano this evening?"

"I'd love to," said Mama with a demur smile.

She stood up and walked to the piano. For a moment she stopped to admire it, then sat down and ran her hands reverently over the keys. She began to play. Sitting in that elegant room with the flickering glow of the candlelight dancing along the walls, I had never heard her play more beautifully. We smiled our approval as she played all the traditional Christmas carols, and we sang along with the final one: "Silent Night."

"Bravo!" said Mr. Hardiman, standing up and clapping his hands vigorously.

We all followed his lead, clapping and grinning until the limelight made Mama blush.

"Thank you all, but no encores," she said, returning to her seat.

"You do have a talent, Jessica," Kathleen Hardiman said. "It would be wonderful if you could pass it along to your daughter."

"Oh, yes," Mama said, sipping her wine. "Sarah is taking

lessons already, and doing quite well, I might add. She knows every song in her practice book."

Sarah dropped her eyes and sank into the sofa.

"Might she feel like playing for us?" Kathleen asked, looking at Sarah with the first genuine smile I'd ever seen on her face.

"Of course she would," Mama said. "Wouldn't you, Sarah?"

Sarah shook her head, almost imperceptibly, and looked at Mama with eyes that begged her to stop.

"Go ahead and play for us, Darlin'," Mama said. "I know you can do it. Emiline told me so."

Sarah stared at the floor and sat frozen in her seat. I think we all wished Mama would stop, but she was committed now. She took another drink of wine and walked to the sofa where Sarah and I sat.

"Come on, Baby," she said. "This is the perfect time."

I rose to Sarah's defense, or at least I attempted to.

"I don't think she feels like it now, Mama," I pleaded.

Mama's cold glance told me she didn't care for my help. She took Sarah by the hand, pulled her to her feet, and led her reluctantly across the room to the piano.

Sarah sank to the bench and looked at the keyboard as if it were something to fear.

"All right, Darlin', play anything you want," Mama told her, and walked back to her chair.

Daddy's brow was furrowed, his eyes questioning. I saw him trying to get Mama's attention, but she was focused on Sarah.

"Go on, Darlin', go on and play," Mama urged.

Finally Sarah touched her fingers to the keys and plinked a few notes. The sound seemed to startle her. I could hardly stand to watch.

"Go on, Sarah, play your favorite," I blurted, too loudly. Then catching myself, I spoke calmly. "I know you can do it. Play it like you did for Emiline and me."

That earned me another dark look from Mama, but her face turned to surprise when Sarah began to play. "You Are My Sunshine," Sarah's favorite tune, rang out perfectly. Mama hadn't even known she could play it.

Everyone broke into smiles, even Sarah. Daddy's mouth dropped open in disbelief.

"Oh, Baby!" Mama said, clapping her hands. "Now don't forget to . . . "

The music stopped. Sarah looked at Mama, her hands shaking, her lips quivering, her eyes filled with fear.

"Don't stop!" said Mama. "For God's sake, Sarah. Play."

Sarah turned back to the piano, her eyes filling with tears, and began fingering the keys randomly.

"Sarah?" Mama said quizzically, then covered her mouth in horror as a puddle of water began to form on the bench beside Sarah. The puddle grew, stood quivering in place for a moment, then ran off the bench and onto the floor.

Sarah sat at the piano, her face red with embarrassment, tears streaming down her cheeks, her own water dripping off the bench beside her.

"Oh, my God!" Mama cried, and ran to Sarah. Grabbing her up by the arm, she whisked Sarah across the floor and out the door to the bathroom. The four of us sat in stunned silence, then Kathleen stood up and quietly left the room.

Graydon Hardiman turned to Daddy.

"I think I'm going to have a glass of brandy, Reid. Care to join me?"

"Yes, I certainly would," Daddy said.

When Daddy and Graydon had finished their brandies, the butler opened the door that led to the hallway. Mama stood in the doorway, her face strained and ashen. Sarah stood behind her looking at her feet, her shoulders slumped, her arms hanging at her sides.

"I think it's time for us to go, Reid," Mama said.

"Probably so," Daddy answered.

He and Graydon stood up and walked to the doorway as Mama backed out of it and turned her face away. Kathleen Hardiman stood twenty feet away down the hall; she followed at a distance as we walked to the front door. The butler helped us into our coats, then waited to open the door.

"Good night, Reid," said Graydon, shaking Daddy's hand. "Good night, Jessica, Lucas. And good night, Sarah. Thank you for coming." Sarah didn't look up.

"Good night all," Kathleen managed as we were leaving. The butler closed the door behind us, and we were alone.

Daddy held the car door open for Mama while Sarah and I crawled into the back seat. We sat still as stones. Daddy slid under the wheel, started the engine, switched on the lights, and slowly drove down the shadowy lane toward Robert E. Lee Street. Mama began to cry, lowly at first, then louder and louder until she bent forward in her seat and held her face in her hands, great sobs racking her body.

"Jessica!" Daddy said in alarm.

Mama rose up, her voice ripping the tight air inside the car.

"MY GOD!" she screamed. "I've NEVER been so embarrassed."

"Oh, Jessica. It's not that bad," Daddy said.

"NOT THAT BAD! How can you say that? The worst night of my life, and right there in the Hardiman's parlor."

"I don't think your daughter had a particularly enjoyable evening either," Daddy said. For a moment I thought he might take up for Sarah, but Mama shouted him down.

"All she had to do was play the piano," Mama said, raising her fists in frustration. "That's all; just play. She plays for everyone else—even the maid, for God's sake—but not for me. Not even when it counted the most. And you say it's not that bad, Reid? I wish I were dead."

Daddy didn't answer. Sarah sunk into the seat and clung to her doll.

Sarah never played the piano again, nor did Mama ever ask her to. Mrs. Quitman stopped coming to the house, and the first time Emiline mentioned her playing, Sarah broke into tears. When Emiline asked what was wrong, Sarah wouldn't answer.

The next afternoon I took Emiline aside and told her what had happened at the Hardimans. She covered her mouth in shock.

"Oh, that angel," she said. "That poor, poor angel."

Chapter Five

Since we were out of school for the holidays, on the Monday morning following the incident at the Hardimans Sarah and I asked Mama if we could walk downtown. She had just got up and was sitting at the kitchen table drinking a cup of coffee while Emiline fixed her breakfast.

"Okay," she said sleepily, "but be careful. And get home in good time."

"We will, Mama," I said. We kissed her on the cheek, grabbed our coats, and rushed for the door.

"Take care of your sister, Lucas," Emiline whispered as she closed the door behind us.

It was a clear day, and unseasonably warm for December. Before we had made it halfway down the block, Sarah turned to me and said, "Let's go to the swimming hole, Lucas."

"No," I said. "You know we're not supposed to be going to the swimming hole by ourselves. We already got away with it once, and we'd be in big trouble if Mama ever found out."

To my surprise, Sarah didn't argue. Instead she grew quiet and walked along with her hands in her pockets staring at the ground. A silent block later I stopped and looked into her crestfallen face.

"All right," I said. "I guess we can go to the swimming hole, but we'll have to hurry."

"I'll hurry, Lucas!" she said. She grabbed my hand and bounded down the street, nearly jerking me off my feet trying to keep up with her.

The cotton fields lay brown and bare as we headed for Sorghum Creek, and this time we had nowhere to hide from passersby. That worried me.

"I sure hope nobody sees us and tells Mama," I said.

"Oh, they won't," Sarah said, trying to sound confident. She probably wasn't any more confident than me—just afraid I'd get cold feet and nix the trip.

A few black farmers passed us on the road, but no one we knew, and soon we walked under the grove of trees that marked the swimming hole. All except the live oaks—the giants that retained their green all winter—had lost their leaves.

As if on cue, Jubal stepped from behind the big cottonwood. In one hand he held a small tow sack. It surprised me to see him here again, but Sarah acted as if she had expected him.

"Jubal!" she cried joyfully. She ran to him, reached around his thick leg with both arms, and leaned her head against it. "I missed you," she said.

The sight of Sarah hugging Jubal embarrassed me, even horrified me. This just wasn't done; white children were not supposed to act that way toward black people.

"I missed you too, Sarah," Jubal said, looking down uncomfortably and holding his hands away from his body to avoid touching her. He knew that such displays of affection between the races were not only frowned upon but taboo, especially when they involved a black man and a white girl. At the moment, however, he found himself helpless in Sarah's grasp.

"Sure is a pretty day, ain't it, Mistuh Lucas?" he said nervously.

"Yes, I guess it is, Jubal," I replied, trying to smile.

He seemed to relax a bit. "What you kids been doin'?" he asked.

I told him about going to the Hardimans' house for dinner.

"The Hardimans," he said, nodding. "Was the food good?"

I told him it was.

"Did y'all have fun?" he asked.

"No!" said Sarah, letting go of his leg and clenching her fists at her sides. "It wasn't any fun at all. I hated it."

Jubal looked confused at Sarah's outburst, and at a loss to reply. He held up the tow sack and said, "I brung somethin' for you."

That snapped Sarah out of her anger. "Something for me?" she asked happily.

A smile creased his lips. "For both of you," he said.

"What is it?" Sarah asked, clapping her hands and dancing in anticipation.

Jubal reached into the tow sack and drew out an ancient doll. The doll's face, arms, and legs were black, and stuffed with brittle straw that poked through the fabric in places.

And though the tiny homespun dress looked terribly old, it showed no tears; even the hand-stitching remained intact. Button eyes with painted pupils and a hand-sewn smile lent merriment to the faded black face.

"My grandmama's," Jubal said. "She was a slave."

Sarah stared wide-eyed at the doll, overwhelmed. When Jubal held out the doll to her, she seemed afraid to take it.

"Go ahead, Sarah," he urged. "She's yours."

Slowly Sarah reached out and took the doll in her hands. Holding it as if it might break, she looked into the smiling black face with wonder.

"She be Mandy," said Jubal. "My mama's name."

"Mandy," Sarah said, and hugged the doll to her chest.

Jubal reached into the tow sack again, this time withdrawing a small metal wagon covered with rust. Holding the toy wagon in his right hand, he rolled it back and forth across the palm of his left. The spoked wheels turned freely, and the tongue and front axle pivoted on a hand-wrought rivet. A tiny seat rested on delicate springs, and intricate sideboards fit perfectly into the little bed. The dark rust formed only a thin protective sheen over the iron. I had seen similar toys, antiques, and I knew it had been hand-crafted by a blacksmith, probably in the 1800s.

Jubal looked immensely pleased as he held out the little wagon to me, and I froze.

"Oh, no," I said, backing away. "You must have had it for a long time."

He lowered the wagon to his side, his chin dropping to his chest.

"I brung it for you, Mistuh Lucas. My daddy gived it to me, and I wanted you to have it."

I had never found myself in such a situation, but as I faced Jubal in that awkward moment somehow I knew that to refuse the gift would hurt him deeply.

"I'd like to have the little wagon, Jubal," I said. "I'd love it."

His eyes lit up again, and he handed me the ancient treasure.

"Thank you," I said, turning each wheel slowly. "I'll keep it forever."

"You's welcome, Mistuh Lucas. You's more'n welcome."

Then as Sarah stood clutching her doll and I admiring my wagon, Jubal raised his hand and said, "Bye, Sarah. Bye, Mistuh Lucas. I gots to be goin' now," and he disappeared around the big cottonwood.

I looked at Sarah in wonder.

"How did you know he'd come?" I asked her. "How did you know he wouldn't be in town making deliveries?"

"He doesn't go to town till after noon," she said. "And if anybody goes to the swimming hole in the morning, he knows it."

Mama never learned about our going to the creek that day. Fondling my little wagon on the way home, I said: "We'll have to hide these from Mama."

"I know," Sarah said. We hid the gifts under our beds and covered them up with other toys.

Later that week we went to the country for our annual holiday dinner with Grandma and Grandpa Dunaway. Eating at their house was relaxing compared to dining with the Hardimans, and far more enjoyable.

Grandma and Grandpa's farmhouse, a simple two-story painted a warm shade of blue, sat half hidden in a grove of tall oaks at the end of a dirt road. A faded red barn and several outbuildings sat farther back in the trees, invisible until one drove into the yard. A welcoming committee of variously colored dogs—large, small, and every size in between—barked at our approach and ran out to greet us. The only thing the disparate array of dogs had in common was a friendly nature; Grandpa wouldn't tolerate an unfriendly animal on his place.

"Hello, folks," Grandma said. "How's my sweethearts?"

She stood at the door with her arms open wide, a white apron covering the front of a gaily flowered dress. Sarah and I ran to her as she bent down to give us a hearty hug.

John Dunaway, who had been standing ramrod straight a few feet behind Grandma, squatted down and hugged us too, the hint of a smile creasing his stern face. He looked us up and down and stared us directly in the eye.

"How are you kids doing these days?" he asked.

"We're fine, Grandpa," Sarah said merrily, hugging his neck until he gently pried himself loose from her grasp. Grandpa's serious air made me a little wary of him when we were little, but it never bothered Sarah. She'd cling to one of his legs when he was standing, and climb onto his lap every time he sat down. And even when Grandpa was holding a conversation with someone or concentrating on something else, I'd notice him absentmindedly patting her on the head or stroking her hair.

Daddy's brother, our Uncle Robert, brought his family to dinner on the same day. We had seen his mule and wagon standing beside the house when we arrived; he didn't own a car. Despite the example that Grandpa had worked hard to set for his children, Robert hadn't managed to avoid the redneck trappings of their poverty-ridden childhood as Daddy had. Robert dropped out of school in his early teens and became a sharecropper himself before the age of twenty.

He was lanky like Daddy but not as tall, and he wore bib overalls and a straw hat every day of the year. And having gained a bucktoothed wife named Mona and six country-shy kids, Robert showed no signs of ever rising above the simple existence he chose.

Daddy's two sisters, Eunice and Esther, were several years older than he and Robert. Both had married farmers; one was a sharecropper and the other ran a small cotton operation of his own. I never could keep track of how many kids they had, but they had plenty. Because Grandma and Grandpa's house wasn't large enough to accommodate all of their children and grandchildren at once, Aunt Eunice and Aunt Esther brought their families to dinner on a different day during the holidays. Since Daddy and his sisters had never been close, this arrangement seemed to work fine for everyone concerned.

Daddy and Uncle Robert didn't seem close either, although judging from the boyhood stories Daddy told on the two of them they must have gotten along well as young-sters. Apparently having a brother as smart and studious as Daddy and watching him go off to school in town, become a star athlete, marry a beautiful girl, and land a well-paying job had created an uncomfortable distance between him and his siblings. After I got old enough to consider such things I found it interesting that none of them ever attempted to span that distance; I suppose they didn't understand it well enough to know what to do about it.

Grandma and Grandpa's house was plainly furnished but clean and warm. Family pictures hung on every wall; Grandma's mementos and knick knacks rested here and there on sideboards and end tables; and Grandpa's double-barreled shotgun occupied a place of honor above the mantle. It felt like more than a house—it was a home, and I loved it.

The downstairs consisted of a small bathroom, a large kitchen, and a combination front room and dining room that gave the interior a more open look than most houses I'd seen. We called it the big room. The bedrooms were all upstairs, all but one unused now that Grandma and Grandpa were the only ones living there.

Mama and Mona helped Grandma in the kitchen while Grandpa, Daddy, and Uncle Robert visited in the big room. A tree decorated with handmade ornaments and garlands of popcorn strung on sewing thread filled one corner. Sarah rested on Grandpa's lap while the men talked, and I sat and read the book I had brought.

"Where are all those kids of yours, Robert?" Grandpa asked. "I've hardly seen any of them since you got here."

"Oh, they're runnin' around outside somewhere, probably down in the woods," Robert said. "They don't spend much time in the house. Run around like a bunch of wild rabbits at home."

Grandpa chuckled.

"Sounds like a couple of boys I used to know." Robert and Daddy looked at each other and exchanged a grin.

From my chair I could see into the kitchen where Mama was attempting to make small talk.

"Well, what have you been doing lately, Mona?" she asked Robert's wife, who looked suspiciously pregnant again.

"Oh, tendin' the garden, feedin' the hogs and chickens, keepin' track of the kids, and tryin' to see that we got enough food on the table to make a meal," Mona said, a perpetual sigh in her voice. "And what do you spend your time at, Jessica?"

"I meet regularly with my garden club and quilting group," said Mama. "And I work with several church and social groups in town as well—volunteer work such as visiting the elderly and infirm, all sorts of things like that. And I work in my flower garden, of course. There just doesn't seem to be enough time in the day to get it all done."

From the look on Mona's face Mama might as well have said she spent her time walking on the moon.

Robert's kids magically showed up just before time to eat. They all came in the back door and started filing through the kitchen, until Grandma noticed them tracking mud across her floor.

"Get yourselves out of this kitchen!" she hollered,

grabbing a broom and swatting the bunch of them back outside as fast as they could crowd through the door. "Y'all clean them feet off out there," Grandma said, "then get back in here and wash your dirty hands before you sit down at the table."

Robert looked at Grandpa and shook his head.

"Mom's still got the old fire, ain't she?" Grandpa just smiled.

Everyone drank sweet tea at dinner, and Grandma's turkey tasted every bit as good as the Hardimans'. It was next to impossible to get the piece you wanted, however, with Robert's kids digging in with both hands.

"Eat with your silverware," their mother admonished them several times, but judging by the clumsy way they hefted their knives, forks, and spoons and sneaked looks at the rest of us for clues as to how to operate the instruments, I was sure they didn't use them at home.

The second time one of the boys reached for the turkey with his hand, Grandpa rapped him across the knuckles with the back of his knife—not hard, just enough to get his attention. It scared the kid so bad he didn't eat any more turkey.

We finished eating early in the afternoon, topping the meal off with pumpkin pie and whipped cream, then everyone moved to the big room. All the kids sat on the floor while Grandma Dunaway handed out gifts, one to each grandchild. Unhappily, we could only look at the colorfully wrapped packages and try and shake them a bit; we had to take them home and open them on Christmas Day.

After the gift giving, Robert herded his kids outside and

into the wagon bed. He helped Mona (who had confided at dinner that she was indeed pregnant again) up onto the seat, then climbed up himself.

"Got to get home and get the chores done," he said cheerfully, and drove the mule and his growing brood off down the road.

We went back in the house and sat down to visit with Grandma and Grandpa awhile longer. When Mama could no longer keep from yawning and Sarah had fallen asleep on Grandpa's lap, Daddy said it was time to go.

"I love you, Grandpa," Sarah said sleepily as John Dunaway gently lowered her onto the back seat.

"I love you too," said Grandpa.

Christmas morning at our house was much the same as previous years. Mama got a new coat and a red satin blouse that probably cost more than Daddy could afford; Daddy got two books as well as shirts, socks, and other Daddy-type Christmas things; I got several books and a shirt that matched one of his; and Sarah got two dolls—a rather plain one made of white cotton fabric and a striking one with a porcelain face and a green velvet dress. And though Sarah and I were pleased when we opened our packages, the gifts that Jubal had given us at the swimming hole far outshone any we received that morning.

Grandma and Grandpa Tolliver came to our house for dinner that afternoon. Emiline didn't complain about having to work on Christmas Day; nearly every black servant in town worked on holidays. Mama gave Emiline a new work dress, and she seemed genuinely pleased when she opened the package.

During dinner Grandma smiled at Sarah and said, "I hear you've been taking piano lessons, Sarah. Would you like to play something for us after dinner?"

Sarah's eyes darted nervously at Mama then back at her plate.

"She's not taking lessons anymore," Mama said curtly. Grandma frowned, glanced back and forth between Mama and Sarah, then let it drop.

After dinner Sarah went to our room to play with her new dolls while Mama and Grandma sat and visited at the dining room table. Grandpa Tolliver, Daddy, and I retired to the front room, where Grandpa lit up one of his infernal cigars. He leaned back on the sofa and said, "Hear about that bunch killin' them two coloreds over by Hunter Springs last week, Reid?"

I was seated across the room from them looking at one of my new books. I kept my head down and pretended to be reading, and I guess Daddy thought I couldn't hear their conversation.

"Yes, I heard about it," Daddy said, the disgust apparent in his voice. "People always seem to talk about such things at the Mercantile."

"Raped a white girl," Grandpa said. "Goddamn black heathens. Them Cheetham County boys got them good, though. Heard they tied them to trees first and whipped them raw. Then, before they strung them up, they chopped off their fingers and toes and passed them around for souvenirs. Cut off their ears and held an auction for them right there on the spot; somebody paid five dollars for one of them. And after they hung the niggers they built a big fire and burnt the bodies."

"Yeah, I heard all that too," Daddy said. "Nap Canfield and Herman Slocum bragged about being there, and others sounded proud that some of their relatives had participated in it. I also heard that nobody had any proof those Negroes had ever been near that girl—only her word that it happened."

"Aw, hell, you know they done it," Grandpa Tolliver said. "A nigger will do that ever chance he gets. Ought to string up more of them black devils than we do. Helps keep them in their place, you know."

Chapter Six

We started back to school after the holidays, and life pretty much returned to normal. It was Sarah's first year, and because she acted so shy around other kids I took on the role of protective big brother. Since I never particularly cared to hang around with boys my age anyway, it was an easy role to assume. I even kept watch on my sister at recess.

It wasn't out of shyness that I avoided making friends with other boys in my class, nor was I consciously aware that I avoided them at all. I liked most people and had a natural tendency to try and get along with everyone; I simply had different interests than most kids my age.

I'm sure I was considered a square, but that didn't bother me. And unlike most squares, I wasn't bothered by bullies. Daddy taught me something that helped me deal with belligerent people. Bullies can smell fear, he said, and if they sense that you're not afraid of them it takes all the fun out of picking on you.

Daddy was right; I was in third grade the first time an

older kid put his hands on my chest and shoved me back-wards, nearly knocking me off my feet. His regular gang of followers stood laughing at my humiliation until I slugged him in his sneering face and knocked him flat. He ran away, holding his hands over his mouth and wailing like a girl. After that the bullies left me alone.

Sarah and I walked back and forth to school together, and although I knew she didn't like to talk about school, occasionally I'd ask her how things were going. The con-versations were usually short, and invariably one-sided.

"What did your teacher talk about in class today, Sarah?" I'd ask.

"Nothing much," she'd reply.

"Nothing?"

"Oh, ABCs, how to spell words, stuff like that."

"Does the teacher ever ask the class questions?"

"Sometimes."

"Do you hold up your hand to answer them?"

"No."

"Does she ever call on you to answer a question?"

"Yes."

"What do you do then?"

"I don't say nothing."

"Why not?"

"'Cause when I do everybody laughs at me."

"Don't they laugh at the other kids the same way?"

"No. Just at me."

One afternoon as we were walking home from school

Sarah and I saw Mama's car pull over to the curb a block up the street. Mama got out and slammed the door as we approached, then she stomped around and looked down at the right front tire with a scowl.

"Damn, flat tire!" we heard her mutter as we walked up.

"Hi, Mama," I said. "Got a flat?"

"Yes, and I'm due at a meeting at Viola Bridge's house right now," she said. Sarah took my hand when she heard the tone of Mama's voice.

"Why don't you call Daddy?" I said. "He could come and fix it."

"Oh, I'd miss the whole party by the time he got here and changed it," she said, looking up and down the street in frustration.

A black man happened to step out the front door of a shop across the street at that very moment.

"Hey, Boy," Mama hollered.

The man looked at her with a question on his face.

"You, come over here," she said, jerking her arm impatiently.

The black man was several years older than Mama, and neatly dressed in a dark suit, a white shirt, a gray felt hat, and a tie. As he was crossing the street I recognized him.

"Yes, Ma'am," the man said, removing his hat and smiling at Sarah and me as he avoided Mama's eyes.

"I've got a flat," Mama said, pointing at the offending tire.

"Yes, Ma'am, I can see that you do," he said, nodding his head in concern. "Well, I need it changed," Mama said.

Holding his hat in his hand, the man glanced nervously down at his clothes. "You want me to change that tire, Ma'am?" he said.

"Yes, I want you to change that tire, Boy, and hurry it up. I'm late for a meeting."

I felt embarrassed for him. "Ma'am," the man said, "do you mind if I lay my hat and coat on the hood of your car while I work, so as not to get them dirty?"

"No, go ahead," Mama said.

After carefully laying his coat on the hood and his hat on top of it, the man tucked his tie into the front of his shirt. Then he opened Mama's trunk and lifted out the spare tire, jack, and lug wrench.

Sarah and I stood holding hands on the sidewalk as the man sat down in the dirt and reached under the car to position the jack. Mama looked down at us as if she might have just noticed us.

"Well, how was school today?" she asked.

"It was good," I said eagerly. "Mrs. Chambers talked about Mark Twain."

"And how about you, little girl?" she asked Sarah.

"It was okay," Sarah said, looking at the sidewalk.

"Okay?" Mama said sarcastically. "Just okay? What did you study?"

"Nothing much," Sarah replied.

"Nothing much?" said Mama, shaking her head.

Then she turned her attention back to the black man working on her car. He was squatting down fitting the spare tire onto the lugbolts, his trousers wrinkled and dusty, his white shirt streaked with grease, his hands and arms covered with grime.

"Are you about done, Boy?" Mama demanded.

"Yes, Ma'am. Just about done," the man said.

He finished quickly, put the flat tire in Mama's trunk, and closed the lid.

"There you are, Ma'am; it's ready to go."

He retrieved his hat and coat from the hood of the car, nodded at Sarah and me, and walked away. Mama didn't even thank him.

I couldn't contain myself any longer.

"That was Mister Chaney, Mama, the principal of one of the Negro schools!"

"*Mister* Chaney?" she said sarcastically. "What do I care if he's principal of a *Negro* school? I don't know why we send them to school anyway. What good's it going to do to teach them anything?"

Mama leaned down into our faces. "What am I raising here, a couple of nigger lovers?" With that she got back in the car, started the engine, and drove off with a roar.

That was the first time I remembered smelling whiskey on her breath.

It seemed to me that life went from good to bad overnight, but considering that Mama had been more vocal in her disagreements and generally more opinionated and argumentative for some time, the change was probably more gradual than my child's perception of it. I became aware of

Sarah's fear and her withdrawing from Mama and trying to reach out to others for protection. I may have been subconsciously aware of it before, and perhaps therein lay the roots of my own protective instincts.

Daddy made fewer jokes now, and Mama seldom played the piano in the evening. When she and Daddy sat together in the porch swing, which wasn't often, they had little to say to one another. Sometimes Mama would fall asleep in a chair or go to bed earlier than Sarah and I. Daddy wouldn't say anything when she disappeared into the bedroom, grasping the door frame to keep her balance, and afterwards he'd tuck us into bed and try to pass it off lightly.

"Mama was real tired," he'd say. "I guess she just fell asleep. I'll tell her you said goodnight when I go to bed."

Sarah would cling tightly around his neck. "I love you, Daddy," she'd say, and hold onto him as long as she could.

"I love you too, Sweetheart, and now Daddy's got to go to bed."

But Daddy wouldn't go to bed. Sometimes I'd wake up after midnight and see a bead of light in the crack beside the door. I'd peek out and see him asleep in his reading chair.

Mama's behavior toward Sarah and me became erratic, unpredictable. One day she might shrug off some minor infraction and the next day react violently to the same thing. Sarah grew especially wary of her. Mama would turn on her more readily than me, I suppose because Sarah didn't measure up to her expectations. I remember feeling guilty about Sarah being judged so harshly, blaming her problems with Mama on my own good grades.

We carried our report cards home one afternoon, sealed in envelopes, and handed them to Mama. She opened mine first, and smiled proudly at every grade I'd got. When she opened Sarah's her eyes darkened.

"What are you doing in school, girl?" she practically screamed. "It says here you don't participate in class. You don't answer questions and you hardly ever pay attention. Do you want to flunk first grade?"

Sarah stood perfectly still, staring at the floor.

"You're a beautiful girl," Mama said, "but you don't care about yourself. You don't care about anything." She grabbed Sarah by the shoulders and began shaking her. "You could have the world by the tail, but you won't do your schoolwork, you won't play the piano, you won't do anything but play with those damn dolls!"

Sarah didn't make a sound. As Mama's temper raged out of control she shook her harder and harder. Sarah's hair flew wildly back and forth and her head flopped as if her neck was made of rubber.

Sarah began to scream. "I'm sorry, Mama! I'm sorry!" I'm sorry!"

I could hardly understand Sarah's words as Mama dug her fingers into her shoulders and shook her violently. I feared her neck might snap.

"Stop, Mama! Please!" I pleaded, pulling at her skirt. "You're going to hurt her, Mama! You're going to hurt her."

That seemed to snap her out of it. Mama stopped shaking

Sarah, let go of her shoulders, and walked to the kitchen. When we heard her open the pantry we went to our room and shut the door.

After Sarah stopped crying she lay down on her stomach and crawled under her bed. A minute later she crawled back out with Mandy, the slave doll that Jubal had given her. And though Sarah and I had agreed to keep Jubal's gifts under our beds and covered up at all times, I didn't say anything.

Sarah sat in the floor and hugged the black doll softly, rocking back and forth and humming a nameless song, her face expressionless, her eyes blank.

After a few minutes, I said, "You better put Mandy away, Sarah. We don't want Mama finding her."

She nodded, kissed Mandy on her ever-smiling mouth, and put her back under the bed.

A short while later I was lying on my bed reading while Sarah sat on the floor playing with her rag dolls. Mama came to the door, opened it gingerly, and looked down at Sarah. Tears welled in her eyes.

"I'm sorry, Darlin'," she said with a boozy slur. "Mama didn't mean to hurt you."

She teetered into our room and dropped clumsily to the floor. She draped her arms around Sarah's neck, lay her head on Sarah's, and began to sob: "Oh, Baby, please forgive me. Mama didn't mean to get so mad."

Sarah sat erect and said nothing as Mama apologized repeatedly. After several minutes Mama gave her a final hug and went back to the kitchen. We heard the pantry door open again.

When Daddy came home Mama was asleep in a chair. He smiled and helped her to bed as if nothing was wrong. That was the first time he served our supper.

Later that night, as Sarah was putting on her pajamas, I saw purple welts creasing her shoulders where Mama had gripped them. When Daddy leaned over to kiss her good-night he spotted the bruises.

"What happened, Sweetheart?" he asked. Sarah turned away and began to cry. Daddy looked at her helplessly, then glanced over at me.

I felt guilty telling on Mama, but it seemed necessary. "Mama did it," I said.

"Your Mama did this?" Daddy said. "How did she do it?"

"Mama was shaking her, because of her report card."

"Oh, Sweetie," Daddy said, cradling Sarah in his arms as she sobbed on his shoulder. A pained cry escaped his lips.

Daddy was quiet the next morning at breakfast, and all day at school I dreaded evening coming. I expected a confrontation between him and Mama when he got home from work. She was already a little woozy by the time he walked in the house, and instead of confronting her, Daddy maintained the same quiet as he had that morning. Sarah's bruises were never mentioned.

Every night I sat in the front room or at the dining room table and read while Sarah played with her dolls, mostly in the bedroom by herself, and we eagerly awaited morning and the arrival of Emiline in our lives. Daddy didn't kid Emiline as much at breakfast now, and she became more attentive to all of us, especially Sarah.

"How's school goin', little gal?" she'd say, and Sarah wouldn't answer. "Come on, Angel, how's school goin'?" Emiline would repeat and pinch her on the cheek.

"Oh, school's okay," Sarah would finally say with a reluctant grin.

"Now that's more like it," Emiline would chime. "You got to turn that frown upside down, girl. Turn that frown upside down."

It was one of her favorite sayings, and she laughed every time she said it.

Although it was a particularly cold winter, Sarah and I walked around town every weekend, and she looked for Jubal constantly. When we saw him pulling his wagon by I could hardly restrain her; she always wanted to run to him, and I'd have to explain once more why she couldn't. She'd wave to him nonetheless, sometimes quite conspicuously, and flash him a smile. He never failed to smile back as he continued on his way.

Every time we left the house Sarah wanted to walk to the swimming hole, but the weather was too cold for that. Besides, I was afraid of what Mama might do if she discovered we had met Jubal in secret.

The weather finally began to warm in early spring, and one clear Saturday morning found us sitting on the square eating cinnamon rolls from Dinkin's Bakery. Mr. and Mrs. Dinkin called us into their shop and gave us a goody of some kind every time they saw us, and we always made sure they did.

We'd been watching for Jubal ever since we arrived down-town, but hadn't seen him yet. The square was alive with townspeople and country folk taking advantage of the warm weather to catch up on shopping and gossip. Sheriff Turnbull was standing on the street side of a parked car chatting with its occupant, one foot propped up on the running board as he idly watched Mama Jingles shuffle slowly across the street a block away. Bent nearly double, her gray head bobbing as if suspended on a spring, the ancient black woman was con-versing loudly with voices that only she could hear.

A wagon stacked with several bales of hay sat double parked in the street halfway between the sheriff and Mama Jingles. A pair of spirited horses stood hitched to the wagon while a white woman sat on the seat holding the reins loosely in her lap. Two young girls in bright going-to-town dresses and wide sun hats sat on either side of the woman, waiting for their father to finish his business in one of the stores. The woman and the two girls watched Mama Jingles stop in the middle of the street half a block in front of them, raise her head slightly, and begin an unintelligible tirade that everyone on the square could hear.

I had just heard one of the girls say "Crazy old woman" when a dilapidated Model T chugged up beside the wagon and drowned out her voice. The team of horses started to shy away from the noisy car, which happened to backfire just at that moment, and all hell broke loose.

The horses reared up on their hind legs, snorting and pawing the air, as the woman jerked back on the reins in a vain attempt to control them. The driver of the car, fearing the team might jump in front of him in their frenzy, slammed on the brakes and stopped. The car backfired again as the engine died. The horses broke and bolted down the street, the woman hollering and jerking the reins as the girls screamed and fought to hold onto the madly bouncing seat.

Sheriff Turnbull yelled down the block, "Mama Jingles, look out!"

But the old woman stood yammering to herself in the middle of the street, oblivious to the runaway horses and wagon hurtling down upon her.

"Get out of the way, Mama Jingles!" the sheriff yelled, waving his hat in the air and running down the street in a futile attempt to get the old woman's attention.

Off to the right of the horses a dark blur emerged from a side street. "Jubal," I muttered, as Sarah dug her fingers into my arm. He was running, sprinting, faster than I'd ever seen a human move. As he angled his run to connect with the charging horses, they shied in the opposite direction and began turning to the left.

A bale of hay bounced out of the wagon, hit the street, and burst. An oncoming car swerved, ran up over the curb, and smashed a bench as panicked spectators abandoned their seats and ran for cover.

Jubal reached the heads of the galloping horses, grabbed the bridle of the nearest with his left hand, threw his body in front of them, and caught the other's bridle in his right. The horses drove him backward down the street, dragging his heels in the dirt as they bore down on Mama Jingles.

Sheriff Turnbull stopped half a block away and stared in

disbelief. Jubal, chopping his feet into the ground and jerking the horses' heads to the side as they propelled him backward, forced the team further and further to the left. Like a runaway locomotive, the lathering horses, careening wagon, and screaming women thundered by Mama Jingles, missing her by inches.

Jubal continued dragging his feet and chopping them into the ground as the horses struggled against him. "Whoa," he said, pulling their heads downward. "Whoa, boys. Whoa." And the horses began to slow.

"Easy, now," he said, talking to them until they stopped. Everyone on the square stood frozen in place as Jubal rubbed the horses' frothing noses and soothed them with soft words.

The woman in the wagon had screamed herself hoarse. She sat shaking violently while the terrified girls continued to wail. "Daddy!" they screamed, as their father ran up beside them and slid to a stop.

"Y'all all right?" he hollered. His wife looked at the girls, wrapped her arms around their trembling shoulders, and nodded.

The man glanced at the panting horses, then ran forward to where Jubal stood holding their heads. Taking the bridles in his own hands, the man looked at Jubal, shook his head, and grinned broadly.

"That was a hell of a thing, Dummy. Hell of a thing. Never seen nothin' like it in my whole life."

"Yes, suh," Jubal said, then turned and walked up the

street toward Mama Jingles. I held onto Sarah as Jubal took
the old woman by the arm, walked her to the far curb, and
stood listening to her prattle.

"I'm glad he had his shoes on," Sarah said, her voice
quivering with fright. "Do you think he's okay, Lucas?"

"I don't know. Let's go ask the sheriff."

Sheriff Turnbull was standing by the wagon talking to
the man who owned the team. Sarah held my hand as we
approached the men.

"Sheriff, sir," I stammered, "my sister and me are worried about Jubal. Is he okay?"

Sheriff Turnbull broke off his conversation with the man,
smiled, and squatted down in front of us.

"Yeah, Jubal's okay, kids," he said. "He's just fine."

Sarah bubbled about Jubal all the way home.

"Did you see how Jubal ran out and caught those horses,
Lucas? He ran like a deer. Turned that team around Mama
Jingles and stopped them dead in their tracks, he did."

"I know, Sarah," I said for the tenth time. "I saw it too,
you know."

I didn't really mind listening to her; it felt good to hear
her excited about something.

At home we found Mama passed out on the sofa. Later
Daddy dished up our supper and tucked us into bed.

Chapter Seven

Prohibition laws made alcohol illegal in those days, but they really did little to stem the flow of liquor. The laws just caused bootleggers to proliferate, and though only rich people like the Hardimans could obtain fine drinks such as wine, Mama had no problem obtaining all the moonshine whiskey she wanted.

She drank every day now, sometimes heavily, but on the surface she managed to keep her life pretty well in order. She dressed well, brushed her hair regularly, and attended church and social events with Grandma Tolliver. And though I occasionally smelled whiskey on her breath early in the day, she normally stayed sober until evening. She still served our supper most of the time and cleaned up the dishes afterward, but by then it was usually obvious she'd been drinking.

For a woman to develop a drinking problem was unheard of in those days, especially a woman of Mama's social standing. It did happen, of course, and through the grapevine that kept track of virtually everything in town, such things usually became well-known facts. They were never discussed openly, however. Never allowed to exist. And I guess Daddy was satisfied to keep it that way—keep Mama's reputation intact however transparent the facade may have been. Or perhaps he was simply incapable of facing it, of admitting to himself that the love of his life had become a drunk.

Mama's world received a shattering blow that spring. The phone rang one Saturday morning, and she picked it up and gasped in horror.

"Oh, no, Mother. Oh, no!"

Then as she stood listening to Grandma Tolliver, her eyes darkened and she gathered a steely composure.

"Sit down, Mother," Mama said. "Stay calm. I'll be right over to get you."

When Mama hung up the phone, she dashed into the kitchen, threw open the pantry, and took several big swigs— Sarah and I could hear her gulping from the front room. She slammed the pantry door and ran past us and out of the house, hollering over her shoulder: "Get in the car, kids. Hurry! Grandpa Tolliver's been hurt, down at the shop."

We hurried after her and jumped in the car just as she was taking off. We rushed to pick Grandma up, then raced to the shop.

A heavy wagon had fallen off of a jack, pinning Grandpa Tolliver under it. He'd tried to steady the wagon as it teetered on the tall jack while one of his mechanics fought desperately to fasten the wheel onto the hub before it fell. When the wagon started to fall, the mechanic dropped the wheel and jumped out of the way. The hub crushed one side of Grandpa's chest, breaking several ribs and puncturing a lung. The axle broke his pelvis in three places.

The mechanic ran down the street to summon help, bringing back several men who lifted the wagon off of him. Doc Armstead arrived a few minutes later. Doc, a lean middle-aged man, stern and erect, was one of the most respected men in Linville. By the time we arrived at the shop, Doc had his tie thrown over one shoulder and was kneeling beside Grandpa. I saw him lean over and listen to Grandpa's chest with a stethoscope, but mostly he just watched him.

"Stand back, boys. Give him some air," Doc said, and the men all moved back.

Grandpa's breath was coming in loud, broken wheezes, and bubbles of blood gathered on his lips. Grandma leaped from the car screaming, "Burris, Darlin'!" and charged into the shop.

Doc Armstead arched his body protectively over Grandpa's.

"Stop her, you men!" he said. "Don't let her touch him."

Several men grabbed Grandma and stopped her, but she fought them furiously.

"Hold her," Doc commanded. "Don't let her come any closer."

Mama caught up with Grandma and helped settle her

down. Doc stood up, ordered one of the men to call an ambulance, then walked over to Grandma.

"I'm sorry, Tessie," Doc said. "Burris is hurt real bad. I can't even tell you for sure that he's going to live, but I do know that if anybody were to grab hold of him right now it might kill him. I can't let you touch him."

Then Doc shifted his gaze toward Mama. "Jessica, it's awfully early in the day for your breath to be smelling like that," he said. The men turned away in embarrassment. Doc walked back to Grandpa, kneeled down beside him, and wiped the blood off his mouth.

Grandpa screamed in pain as they lifted him onto a stretcher and into the ambulance; then Doc rode with him to the Linville hospital, where he would spend the next two months. Although few surgical procedures had been perfected by that time, he underwent two operations: one to repair his crushed chest as well as Doc Armstead knew how, the other to set his broken pelvis and place it in a cast. Besides struggling to recover from life-threatening injuries, Grandpa Tolliver's body had to fight to ward off infection. For weeks we wondered if he would live.

Although Grandma knew how to drive, she didn't really care to, so Mama took her to the hospital every day to visit Grandpa. Mama never failed to have at least one drink before she went to pick up her mother—sometimes she had several—but to my knowledge Grandma never mentioned it.

Grandpa Tolliver survived the accident, but he went home the same way he'd gone to the hospital, in an ambulance. At home he lay in bed for weeks, smoking cigars, reading every story in the newspaper, bitching about most of them, and hollering at Grandma. It would be months before he could walk, and then with a cane and for only a few steps. Grandpa would continue to use the cane and walk with a pronounced limp the rest of his life, and he never regained the stamina he had prior to the accident.

Tolliver's Grocery continued to do well, but the shop began to fail. None of the mechanics could replace Grandpa. With the Depression in full swing, only his skill and ambition had kept the shop going. It had to close, and he and Grandma's life had to change.

As Grandpa Tolliver lay bedridden and the shop boarded shut, Grandma had to let the gardener go. Sarah and I were visiting at their house the day it happened. Zeke, the gnarled black man who had tended their yard for years, was standing at the back door when Grandma told him. Holding his hat in one hand and a rusty hoe in the other, he stared at the ground as tears filled his eyes.

"What's I goin' to do, Miz Tolliver?" Zeke sobbed. "I's a old man, and been losin' a lot of my work these days. And what's you and Mistuh Tolliver goin' to do, what with him all laid up in bed like that?"

"I'm sorry," Grandma said, dabbing at her own eyes with a handkerchief. "If things don't get better I don't know what's going to happen to all of us."

And although he hadn't done any work that day she handed him two dollars and shooed him away.

"Go on now, Zeke, before Burris finds out I gave you that."

The man probably wasn't more than sixty, but he had labored in the fields until his body could no longer stand the strain. Yard work was all he could do now. Zeke looked a hundred years old as he shuffled off down the street, dragging his hoe in one hand and wiping his eyes with the other.

Grandma had to let one of their maids go too. I wasn't there that day, but I'm sure she didn't mind telling Estella, Grandpa's haughty concubine, not to come to her house again.

As Grandpa Tolliver grew increasingly bitter and demanding, Grandma spent her days rushing to his sickroom every time he hollered. She also fretted over the weeds that were taking over her lawn, the untrimmed hedges, the holes in her shoes, and their dwindling bank account.

Mama loved her father, but she seemed more devastated by her parents' financial demise than by his injury. As her drinking became more obvious and Grandma could no longer afford to entertain guests, the ladies of the town began avoiding them.

Mama tried to talk her mother into attending functions to which they had not been invited, rationalizing it by explaining to Grandma that the hostess had simply not felt it necessary to ask them because she had known them so long. Perhaps in her alcoholic fog Mama was able to convince herself of such a thing, but Grandma knew better. When Grandma refused to go, Mama actually attended several such functions by herself.

Sarah and I knew to stay away from Mama when she came home from some party that she had gone to without Grandma Tolliver. On those days she barely spoke to us on her way to the pantry.

One day Mama conceived a plan to revive their failing social life. In light of all the tribulations that Grandma had endured since Grandpa's injury, Mama decided to host a party at our house to honor her mother. As soon as the idea occurred to her she became obsessed with it. She planned the party for a Saturday afternoon, and called to invite every woman of any social standing whatsoever.

Despite the embarrassment she felt over the Christmas incident at the Hardiman house, Mama even called Kathleen Hardiman. Grandma was pleased that her daughter would put together such an event in her honor, but she seemed less optimistic than Mama about the number of ladies that might attend.

Clearly, her mother's party was to be Mama's big show. She was tireless in the planning, and a tyrant with Emiline, commanding her to clean the house extra well for the event and insisting that she prepare every one of Grandma's favorite dishes. And though she appeared to be drinking as much as usual, she seemed more alert in the evenings than we had seen her in some time.

Daddy grimaced at the expense of it all, but he seemed pleased at Mama's enthusiasm for the upcoming event. He was probably glad to see something interrupt the alcohol-induced depression she kept herself in most of the time. I was glad to see it too; for awhile it seemed like we had returned to our old life—the happy times before Mama started drinking.

To everyone's surprise, on the Saturday of the big party Mama was up early enough to eat breakfast with the rest of us. Daddy had to work that day, and Sarah and I planned to spend the afternoon at the library and the square. The ladies were due to arrive at one o'clock, and Emiline wasn't smiling much that morning.

Sarah and I were glad when Mama told us we could leave the house at noon, and even though Emiline served us sandwiches before we left, Mama gave us money to buy candy or cookies downtown. She didn't know about the free treats that Mr. and Mrs. Dinkin gave us. She kissed us goodbye at the door and said, "I love you both." There was no alcohol on her breath, and as we walked off down the street I felt the world belonged to us.

"Is Mama gettin' better, Lucas?" Sarah asked.

"I think so," I said happily.

Bright shafts of sunlight danced through the trees as we walked the six blocks to downtown. The late spring air was warm, the leaves freshly green. At the library Miss Hawkins advised me on the merits of several authors—a few more than I felt I needed—while Sarah sat at one of the tables and played with her doll. When we left the library we went directly to Mr. and Mrs. Dinkin's shop, and had to walk past three times before one of them looked up and motioned us in. They gave us each two fat glazed dough-nuts hot out of the oven—my favorite, and Sarah's too.

The low point of our afternoon came when Nap Canfield

and Herman Slocum spotted us and made a point of coming over to our bench. Herman didn't say a word, just looked at us out of the corner of his eye and grinned a stupid grin.

"Well, how're the Dunaway kids this purty day?" Nap said, turning his head to squirt a thin, dark stream of tobacco juice between his teeth. The stream hit three feet from his cracked shoes, left a black strip on the sidewalk, and bounced another couple of feet where it lay jiggling in the sunlight.

Sarah leaned against my shoulder and stared at the men's feet. "We're fine, Mister Canfield," I said.

"*Mister* Canfield?" said Nap, louder than necessary. He winked broadly at Slocum. "I ain't been called Mister in a coon's age—probably not since you called me that the last time I seen ya. You just made my day, MISTER Dunaway." Herman grinned at Nap's wit.

I didn't answer, just thanked God when they left. Then to the Dinkins' surprise we walked back into their store. I laid our money on the counter and told Mrs. Dinkin we wanted to buy some doughnuts this time. I don't know if the look she gave me was one of suspicion or respect; I think a little of both.

Shortly after we returned to our bench, Jubal came by with his wagon. Sarah stood up and gave her usual little wave. To our surprise Jubal didn't return the greeting, not at first anyway; instead he looked at us with concern in his eyes. Then he smiled, ever so slightly, and continued on.

Mama had planned for Grandma's party to be over by four o'clock. She told us to watch the clock on Planters Bank so we could get home by 4:30. We walked in the door seven or eight minutes late and found Mama in a black mood.

"Where have you been?" she yelled. Sarah shrunk behind my back.

"We forgot to look at the clock, Mama, but just for a few minutes," I said.

"I guess most of the women we invited to Mother's party forgot to look at their clocks too," Mama said. "Either that or they've all got too goddamn good for us." Then she grabbed me by the shoulders and pulled me into her face. "You're the oldest, Lucas, and you're supposed to be in charge—to keep track of the time. Are you going to start making trouble for me too?"

In an effort to protect me, Sarah tried to explain. "We didn't mean to be late, Mama," she said. "Honest we didn't."

"Didn't mean to!" Mama screamed. "Didn't *mean* to! Nobody ever means to do anything around here, and I'm always the one who pays."

"I'm sorry," Sarah said, her eyes dropping to the floor.

Mama lost the last of her self-control. She swung at Sarah open-handed, slapping her so hard it knocked her off her feet. Sarah's head hit the floor with a loud thump and she lay deathly still, long enough for me to wonder if she was conscious. Then she reached up and covered the side of her face with her hand, but that's all she did. She continued to lie there with her head on the floor and her hand against her face, not making a sound.

Mama turned to me. The fury in her face made me

cringe, and for a moment I thought she would turn her rage on me. Instead she whirled, stomped to the kitchen, and threw open the pantry. I helped Sarah up off the floor, walked her to our room, and closed the door.

Both the dining room table and the kitchen table were full when Daddy got home from work, every tray and bowl of food from the party left sitting open. Mama lay asleep in a chair, reeking of whiskey. Sarah and I remained in our room with the door closed.

"What's going on, kids?" Daddy said, pushing the door open cautiously. He glanced first at me and then at Sarah. Sarah sat in the floor looking down, her hands folded in her lap. She wasn't even holding a doll. Slowly she turned and looked up at Daddy. The entire left side of her face was blue. Her cheek was bruised and swollen, her eyelid drooped, and the eyeball was streaked blood red.

Daddy's eyes widened in shock, then narrowed, then turned a smoldering black.

"Did she do anything to you, Lucas?" he said. "Did Mama hurt you too?"

"No," I said, choking back tears.

Daddy whirled, flew out the bedroom door and across the room.

"Jessica!" he roared. He grabbed Mama by the arm and gripped it like a vice. "Jessica! Get up!"

Mama's eyes opened blankly, confused at first, then frightened.

"Do you know what you did to our daughter, Jessica?"

Daddy bellowed. "Have you seen her? Or were you too drunk to notice, or care?"

He jerked Mama out of her chair and dragged her to our room.

"Look at our beautiful daughter, Jessica. Look at her! What in God's name would make you do something like that?"

His voice sounded like a man out of control.

"I'm sorry," Mama stammered, her face falling as she looked at Sarah. Then she tried to explain. "Nobody came to Mother's party. Only a few women showed . . . ."

"Party?" Daddy bellowed, and propelled her back into the front room. His face an inch from hers, he clenched his teeth and growled, "I don't give a good goddamn about your party, Jessica."

Daddy released her arm from his grasp and clenched his fists at his sides; his eyes darted around the room uncontrollably. Mama stepped back and raised her hands to her face as if to protect it.

He finally regained control of himself, and spoke in a voice cold as ice. "I've put up with a lot, Jessica, far more than I ever should have. But no more. I won't have you beating my children. You hear me, Jessica? I will not have it."

Chapter Eight

Sarah stayed out of school for a week after Mama bruised her face, but even so her teacher asked what had happened when she saw her.

"Nothing," Sarah told her.

Mama stopped drinking the night Daddy lost his temper, and since her social life had pretty well come to an end with the failure of Grandma's party, she was there when we got home from school in the afternoon. And another pleasant change: she always asked how our day had gone. She served our supper, joined in the conversation while we ate, and even started playing the piano again.

Despite the change in Mama, Sarah became quieter and more reserved after the incident. Even her face lit up, however, the night Daddy took Mama's hand and led her out to the porch. As the two of them sat swinging and talking lowly, I peeked out the living room window and saw them holding hands. I looked at my sister, sitting in the front room floor surrounded by her dolls, and asked: "Are you having fun, Sarah?"

"Uh-huh," she said.

Sarah's face healed without scars, and as spring became summer Mama nursed her flower beds back to life. Brilliant roses and azaleas adorned our house once more, and Daddy gave it a new coat of paint for good measure. He stood up on the ladder and hollered and waved at everyone who passed by.

As usual, Sarah and I enjoyed exploring the town and visiting Daddy at the Mercantile, and once we even walked out to see Grandpa Tolliver's boarded-up shop. We went into Tolliver's Grocery too, but the man working there hardly acknowledged us. We stood looking through the glass at the candy longer than we should have, and finally realized he wasn't going to give us any.

Daddy burst into our room one Saturday morning, waking us out of a sound sleep.

"Get up, kids," he said, loud enough to wake the neighbors. "Those fish'll be filling up on something besides our bait!"

The first thing that registered in my sleep-filled eyes was his floppy hat, and suddenly I came alive. I jumped up and began pawing through my drawers, looking for my cutoffs and Huck Finn hat.

"Come on, Sarah," I said. "We're going to the swimming hole."

Sarah grinned at Daddy, then pulled the covers up over her head. He tickled her ribs through the covers, causing her to laugh and roll around in a futile attempt to escape his playful torture.

"I give up!" she said, crawling out of bed and shaking a warning finger at Daddy.

It was a warm, sultry day, the Delta a sea of cotton that stretched forever. As we drove through the fields, we all rolled our eyes when Daddy started to sing. *"She'll be comin' round the mountain when she comes!"* he wailed loudly and hideously off key.

Bobbing his head from side to side and whipping the steering wheel back and forth at the same time, he veered the car wildly from one shoulder of the road to the other. The wide brim of his straw hat flopped up and down like the pumping of a blacksmith's bellows. Mama grabbed hold of the door handle, grinning as she bounced all over the front seat; then she broke into laughter.

Sarah let out a jouncing giggle as Daddy sang, *"Oh, we'll all have chicken and dumplings when she comes!"* his voice wavering in a ridiculous parody as the car veered crazily down the road. *"Oh, we'll all have chicken and dumplings . . . ."*

Mama clung to the door handle with both hands, laughing hysterically as her body pivoted from the dashboard to the seat.

"Stop, Reid," she wailed, "before you make me wet my pants!"

Sarah went into spasms when Mama said that, and Daddy sang even louder, his hat bouncing in wild undulations.

We finally reached the swimming hole, much to Mama's relief. Daddy got down our fishing poles and baited Sarah's hook, then he joined Mama on a blanket while we dangled our feet over the creek bank and concentrated on our bobbers.

I looked around at the big cottonwood several times, and after a while I whispered to Sarah: "Do you think he'll come?"

"No," she said. And he didn't.

The fishing was lively for a while, then it began to slow. Right on cue, Daddy leaped over our heads and hit the water with a great sploosh, drenching us. Sarah and I jumped in and we laughed, swam, and splashed while Mama smiled and watched. Afterward we ate our lunch in the shade of a great oak.

When we finished eating we all sat and talked awhile, then we went for a walk on the path that ran alongside the creek, the one that Jubal used to get to the swimming hole. We walked downstream, however, in the opposite direction from Jubal's house. The creek bed tightened just beyond the swimming hole, and we found ourselves walking along the bottom of a narrow ravine with steep banks on either side. Mama and Daddy were tall enough to see out, but Sarah and I had to run up the side of the creek bank to look out over the fields. We used up a lot of energy chasing each other up and down the banks.

The path played out within a quarter of a mile, so we reversed our steps back to the swimming hole. The sun hung low on the horizon as we drove away. Sarah lay asleep on the seat beside me, and Daddy's hand rested on Mama's shoulder.

Mama had followed her mother's lead all of her adult years, relentlessly pursuing a social status that somehow seemed to elude them both—a golden ring that hung tantalizingly beyond their grasp. With that frustration gone from her life, Mama seemed happier than she ever had before. She and Daddy laughed and enjoyed each other immensely. Seeing them together now was a joy I had never experienced, and something I had difficulty comprehending. Although Sarah never mentioned it, I'm sure she shared my confusion over this new side of Mama that we had never known.

Emiline read our thoughts, as usual, and one day when Mama was gone she sat us down on the front room rug, took a seat on the sofa, and started explaining as if we might have brought up the subject ourselves.

"You children ought to have seen that mama of yours when she and your daddy first got married. She was the prettiest young colt I ever seen, and oh, so happy."

The smile on Emiline's face mirrored the fondness of the memory.

"Mistuh Reid was forever clownin'," she continued, "and your mama just couldn't get enough of it. I swear, they was the funnest pair I ever knew. He was your mama's hero, and she his queen."

With that, Emiline stood up and started toward the dining room, but I wanted to know more.

"What happened?" I asked. "How come Mama stopped laughing?"

Emiline looked thoughtful, and perhaps a little wary, then she sat back down.

"I probably already run my mouth off too much," she said. "You kids won't never tell your mama what I told you today, will you?"

"No," I said, and Sarah nodded her head in agreement.

"After your mama got pregnant with you, Lucas, she

started goin' to more and more of them society doin's with her mama, Miss Tessie, and somehow she just got too serious about it all. That's when she stopped laughin'. It's all over now, though. Your mama's back, and your folks is happy again. And you, little girl," Emiline said, pointing a finger at Sarah, "you got to believe that. You got to turn that frown upside down."

That drew a smile out of Sarah, and Emiline stood up again.

"Okay, kids, run along now," she said. "I already talked more'n I should of about white folks' business. Remember, don't tell your mama what I said today."

"We won't," I promised.

So we finally got to know our mother, the one who had fallen in love with Daddy. And Daddy—charming, lovable, entertaining Daddy, whose one fault was trying too hard to avoid a fight—got her back.

I loved our new life, and readily accepted the change. With Sarah it was different. Sarah had withdrawn inside herself when Mama became abusive, and she seemed unable or unwilling to come out again when it ended. She remained wary of Mama, shying away from her at the slightest provocation and returning her affection with a stiff silence. She was Daddy's girl, more now than ever before it seemed.

Grandma and Grandpa Tolliver's remaining maid, Pernella, had been with them much of her life. When it became apparent that Grandpa would never have the strength to work again, Grandma had to let Pernella go. She also couldn't afford to keep full-time help at the store, and so cut her one employee's hours and started working at Tolliver's Grocery several hours each day herself.

Although Grandma was unaccustomed to working for a living, she gamely rose to the occasion, perhaps feeling the same relief as Mama at no longer having to worry about what appeared on the society page. Sarah and I were happy that Grandma started working at the store; once more we had a source of free candy on that side of town.

Between Grandma and the Dinkins, Sarah and I had an abundant supply of sweets that summer. And what a summer it was. We learned every street in town, except those across the tracks, of course, and everyone we saw waved and spoke to us. We often saw Jubal passing by with his wagon, and one morning Sarah talked me into walking to the swimming hole again.

Jubal met us there just as she had known he would. He seemed concerned about us, and asked how we had been. I told him we were fine, and Sarah nodded her agreement while clinging to his big hand and looking up at him in adoration.

Jubal even looked me in the eye when we spoke, albeit rather shyly, and only then did I realize he'd never done it before. And although I realized what a social taboo it was, somehow I felt honored.

The long summer finally passed and we returned to school. I started fifth grade that fall, and Sarah was in second. Somehow she had managed to pass first grade, though nobody quite knew how. Nobody was asking, either. I felt happier than I could remember, and I think Sarah did too.

Mr. Tarver, the school principal, came and got me out of class one morning just before noon. As I followed him out the door, he glanced at me quickly, then looked away and spoke in a curt, businesslike manner.

"Come to the office with me, Lucas," he said, then turned and hurried down the hall. I practically had to run to keep up with him.

Mr. Tarver was a small, dapper man who loved children, and he took the job of educating us seriously. As I quick-stepped down the hall behind him, he suddenly stopped, turned, and looked down into my questioning face.

"You're not in any kind of trouble, Lucas," he said. "It's nothing like that."

Before I could reply he whirled and took off again.

Mr. Tarver held his office door open for me, and when I walked in I saw Sheriff Turnbull standing in front of the desk, holding his hat in his hand. Sarah, looking frightened and confused, stood beside him.

"Hello, Lucas," the sheriff said with a weak smile. "I'm going to give you and your sister a ride home."

I looked at the principal, who had a far too serious look on his face.

"What's wrong, Mister Tarver?" I asked.

His eyes dropped to the floor, then lifted back to mine.

"I'm sorry, Lucas," Mr. Tarver said. "I can't tell you why, but you and Sarah need to go with Sheriff Turnbull. He's going to take you home."

We followed the sheriff out to his car, where he held the door open for us. Sarah climbed into the middle of the front seat and I climbed in beside her. The sheriff walked around and slid under the wheel, looked at us with that strange half smile again, and started for our house.

The silence hung heavy in the air as we drove along, and after a block or two Sheriff Turnbull seemed compelled to say something.

"How've you kids been?" he asked. "I see you downtown pretty often."

"We're okay, Sir," I said. "Why are you taking us home?"

He turned toward me and started to speak, but when he opened his mouth nothing came out. His face reddening in embarrassment, he turned his attention back to the street. We rode the rest of the way in silence.

At least half a dozen cars were parked near our house and across the street, along with a wagon and mule that I recognized as Uncle Robert's. Sheriff Turnbull had to park a few doors away, and I could see curtains parting in the neighbors' windows as we followed him to our front gate.

Sarah hadn't said a word since we left the school. Halfway up the front walk she stopped and shook her head. "No," she said in a small, trembling voice, and turned her back on the house.

Sarah stood facing the street, her chin turned down in a pout, her arms hanging at her sides.

"Come on, Honey," Sheriff Turnbull said. "Take my hand."

She took the sheriff's hand and reluctantly followed him to the door.

I remember the moment as if it were yesterday. Mama was standing at the door when it opened, and beyond her I could see a number of people throughout the house. I recall the front room exactly as it looked: the sofa at my fingertips on the left, the wooden rocker on the right, the piano against the left wall, Daddy's big reading chair in the far right corner, Mama's Persian rug covering the floor—every lamp, every piece of woodwork, every picture that hung on every wall.

I looked up into Mama's face. Her cheeks were puffy, her eyes red, and I knew she'd been drinking. Behind her, filling the front room and dining room, stood every member of the family. Fleeting glimpses registered in my mind: Grandma and Grandpa Dunaway, Uncle Robert, Aunt Eunice, Aunt Esther, Emiline, Grandma Tolliver. Even Grandpa Tolliver was there, hollow-faced and leaning on his cane.

"Oh, Lucas, Sarah," Mama said, bending down and wrapping her arms around us. "It's your daddy."

I remember several people sobbing when she said that.

"Your daddy . . . ." Mama said again, and choked on her words. She leaned heavily on Sarah and me and began reeling on her feet. Someone helped her to a chair.

Grandma Dunaway took Mama's place. Grandma squatted down in front of us, laid a gentle hand on each of our shoulders, and looked into our eyes.

"There's been an accident. Your daddy's gone."

"Gone?" I said.

Grandma bit her lip, and something in her eyes made me think she might faint.

"Your daddy's been killed," she said. "There was an accident at the Mercantile, and he's gone."

The rest of the day remains a blur—people filing in and

out, crying, hugging, talking, fanning Mama. Emiline setting out food and holding me close, her hot tears wetting my cheeks. Mama going to the bathroom, too often, opening the pantry door every time. Occasional glimpses of Sarah, clinging to Grandpa Dunaway.

The brake had come loose on a loaded wagon parked behind the Mercantile, setting it rolling downhill toward the loading dock. George Holland, a fellow employee of Daddy's, stood facing the dock unaware of the perilous load bearing down on him. Daddy leaped and shoved George out of its way, only to be caught between the wagon and the dock himself. The tailgate of the wagon crushed his chest, killing him instantly.

How does one describe the death of a parent at the age we were, or define it, or comprehend it? I don't know if I really believed Daddy was gone forever; somehow it didn't seem possible. Still, I remember thinking over and over that I hadn't got to tell him goodbye.

When Grandma and Grandpa Dunaway started to leave that evening, Sarah wouldn't let go of Grandpa's hand. And although she was seven, he picked her up in his arms as if she were a small child. She lay her head against his and clung to his neck.

"Don't you want to stay here with your brother and me?" Mama asked her.

Sarah shook her head.

"All right, Darlin'," Mama said. "You can go with Grandma and Grandpa, if they don't mind."

They nodded, and Mama gave Sarah a boozy kiss, which she didn't return.

Although Grandpa Burris grumbled about having to spend the night alone, Grandma Tolliver insisted on staying with Mama and me that night. A few minutes before Sarah and I went to bed we heard Mama opening the pantry door. Grandma got up from the sofa and walked to the kitchen.

"I've never said anything about this, Jessica," I heard her tell Mama. "You were always too stubborn to listen to me anyway, and besides that I figured it was between you and Reid. It's different now, and all the whiskey in God's creation isn't going to bring him back. You've got Lucas and Sarah to think of. Maybe you don't care if this stuff ruins your life, but you can't let it ruin theirs."

Mama didn't answer. A while later Grandma helped her to bed.

I lay awake for hours that night. Whenever I closed my eyes, Daddy's smiling face would come to haunt me. Sometime after midnight I finally dropped off, and when I woke the next morning I thought maybe he hadn't really died; perhaps it had just been a bad dream. Then I remembered coming home in Sheriff Turnbull's car, and I knew it was true.

The First Methodist Church, a tall stone structure with twin spires and stained-glass windows, bulged with people, more than I'd ever seen in one place. The crowd filled every seat, the back of the church, the space in the balcony behind the choir, and spilled out onto the lawn.

Although blacks were not allowed to enter white

churches, a large crowd gathered around the perimeter of the yard under the oaks. They stood solemn and quiet, Bibles in hand, the women in white dresses and thin veils that hung from the front of their wide hats, the men in dark suits and ties. Some clothes were patched and worn, but assuredly were the best they owned.

Pastor Clifton Hogan walked to the pulpit and gripped it with both hands. He turned and looked at Daddy, lying in the casket as if he were asleep, gave a sympathetic nod to Mama, Sarah, and me, then looked out over the multitudes packed into his church. He was a large, dignified man who spoke with authority.

"A crowd such as this will gather at a funeral for one of three reasons," the minister's voice boomed. "One—if the deceased was rich. Two—if the deceased was powerful. Or three—if the deceased was true. Though it is a fact that few people can claim to be rich or powerful, the first two remain commonplace compared to the third. The third is rare indeed. Reid Dunaway was not rich, nor was he powerful. Reid was one of those rare human beings. He was true."

George Holland, his face ashen and drawn, sat near the front beside Graydon Hardiman. The rest of the Mercantile employees filled the row. When Pastor Hogan talked about Daddy's untimely death and how he had given his life to save that of another, George broke down completely. Graydon reached over and rested a hand on the sobbing man's shoulder.

Sarah and I sat on either side of Mama. I remember hearing our names spoken more than once during the service but I don't recall much else that was said. Mama wrapped her arms around us and we held hands across her lap as the choir sang "Amazing Grace," Daddy's favorite, then we filed past his casket. I looked first at his face and then at his hands, an experience that for the longest time seemed as if it had occurred in a dream.

Sarah had remained silent throughout the service, but when she looked in his face she screamed, "Daddy!" and reached out to touch him. Mama grabbed her and pulled her back, but she fought like a demon.

"Daddy!" she screamed again, her voice filling the church. Grandma Dunaway rushed up and kneeled down beside her. She reached out and encircled Sarah in a loving embrace, pinning her flailing arms to her sides in the process. Slowly Sarah stopped struggling, and lay her head on Grandma's shoulder. She turned away and refused to look at Daddy again.

Grandma stood up, looked at her son one last time, and walked Sarah down the aisle and out the door. Mama and I lingered at the casket until she leaned over and kissed Daddy on the forehead, then she took my hand and led me out.

Outside, I saw the blacks congregated off to one side of the yard. Emiline stood in the front row, tears streaming down her sunlit cheeks. I noticed Jubal's wagon parked under a tree, and near the back of the crowd his head towered above the others. Our eyes met momentarily, then he looked away. When the graveside service ended and we were leaving, we passed him on the road. He was walking with his head down, pulling his wagon.

Daddy was killed on a Wednesday, and we buried him the

following Saturday. Sarah remained at Grandma and Grandpa Dunaway's until the funeral, then she came home to stay with Mama and me. After one more night of sleeping on our sofa, Grandma Tolliver went home too. That left the three of us, and Emiline, during the day. And though Sarah and I stayed home from school the following week, Emiline came at her regular time Monday morning and fed us breakfast while Mama slept in.

When Mama got up that morning she barely spoke to any of us. A few times she tried to talk to Sarah and me about some everyday thing, but she never mentioned Daddy or the funeral. By the time Emiline left in the afternoon Mama reeked of alcohol. She fell asleep on the sofa early that evening.

I read for awhile after Mama fell asleep, then I went to the kitchen and got two plates out of the cupboard and two sets of silverware from the drawer. Sarah stood by the sink and watched while I set the kitchen table, took our supper out of the oven, and sat down in my regular place.

"Sit down, Sarah," I said. "It's suppertime."

Sarah sat down, reluctantly, and stared disinterestedly at her food. I didn't know exactly what was bothering her, but I knew it had to do with Daddy.

"Come on, Sarah," I said. "We have to eat supper."

"Lucas, when people die, do they ever come back?" she asked.

"I don't think so," I said.

I served our supper every night that week, and cleaned up

afterward as best I could. Emiline frowned each morning when she looked over the kitchen, but she didn't ask how it came to be in such a condition.

We always woke Mama before we went to bed. She'd stagger into our room and kiss us goodnight, then into the kitchen to have another drink. One night she leaned over my bed and stroked my face.

"Oh, my handsome Lucas," she said. "You're so like your father."

Then she switched off the light and hurried out the door.

When the door closed behind Mama, Sarah spoke into the darkness.

"I wish Daddy could tell us goodnight."

"Me too," I said.

I'd been having nightmares, nearly every night it seemed. Some I remembered well, others only vaguely, and some I suppose I didn't remember at all. One night Sarah woke me up, crying. I got up, stepped over to her bed, and took her hand

"Did you have a bad dream?" I asked.

"Yes," she said, choking on her tears.

"About Daddy?"

"Yes. I saw him getting run over like I heard people talking about."

I wanted to comfort her, to say something to make it better, but I didn't know how.

The following Saturday morning we asked Mama if we could go for a walk. She looked at us with a distant, detached smile and said it would be all right. She'd already had several drinks by the time we left the house.

Before we had even reached the front gate Sarah asked, "Can we go to the swimming hole, Lucas?"

"Okay," I said without argument.

The day was gray and overcast, the first hint of fall in the air. We walked in silence and didn't worry about hiding from passersby. When we reached the swimming hole, Sarah stood under the trees and looked around hopefully for several minutes, then she dropped her eyes and walked dejectedly to the creek bank. She sat down, hung her feet over the edge, and folded her hands in her lap. I sat down a couple of feet from her, in the same spot from which I'd always fished, and stared out over the water. It didn't seem like the swimming hole at all—just a bleak, gray pond in a turn of the creek.

He was close behind when we sensed his presence, but neither of us were startled. We looked up into his sad face, reached out, and took his hands in ours. He eased his large frame down between us, looked into Sarah's eyes, then into mine. She laid her head against his side and reached her arms around his middle. I did the same. He wrapped an arm around each of us and began rocking to and fro. His sides resonated as we rocked, and a mournful hum touched our ears. We held tightly to him, and cried.

Part III
Chapter Nine

Daddy had done well for a working man trying to raise a family during the Depression, but he hadn't managed to put much money in the bank. He had been a big believer in insurance, however, and with that he left us financially secure. A burial policy paid for his funeral, plot, and headstone, and his life insurance enabled Mama to keep the house. We were able to keep Emiline working for us too, thank God.

Mama remained in a morose state for weeks following Daddy's death. She slept odd hours day and night and wore nothing but a nightgown and robe around the clock. She drank most of her waking hours, and seldom even combed her hair. She withdrew from the world, and from Sarah and me.

Although Grandma Tolliver had virtually no time to herself now, she took a few minutes to stop by our house one evening. Finding Mama asleep on the sofa and reeking of alcohol, Grandma just shook her head. Then she hugged the two of us and asked how we'd been. We told her we were all right, and thanks to Emiline she could see that we were clean and well fed. Grandma kissed us goodbye, looked at Mama again with a disgusted sigh, and left.

For all intents Emiline became the only parent we had during that period. She got us up in the morning, fed us, sent us off to school clean, then met us at the door in the afternoon and gave us treats as she always had. She set out meals for Mama too, most of which were never touched, and simply went about her work as if Mama weren't there. Mama treated Emiline the same, seldom acknowledging her presence.

Then one afternoon when we got home from school she wasn't there.

"Where's Mama," I asked Emiline.

"Well, your Grandma, Miss Tessie, stopped by to see her a couple of times lately," Emiline said. "Got pretty fussy with her too. And today your Mama got out of bed, prettied herself up, and went over to the store to help Miss Tessie out. She looked real nice when she left."

What a relief I felt. When Daddy died it seemed we'd lost Mama too, but from what Emiline was saying we might have gotten her back. When she came home that evening the change was amazing. She had on a pretty red dress, her auburn hair was glistening, and her eyes were clear and alert. Our Mama was beautiful again.

"There's my babies!" she said, bouncing through the door. "Come here and give your Mama a hug."

I ran right to her, but Sarah hung back.

"Come here, Darlin'," Mama said, reaching toward her with outstretched arms. "Your Mama don't bite."

Sarah walked across the room and joined us.

Tears welled in Mama's eyes as she hugged the two of us. When she let go of us I broke down. "Sometimes we have nightmares," I said, "about Daddy. And sometimes we can't sleep at all."

"I'm sorry, Lucas; I'm so sorry," she said. "I know I went away and left you for awhile, but now I'm back."

She hugged me again as Sarah stood beside us in silence.

Mama served our supper that night, and sat down and ate with us and asked us all about school. And she didn't get on Sarah about anything. After supper she played the piano while Sarah and I sat on the sofa and listened. I smelled whiskey on her breath when she kissed us good-night, but it wasn't as strong as I was accustomed to.

After Mama turned out our light and closed the bedroom door, I whispered: "Isn't it great, Sarah! Mama's just like she always was. Things will be a lot better now."

I lay in the dark waiting for a reply, but Sarah didn't answer.

"Aren't you happy about Mama?" I asked.

"Yes," she said.

Mama started working at Tolliver's Grocery regularly. Sometimes she tended the store by herself and other times she worked with Grandma. She didn't stop drinking altogether, but she did wait until evening, and most nights she only had a few. Occasionally she'd have enough to make her woozy by the time we went to bed, but that didn't happen often.

I missed Daddy every day, and at times I felt a great need to talk about him. Whenever I mentioned him, though, Mama would interrupt me and change the subject. Finally, one night I tried to press the issue.

"I miss Daddy a lot, Mama. I think about him all the time. Do you miss him?"

"Do I miss him?" she snapped. "Of course I miss him."

She sat and stared at the floor for several minutes, then she got up and went to the pantry. I never mentioned Daddy again.

The first time Sarah and I stopped by Tolliver's Grocery to see Mama and Grandma the store looked tidier than I'd ever imagined it could. When Grandpa Burris ran it, the store had been a cluttered space with cobwebs on the ceiling, spirals of ancient flypaper dangling overhead, and a pile of dust in every corner. Grandma hadn't had the energy nor the inclination to clean it up. Mama, being neat by nature and obsessive in everything she did, set about cleaning and straightening the store the day she started work. She added a badly needed splash of color by hanging red and yellow curtains across the tops of the windows, and she even cleaned the thick smudge off the smoke-dimmed panes, a job that had needed doing for years.

I was always the optimist; when Mama came out of her depression and cut back on her drinking, I believed the change was there to stay. Sarah remained skeptical, and, unfortunately, she turned out to be right. Mama began to drink more in the evenings and grew sullen again. And though the use of tobacco was considered a terrible habit for women of breeding, she started smoking cigarettes. I hated the dirty ash trays and the smell it left in the house, but I knew better than to mention it.

One night while Sarah was helping Mama clean off the kitchen table she dropped a glass and broke it. I was sitting in the front room reading when it happened.

"My God!" I heard Mama scream. "Can't you do anything right?"

Before Sarah could answer, Mama grabbed her by the hair and slammed her in the jaw. I ran for the kitchen, where I found Sarah holding her chin and staring at the broken glass on the floor. Mama smacked her again, this time across the top of the head, then she looked up and saw me in the doorway.

"Get you sister out of here," she said, "before she messes something else up."

I took Sarah by the arm and led her to our room. She sat down on the floor, pulled her dolls next to her, and rubbed her jaw. She didn't make a sound; she didn't even cry.

Sarah's jaw was swollen the next morning, and horribly black and blue. Without asking what had happened, Emiline gently touched the side of Sarah's face and asked, "Is that as sore as it looks, Angel?"

Sarah winced and nodded.

When we sat down for breakfast, Emiline said, "Better open your mouth, girl, if you can, and let me check those teeth."

Sarah could only open her jaws part way, but Emiline reached a finger in and ran it over her teeth.

"Feels like everything's okay—no loose ones." She leaned over and kissed Sarah on her bruised face. "I loves you, Angel," she said.

On the way to school that morning I thought Sarah might need some advice on how to handle the day.

"When Mrs. Roberts asks about your jaw, you better tell her you ran into something," I said.

"Why?" she asked.

"Because you can't tell her what really happened."

"I know that."

"What did you tell the teacher the last time Mama hit you?"

"Nothing."

"You didn't tell her anything?"

"No, I told her nothing happened."

"I don't think you ought to tell her that again. She's not going to believe nothing happened."

"Okay," Sarah said, sighing. "I'll tell her I ran into a door."

Mama was sleeping later in the mornings and working less at Grandma's store, and I'm sure she and Grandma weren't getting along as well as they had been. Although Mama still served our supper in the evening, she didn't always eat with us, and when she did we seemed to have little to talk about. And though neither Sarah nor I realized it at the time, we would never hear Mama play the piano again.

A week or so after Mama bruised Sarah's jaw, Emiline confronted us when we arrived home from school.

"I was cleanin' under your beds today, and I found an old slave doll and a little bitty wagon. Where'd you get them things?"

We were standing in the middle of the front room, and I knew Mama wasn't home. Sarah and I exchanged a furtive glance out of the corners of our eyes, and neither of us answered. Emiline walked into our room and returned with Mandy and the little wagon in her hands.

"Come on now. Where'd you kids get these things?" she said, holding them out and staring a hole through us.

I couldn't stand it.

"Jubal gave them to us," I said.

"Jubal?" she said, frowning.

"You know—the big black man."

"You mean Dummy?" Emiline asked. "He gave you these?"

"Yes, he did," I answered, and Sarah nodded to confirm it.

"Why in the world would he . . .?" Emiline started to ask. Then she stopped and stood thinking before she continued. "Your Mama don't know about these, does she?"

"No," I said. "She's never seen them."

Emiline studied the toys gravely. "If she found these in this house, there'd be hell to pay. You know that, don't you, Lucas?"

It was the first time I'd ever heard her use such language.

"I know," I said, "but we didn't know what else to do with them."

"You better let me take them to my house and keep them for you," said Emiline. "Might save a lot of trouble around here."

I glanced at Sarah. She didn't say anything, but nodded.

"Okay," I said. "Maybe you should take them home with you."

Emiline turned and started walking toward the kitchen.

"Can I see Mandy before you take her?" Sarah asked, her tone nearly a plea.

"Mandy?" Emiline said. "Oh, the slave doll. That's a good name for her. Where'd you get a name like that?"

"Jubal told me that was her name," Sarah replied. "He said it's his mama's name."

"So it is. Mandy is his mama's name," said Emiline,

handing the doll to Sarah. "I don't know how you two come to know that man so good, and maybe I don't even want to know, but you should be careful who you go makin' friends with."

Sarah held Mandy up, kissed her smiling black face, and handed her back to Emiline.

"Jubal's my friend," she said. "He's my best friend."

We sneaked off to the swimming hole again one Saturday morning, and Jubal met us there as usual. Sarah ran to hug him around the waist as soon as he appeared. I felt happy to see him too, but I just shook his hand. He took my hand in both of his and smiled. Although shyness remained his natural manner, he talked to us easily and looked us in the eye when he spoke.

"We let Emiline take Mandy and Lucas's little wagon home with her," Sarah told him. "She said Mama would get real mad if she found them in our house."

"Yeah, she probably would at that," Jubal said. "Emiline'll take good care of them for you."

"You know who Emiline is?" Sarah asked incredulously.

"Yes," he answered, "I knows who near everybody in town is."

"Emiline knows your mama's name is Mandy."

"Most everybody knows who my mama is," Jubal said. "Would you like to know her."

"Your mama? Sure, I'd like to know her!" Sarah said, before I even had time to consider what he had asked.

"You can follow me to our house if you wants to," he said.

"Right now?"

"Yes, right now," he said, grinning at her exuberance.

"Come on, Lucas," Sarah said. "Jubal's gonna take us to his house to meet his mama!"

I was dumfounded at the invitation. I didn't really think it was something we should do, but the ecstasy on Sarah's face was too much for me. And I also couldn't bear to hurt Jubal by turning down his hospitality.

"Okay, Jubal. Lead the way," I said.

He smiled like a pleased child, then turned and led us to the big cottonwood where he always appeared. We followed him around the enormous trunk and onto the path that sloped down the side of the bank into the creek bed. The path had partially grown over from lack of use, but still it made the walking easy.

Jubal could see out over the fields, but Sarah and I found ourselves moving along the bottom of a deep trough the same as we had on our walk with Mama and Daddy the previous spring. And to our surprise Jubal stretched out at a brisk pace, unlike the slow trudge with which he always pulled his wagon around town. Sarah and I practically had to run to keep up with him.

With the stream bubbling beside me and Sarah bounding along in front, I felt happier than I had in a long time, and I was looking forward to meeting Jubal's mother. After we'd gone about half a mile Jubal sensed that we were tiring, and he slowed down to a regular walk.

It felt good after the fast pace we'd been going, and I found myself lost in thoughts of Daddy—the first pleasant thoughts I'd had about him since he died. I imagined him walking along with us, his long legs making those great easy strides, his smile brightening up the whole outside.

"There's my house," Jubal said, pointing ahead and off to

the left. I couldn't see it at first, only a grove of trees jutting out from the ones lining the creek bank. Looking closer, I found it: a small shack resting among the trees, their shadows merging with its irregular lines to form a near-perfect camouflage. As the path led us up the bank and closer, details began to emerge from the shadows.

The shack was built of hand-hewn boards, their beveled edges darkened by remnants of the original bark. A flat metal roof, extending out over the front to cover a small porch, sloped downward toward the back. Four twisted poles supported the porch, their irregular form reminding me of carved walking sticks. A number of chickens pecked, scratched, and chased each other around the shack and among the trees.

On the far side of the shack lay a wider path that led toward town, just visible in the distance. The path had been worn smooth by Jubal's feet and the wheels of his wagon. The grove of trees—being situated on an extension of the creek bank and the natural levees the stream had built—caused the shack to sit four or five feet higher than the surrounding countryside. A gentle berm sloped up into the yard from the field in front.

Nestled close to large trees on either side and butting tightly against them in back, the crude shack blended easily into its surroundings. Adding to its natural look was a total lack of straight lines. Although it was not apparent at first glance, as we neared the shack I began to think it looked somehow askew. First, the boards on the sides seemed misaligned, then every line on it began to look slightly out of kilter.

A large cottonwood, a monster, stood twenty feet in front of the shack, its limbs draped over the porch and shading the yard. In the shade of the big tree stood a hand-operated pump, its curved handle pointing at an angle toward the ground. Beneath the spigot rested a huge iron pot, its sides scorched black by the hundreds of wood fires that Jubal's mother had built around it over the years—her only source of hot water for the mounds of washing she did every day. Two clotheslines, hanging heavy with wet garments, ran from the corners of the porch to the big cottonwood. Several wooden tubs filled with soaking clothes rested on benches beside the porch.

An ancient rocker sat on the porch. In the rocker lay a white cat and four multicolored kittens of questionable ancestry. A black woman, small and stiffly erect, stood in the doorway.

"This is my mama," Jubal said proudly. "Mama, this be Lucas and Sarah."

With that introduction I learned a valuable lesson: I discovered how totally wrong a preconceived notion could be. I knew her name was Mandy, but to me this lady could never be a Mandy. She would forever be Miss Amanda.

Miss Amanda's skin was dark like Jubal's, her face thin and taut, her eyes disconcertingly alert. Her hair was short and neatly trimmed, the faded cotton dress worn but clean.

However small she may have been, Miss Amanda seemed to fill the doorway. She possessed a presence that would not be denied—a dignity that neither poverty, hard labor, nor the insults of others could degrade.

She looked first at me and then at Sarah, her gaze effecting a melting assessment.

"Come in," she said, and stepped back from the doorway. Neither of us moved until Jubal urged us forward. Then we walked tentatively onto the porch and through the door. Jubal followed us in, picking up the white cat as he passed the chair and cradling it in his arms.

Crossing the plank floor, I felt I was walking on an uneven surface, and again I had the odd feeling that the shack was somehow twisted or off-center.

Miss Amanda pushed a handmade table into a corner to make room for us, then pointed to a pair of crude chairs.

"Have a seat," she said.

As Sarah and I settled uneasily into the chairs Miss Amanda sat down on a narrow bed, the far side of which rested against a sheet that hung across the back of the room to form a makeshift curtain. Jubal sat down on the bed beside his mother and began stroking the cat. The cat stood up in his lap and rubbed against his chest, her gentle purr filling the room.

The walls were covered with newspaper. Tacks, driven through the paper about two feet apart, held it up. The ancient paper sagged in places and billowed in others as if pockets of air had been trapped behind it. The shack had two windows: one in front beside the door and another in the left wall. A cast-iron stove stood beside the window on the left, its black pipe passing through a tin-lined hole in the ceiling. A tall bench served as a kitchen counter while a shelf beneath it held buckets of water.

A wooden orange crate sat on end near the head of the bed—a makeshift bedside stand. On the crate stood a Bible, a kerosene lamp, and a single photograph in a hand-carved frame: a faded portrait of a smiling black man.

While I shuffled my feet, looked at my hands, and tried not to stare at the inside of the shack, Sarah gawked around in wonder. I could feel the intensity of Miss Amanda's gaze, and I dared not look in her eyes. Finally she spoke.

"Jubal talks about you two all the time. I swear, you'd think you was some of his own."

I didn't know what to say, but Sarah had no problem.

"Jubal's my best friend," she said proudly.

"I guess he's my best friend too," I said, surprising myself with the statement. Jubal smiled shyly and looked at his mother.

"Jubal gived you the Mandy doll and his little wagon, two of the things he loved most in this world," Miss Amanda said.

"I know he did," I replied, and for some reason found myself groping for my best English. "It was an honor when he gave them to us."

Miss Amanda looked at me coolly, and I thought I saw the hint of a smile in her eyes.

"Jubal's got a little spyglass that he can see a long ways off with," Miss Amanda said. "He can see to the road from here, the one you takes to get to the swimmin' hole. He watches the road every mornin' to see if you's goin' there."

"How long have you lived here?" Sarah asked.

"A long time, Sarah," Amanda said. "We lived here ever since Jubal was a baby. That's his Daddy in the picture here beside my bed. His name was Rufus."

Jubal glanced uneasily at the picture of his father, then quickly asked, "You want to see where I sleeps?"

Before we could answer, he stood up and pulled aside the

sheet that curtained off the back one-third of the house. A second narrow bed rested against the back wall, and another orange crate served as a bedside stand. A kerosene lamp stood on this crate as well, along with a number of books arranged neatly on end. Books also filled the shelf formed by the middle partition of the crate and more yet were stacked in the bottom. The books appeared worn, well-used, and strangely out of place

"Whose books?" I asked.

"They belonged to Jubal's daddy," Amanda said. "He knew how to read and write, and he left them for Jubal."

With that mention of his daddy, Jubal set the cat on the bed and walked out the door. Sarah and I looked after him with concern.

"It's okay," Miss Amanda said. "Jubal's daddy died when he was just a little boy, and he don't like to talk about him. But he was my husband, and I do like to talk about him some-times. Rufus was a fine-natured fella—always talkin' about what a pretty day it was, sometimes even when it wasn't."

"What happened to Jubal's daddy?" I asked.

"Oh, you's too young to hear such things," Miss Amanda said, reminding me of a similar answer I'd got when I posed the question to Emiline.

"Our daddy died," Sarah said, looking at the floor.

"I knows, Honey," said Miss Amanda, her stern eyes sud-denly soft. "I knows." Then she changed the subject.

"I seen you lookin' funny at the floor when you walked in, Lucas. I bet you wonderin' how come this old shack don't set just right, ain't you?"

"Well, sort of," I admitted.

"Rufus built it himself," she said, "before Jubal was born. Rufus was a smart man. He put the shack up here amongst these trees so we'd have the shade and so it'd be on high ground in case a flood come. It used to set a little ways out from them trees in back, before the big flood of '27 come. The water shoved it clean back against the trees and twisted it up so it don't set straight anymore."

Daddy had told me about the great Mississippi flood of 1927, and I learned more about it later in life as well. It was the biggest flood in the history of the river, the one that left highwater marks on the sides of many of the houses and stores in Linville. Even the courthouse bore a distinct line ten feet above its foundation.

I had been just two and a half at the time, and Mama was pregnant with Sarah. Daddy sent us away in the early spring for fear the levee would break, which it did a few weeks later. Before it broke, Daddy rolled up Mama's Persian rug and stowed it in the attic. And with the help of several strong men, some heavy wood, and a great amount of ingenuity, he built a scaffolding, laid the piano on its back, and hoisted it to the ceiling. It barely survived when the water filled the house.

Rain had fallen week after week and month after month until it soaked the entire drainage basin of the Mississippi River, an area covering a huge portion of the United States and extending into Canada. When this enormous valley flooded, the river swelled to the tops of the levees, uprooting forests and carrying trees, mules, hogs, barns, houses, and human bodies in its surge.

By the time it reached the Delta, the river had become a

raging torrent tens of miles wide. Black men were rounded up by the thousands and made to work on the levee, laboring day and night to buttress its bulging backside with sandbags by the million.

The levee finally broke several miles north of Greenville. A hundred-foot wall of water roared through a crevasse three-quarters of a mile wide, killing hundreds of black men who were sandbagging it as it broke. Twice the volume of Niagara Falls poured into the Delta and began filling it up like a giant soup bowl.

Within ten days the river filled the Delta and broke back through the levee at Vicksburg on the southern end, drowning thousands of head of livestock and hundreds of humans in its wake and leaving ten feet of water standing over the entire Delta. Five thousand square miles remained under water for weeks.

The Delta returned to virtual slavery during that period. Staring down the barrels of National Guard rifles with fixed bayonets and shotguns in the hands of redneck farmers, thirteen thousand blacks were forced to work and live atop the levee—a sinuous city of bottomless tents that snaked eight miles long by eight feet wide, the width of the levee crown—a disease-ridden colony where men shivered twenty-four hours a day, slept in the mud, and worked within a few feet of the raging water. If one fell in, his body belonged to the river.

"They came and got Jubal and took him to work on the levee," Miss Amanda said, "but before they took him he fixed the shack up so I could make it in the flood. He hung a bunch of water buckets up on nails around the edge of the ceiling.

That way I'd have enough to drink for a long time. He put all his books in tow sacks and hung them up high too.

"Then he stacked his bed on top of mine right here in the middle of the floor where I could stay up high and out of the water—wired the frames together so the beds wouldn't get shook apart when the water hit."

Jubal had been standing outside on the porch. When he heard his mother describing the flood, he came back in. He walked to the bed, picked up the cat, and sat down.

Miss Amanda continued.

"I had some salt pork and canned vegetables and the like, and I hung them up high too. With the buckets of water, we thought it'd be enough to last me through the flood. When the white men come and got Jubal, the last thing he said to me was: 'Mama, if that levee breaks you leave the windows and doors open. If you don't, the water'll tear the shack up when it hits. Just open them up and let it run on through.'

"We had a back door then, you see. That was before the water moved the shack backwards and jammed the door against a tree, like it is now."

I glanced at the back wall as she spoke. There it was, the dim outline of a door that hadn't been opened in years. Miss Amanda paused while Sarah and I studied the door, then she went on.

"Well, they took Jubal to the levee over by Greenville, and I stayed here, waitin' to see what happened. It was just a few days later that the levee broke. It took about three days for the water to get here, and by that time everybody knew it was comin'. I did what Jubal said—opened up the windows and doors and waited for it to come.

"I could see north out the side window and west out the front, and I knew it had to come from one of them ways. I thought I was ready for it, but Lord, when that water come there wasn't no way I could've been ready for somethin' like that. I seen it comin' from both windows and through the front door too. It was a wall of water eight or ten foot high, comin' like the wrath of the Lord, tearin' up trees and roarin' like a steam engine. It would've tore my trees up if they hadn't been so big.

"I climbed up on the top bed, opened up my Bible, and begun to pray. I looked out just before it hit, and there was a whole house headin' straight for me, and two dead cows besides. But the house went by on one side and the cows on the other. And when that water hit the front of this shack, I thought it'd tear it apart. It roared in through the door and the windows and sounded like it was rippin' the place in two. Tore the front door right off its hinges. It knocked the stovepipe down and picked up the stove and carried it right out the back door. Picked up the beds I was on and slid them up against the back wall, but it didn't knock them over, thank the Lord. I felt like I was flyin', and my head hit that wall so hard it like to knocked me cold. I swear I never been so scared in all my life.

"Jubal was right—the water started pourin' out the back door, but not as fast as it was comin' in the front. The place begun to fill up, then I felt the whole shack just lift up and start movin' backwards. That's when it slammed against the trees and knocked my head into the wall again. The shack stopped against the trunks, but it pushed the back door shut when it did. Water started fillin' the place up fast after that, and I thought I was a goner. Then it tore some boards outta the back of the house and found itself a way to get out. I sure was glad to see that."

Sarah and I sat mesmerized. Miss Amanda stared upward, her eyes distant as she relived the flood.

"The shack wasn't movin' anymore now, and when I looked out I could see dead mules, hogs, and trees floatin' by. Porches, roofs, and big pieces of barns and houses were all in the water. Even saw a big old black woman—she was whooshin' along on her back and whirlin' round and round like a windmill, her dead eyes starin' up in the air like she was still scared."

Miss Amanda stopped talking, took a deep breath, and her body seemed to relax.

"And that's how this old shack come to be crooked like it is," she said, smiling at Sarah and me.

My heart was pounding like a racehorse, and Sarah's eyes looked like they might pop out of her head.

"How long did the water stay in the house?" I asked.

"Well, it quit runnin' very much before that day was over, and then it just sat there. The water was about ten foot deep down off the yard, but thanks to Rufus buildin' the shack up on this high ground it was only about half that deep in here. I could stay dry up on the top bed, and even get a little sleep."

Miss Amanda grinned and shook her head.

"Trouble was—that water stayed where it was for weeks and weeks. It wasn't goin' nowhere. Me and Jubal hadn't quite figured on that, and I ended up stuck in here on top of the beds for more'n a month."

"A *month!*" Sarah said. "What did you do?"

"Well, with the beds over against the back wall I near had to swim to get to the water buckets and the food we'd hung up, but that worked all right, for awhile anyway. I had enough water to last me a long time, but I run out of food."

"What did you do?" Sarah said.

Miss Amanda scrutinized the two of us closely, trying to decide whether she should finish her story. She decided to.

"I had to leave the front door and the windows open all that time, else the stink of that dirty water would've killed me dead. The water kept on runnin' through, but just real slow. Ever now and then a dead cow or a mule would bump into the shack and then float on off.

"A bunch of chickens took up roost in here with me. Some of them was my own and some I never seen before. They sat around on anything high enough to keep them out of the water. I propped up the tore-off front door for them to set on, and some of them was always settin' on my bed with me.

"Snakes, mostly cottonmouths, come in lookin' for shelter themselves. The chickens would set up a racket whenever a snake come swimmin' in; which was good, 'cause that way none of them could ever sneak up on me. I had a broom handle up on the bed with me, and I'd use it to kill the snakes. Then I'd cut the snakes open and feed them to the chickens. They'll eat anything, you know."

"What did you eat," I asked.

"Chicken," she replied.

Chapter Ten

We had lost track of the time. We didn't have a watch to go by, and by the time Sarah and I left Jubal's and Miss Amanda's shack, the afternoon sun was low in the sky.

We could have walked to town on the path that Jubal used to make his deliveries. That was a shorter way home but would have taken us through the black part of town and across the railroad tracks, a place white children never went. Jubal walked us back to the swimming hole and told us to hurry home. We hurried as fast as we could, but we knew we were late.

Listening to Miss Amanda's stories had been more enjoyable than anything we'd done since we lost Daddy, but as we neared the house that evening I had to question the wisdom of our visit. When we opened the door and saw Mama's face, we knew the worst.

"Do you know what time it is?" she yelled.

She charged across the room, a cigarette dangling from her lips, and I smelled the booze on her breath before she reached us.

"Where have you been?!" she demanded, bending down and shouting in our faces.

Sarah hadn't said a word since we left the swimming hole; now she shocked me.

"We've been at Jubal's place," she said.

"Jubal's place?" Mama said, the name not registering at first. Then she remembered. "You mean Dummy?"

"Yes," Sarah said defiantly. "We went to the swimming hole, and Jubal took us to see his mama, Miss Amanda."

Mama looked confused, like the entire scene did not compute—neither us visiting Jubal's mother nor Sarah talking back to her made the least bit of sense. Her face went through wild contortions—confusion, bewilderment, then a terrible realization.

"Oh, God!" she said, pressing her temples and staring at us in horror. Then she turned on Sarah.

"You think that's smart don't you, little girl?" she screamed. "Spouting your sassy mouth off at me. You could have been Miss America, or a musician, or anything you wanted. But what did you turn out to be? A goddamned nigger lover!"

Sarah's eyes widened in fear, but she held Mama's gaze, until Mama hit her. Mama swung from the right, slapping her so hard it snapped her head to one side. Before she could regain her balance, Mama hit her across the other cheek with her left hand, then again with her right. Sarah reeled like a prizefighter knocked senseless on his feet.

"Mama, stop!" I yelled. "You're going to kill her!"

I rushed toward them, but Mama whirled and caught me

by surprise. She slugged me hard on the cheekbone, the blow exploding in my ear. I flew across the room, slammed into the door, and slid to the floor.

"You stay out of this," Mama yelled. Then, her eyes blazing like the devil's own, she turned back to Sarah. She grabbed her hair in both hands and drove her face into the wall.

I lay against the door rubbing my cheek, too dazed to get up. Ever since Daddy died I had harbored the notion that I could take care of Sarah. Lying there watching Mama pound her unmercifully, I knew the terrible truth. I could not protect my sister.

The next day was Sunday. As was often the case on the Sabbath, Emiline didn't work that day. My left cheek was purple and swollen, my eye bloodshot and ringed in a dark circle. Sarah looked worse.

Both of her eyes were black, the bruises extending across the bridge of her nose and back along both temples—a cruel mask that might have been hooked behind her ears. Her cheeks were swollen and discolored, her nose too sore to touch.

Mama was already half drunk by noon, and still in a black mood. Sarah and I got dressed, but didn't venture out of our room.

Mama threw our bedroom door open with a bang.

"Come on, you two. We're going for a ride," she said.

Wondering where we were going, we followed her out to the car and climbed into the front seat. She took off with a vengeance, pinning us to the back of the seat with acceleration, and headed for downtown. At the town square Mama slowed and circled the courthouse, craning her neck and searching every street and sidewalk as she drove. We were afraid to ask what, or who, she was looking for.

Failing to find whatever it was on the square, Mama began driving up and down residential streets, scanning the neighborhoods in every direction. Then we rounded a corner and she spotted him. Jubal was half a block away with his back to us, pulling his wagon down the street in the same direction we were moving. Mama clamped her jaw and stomped the accelerator. We moved up on him fast, and for a terrifying moment I thought she intended to run him over. Jubal heard us coming, glanced over his shoulder, and turned toward the curb.

Just before we reached him, Mama slammed on the brakes and slid to a stop. "You kids stay put," she growled.

She leaped out of the car and ran toward him, her hair flying behind her like a madwoman.

In a voice that caused doors to open up and down the block and people to peer out front windows, Mama said, "Dummy! Stop right there, boy."

"Yes, Ma'am," Jubal said. He stopped and averted his eyes to the ground, his arms at his sides, the wagon tongue resting in his hand.

Mama leaned into his face with a blazing stare. He stood perfectly still and concentrated on her feet.

"What do you think you're doing, messing with my children?" she demanded.

Jubal didn't answer.

"I'm talking to you, boy. Answer me!"

"I ain't been messin' with your children, Ma'am. I ain't done nothin' with them."

"You took them to that shithole of a shack you live in, and let them talk to your mama. Don't tell me you *ain't done nothin' with them,*" she said in a mocking tone. "You trying to lie to me, boy?"

"No, Ma'am," Jubal said, then turned his head and risked a glance in our direction. He could see our bruised faces through the car window, and in that moment I saw our own pain reflected in his eyes. He dropped his gaze back to Mama's feet.

"Don't you be looking at my children," Mama said. "I'll take care of them. They're none of your concern, nigger. You hear me—none of your concern."

"Yes, Ma'am," he said.

"Now listen close," she said, inches from his downturned face. "You keep your black ass away from my children. You hear me, boy?"

"Yes, Ma'am."

"You better be hearing me. You know who my Daddy is, don't you? Our men have ways of taking care of niggers like you, you know."

Jubal had remained expressionless until that moment. With Mama's threat a terrible fear gripped his face.

Mama marched back to the car, slid in, and slammed the door. I glanced in his direction as we roared past him. He didn't look up.

Emiline woke us Monday morning, looked at our bruises, and didn't say a word. She gently washed our swollen faces and got us ready for school. At breakfast I looked at her and asked, "Do we have to go to school looking like this?"

"Yes," she said. "You can't be missin' school. You go on, and make the best of it."

I'm sure she wanted us to be seen.

Silence fell as we entered the school, and every kid turned to stare. I felt like some sort of freak on display. My teacher couldn't hide her shock when I walked into class, but she turned away and said nothing. Then walking down the hall at recess I came face to face with the principal. I attempted to sneak past him but he stopped me.

"What happened to your face, Lucas?" Mr. Tarver asked.

"I ran into a door, Sir," I said, avoiding his eyes.

"You ran into a door," he said, shaking his head. "Did your sister run into the same door?"

"I think so," I muttered.

Mr. Tarver stared at me in exasperation. I knew he didn't believe me.

"Sarah's been running into a lot of doors lately," he said. "Now you're starting to run into them too?"

"I guess so, Sir," I answered.

"You two need to be more careful," he said, "about everything you do. Now go on and play, Lucas."

I quickly left him and went outside. Sarah and I stood against the side of the building until the bell rang to call us back in.

Grandma and Grandpa Dunaway came to the house late that afternoon. Mama heard their truck pull up and peeked out around the front drapes.

"You kids get in your room and shut the door," she said. "And don't make a sound."

When Mama answered the front door we could hear every word of the conversation. "Well, hello," she said. "Haven't seen you folks in a while."

"Hello, Jessica," Grandma Dunaway said. "How have you been?"

"Oh, I've been doing well—staying busy at the store and taking care of the kids," Mama said, though she seldom worked at Tolliver's Grocery anymore. She didn't invite them in, and I could picture Grandma and Grandpa standing on the porch looking at Mama uneasily as they talked.

"How are the kids, Jessica?" Grandpa asked. "We heard they got their faces banged up, both of them."

"Oh, that," Mama said, interrupting herself with a chuckle. "They were chasing each other around the house like a couple of wild Indians—you know how kids are—and they both piled up against a door frame at the same time. It didn't hurt them very bad, though. They look worse than they really are."

"Where are they?" Grandma asked. "Can we see them?" I could hear impatience edging into her voice.

"Well, they happen to be over visiting their Grandpa Burris right now," Mama said, "and I was just leaving to go help Mother close up the store."

Mama knew they wouldn't go to the Tolliver's house to check on us; John Dunaway despised Burris Tolliver.

"All right," Grandma said, sounding less than convinced. "Tell Lucas and Sarah we stopped by, and give them our love. You need to bring them out to our place to visit us one of these days, Jessica."

"I'll do that," Mama said, though they all knew there was little chance of that happening. Mama and Grandma had never seen eye to eye even when Daddy was alive.

"Take care of yourself, Jessica, and the kids," Grandma said.

"I will," Mama answered, and closed the door.

We lived like prisoners for the next three weeks. Mama wouldn't allow us to go anywhere except to school, and we had to come straight home in the afternoon. Occasionally she talked to me in the evening and even patted me on the head a couple of times as she walked by, but she never spoke to Sarah. Neither of us dared try to start a conversation with her; she got drunk every night, and we were afraid of her.

Child abuse was a taboo subject in those days; it was strictly a family matter. If people outside the family knew about it or suspected it—whether they be friends, neighbors, or authorities—they stayed out of it.

Mama was a walking powder keg primed to explode at any moment, and I knew Sarah would pay the price when she did. Sarah withdrew from the world, spending most of her time in our room with her dolls. I'd see her whispering to the dolls at times, but other than that she hardly spoke, even to me.

We had no one to turn to. Grandpa Tolliver had neither the strength nor the inclination to help us if he had known the situation, and Grandma Tolliver was not only overworked but Mama kept her at arm's length. Grandma and Grandpa Dunaway were likely suspicious of Mama, but they were uncomfortable with the ways of city folk and reluctant to interfere, and they had a farm to run.

I thought of Daddy every day, and cried for him in the night.

I had read everything in the house, and hungered for a book in which I could lose myself and escape the frightening world, at least for short periods. Just after noon the next Saturday I got up the nerve to ask Mama if we could go to the library.

"All right," she said, "but don't you go to that swimming hole again, and don't be going to the store and bothering Grandma Tolliver either."

"We won't," I promised.

Mama's eyes narrowed, and she shook a finger in Sarah's face.

"And stay away from Dummy too. I better not hear of you talking to that nigger again. You hear me, little girl?" Sarah nodded, and reached for my hand.

Mama told us we could stay out longer than I expected; we'd have time to stop on the square for awhile after we left the library. Sarah didn't seem to care what we did; she just held tightly to her rag doll and followed me.

Miss Hawkins beamed when we walked into the library. "Hello, you two," she said, louder than she ever allowed anyone to talk in her hallowed space. Before we made it five feet inside the door the prim librarian was out from behind her desk and squatting down in front of us.

"Let me see your faces," she said. "I haven't seen you in so long."

I was aware of how fast news traveled in Linville, and Miss Hawkins' motive for looking closely in our faces didn't escape me. Even so, I enjoyed the attention; it felt good to have someone besides Emiline making over us for a change. As usual, Sarah sat at a table and held her doll while I perused the books. More than once I caught Miss Hawkins staring at us with concern in her eyes.

Mr. and Mrs. Dinkin also greeted us grandly. They too scrutinized us closely, and filled a paper sack with twice as many doughnuts and cookies as they'd ever given us before. We took our sweets outside and sat on our favorite bench, the spot where we always watched for Jubal. We tried to act as if we really weren't watching for him, but when he came into view a block down the street neither of us could take our eyes off of him.

He knew to look for us on that bench, and as he drew near we kept expecting him to raise his eyes and share a secret smile with us the way he always did. But this time he didn't. He pulled his wagon past us without a glance in our direction. Sarah leaned back on the bench and hugged her doll to her chest, her tears staining its face.

I'd been serving our supper most nights since Mama started drinking again. As fall turned to winter, she began coming home late, sometimes after Sarah and I had already gone to bed. If we were still up when she stumbled through the door, reeking of booze and cigarettes, she'd look at us with a sneer, as if daring us to ask where she'd been.

She still brushed her hair, applied her makeup meticulously, and dressed well when she went out, but she didn't really look pretty anymore, just hard and severe. Sometimes we went to bed early to avoid facing her return from wherever it was that she was spending her time.

We had known about her bottle in the pantry ever since she started drinking, but she'd always preferred to take her swigs in private. Now she didn't even attempt to hide it. She'd pull out the bottle, uncork it, and take a drink of whiskey right in front of us. Or she might pour herself a glass and sit at the kitchen table sipping it while staring blankly out the window and filling the ash tray with cigarette butts.

Mama was standing at the pantry swallowing a mouthful one evening when Sarah came out of the bathroom and walked past her. I was sitting in the front room looking toward the kitchen when Sarah turned to walk out the kitchen door into the dining room. She turned her head and glanced back over her shoulder at Mama with a disapproving look. Mama saw her do it.

"Who do you think you're glaring at?" Mama screamed, grabbing a broom and racing across the kitchen at Sarah.

Sarah turned toward me and walked calmly out of the kitchen, neither looking back at Mama nor reacting to the sounds of her pursuit. Mama ran out the kitchen door, raising the broom over her head as she rounded the corner, her face twisted in rage. I saw the broom whip through the air and come down in a blur, and heard a loud crack as the handle broke across Sarah's head.

Sarah's face remained expressionless. She took another step, her eyes rolled up into her head, and she sank to the floor. She lay still, her face pressed against the wood. Mama dropped the broken handle, turned, and stalked back to the kitchen. I heard the pantry door open again.

I didn't run to Sarah; I walked. I sat down on the floor beside her and stroked her hair, hoping she was alive. She lay unconscious for several minutes, then I helped her to bed. She could barely walk.

Emiline had a difficult time waking Sarah the next morning, and she wasn't alert when she did wake. The blow hadn't lacerated her scalp, but the bump that protruded from the top of her head was half the size of a tennis ball. Emiline ran her fingers over the lump gingerly, then kissed her on the cheek and told her to go back to sleep.

Pieces of broomstraw and wood lay scattered on the dining room floor. While I ate breakfast Emiline picked up the remains of the broom and carried them out to the trash barrel behind the house. When she returned she looked at me and shook her head in frustration. The question loomed too large to avoid.

"What happened last night, Lucas?" she said.

I was afraid to speak at first, but felt I had to. "Mama broke the broom over Sarah's head," I told her. "It knocked her out cold. I thought she was dead."

"Lord, God," Emiline said, then turned away and continued her work.

At school that morning Mr. Tarver stopped me in the hall. "What's wrong with Sarah?" he asked. "Did she run into something again?"

"No," I lied. "She's sick."

I felt distracted all that day, and walking home that afternoon I kept seeing the broom handle break over Sarah's head and her eyes roll up as she sank to the floor.

Mama was gone when I got home, and Sarah was still in bed. Emiline met me at the door, and I followed her into the kitchen. I still had my books in my hand when the words came tumbling out of my mouth.

My lips trembled as I spoke. "I'm scared, Emiline. I don't know what's going to happen to Sarah and me."

Emiline didn't answer. She didn't even turn her head, just went on washing dishes.

"Emiline?" I said.

She stopped and turned toward me.

"You and Sarah got to be as good as you can be these days," she said. "Your Mama's goin' through a bad time, and you got to keep from rilin' her up."

"But she won't even talk to us," I said. "And she acts like she hates Sarah. Last night I thought she'd killed her."

"I know, Lucas," Emiline said, "and I loves the two of you like you was my own. But you don't understand; there's nothin' I can do. This is white folks' business."

She turned back to her work.

"Please, Emiline, we don't have anybody to help us."

"No, Lucas. No!" she said. "That's white folks' business."

Chapter Eleven

Emiline kept Sarah home from school for a week after Mama hit her with the broom. Sarah slept most of every day, and most of the time Mama didn't seem to even know she was there. Sarah wouldn't say a word, not even to Emiline.

I never learned where Mama was spending her nights, and I guess I never wanted to know. We had no idea what time she might come in; sometimes she'd be there when we got home from school and other times we'd hear her fumbling with the front door lock at two or three o'clock in the morning.

On a few occasions we heard her wandering through the house muttering to herself, either cursing some unknown adversary in bitter tones or crying and calling Daddy's name.

Mama still talked to me on occasion, but she seldom even looked at Sarah. Sarah whispered to her dolls often, and talked to them aloud when only she and the dolls were in the bedroom—and if Mama wasn't home. When Mama was in the house she wouldn't make a sound.

Mama still allowed us to walk downtown for short periods on the weekends, and though we knew she might be gone when we returned, we were never a minute late. We didn't dare go to the swimming hole, and since Jubal would no longer even look at us we figured he wouldn't meet us there anyway. We still harbored the hope that he'd return to us one day, or at least I did; I couldn't guess what was going on in Sarah's head. At the square we always sat on our regular bench and watched for him, though most of the time we didn't see him. The few times we did he simply trudged by as if we weren't there.

Crossing a street on our way home one day, I sensed something, or someone, down the block to our right. Sarah must have had the same feeling; we both turned our heads at the same time. We saw Jubal a block away; he was standing in the shadows of a tree, watching us. His wagon was parked behind him as if he'd been waiting for us to appear. He looked directly at us and remained motionless. I raised my hand and waved, just once. He dropped his head, picked up the tongue of his wagon, and walked away.

My heart sank as I watched the wagon full of clothes recede down the dusty street, his head and shoulders protruding above the load. Somehow he seemed to move even slower than normal. I glanced down at Sarah, and she wasn't even looking at him. I started to call his name, but didn't.

As the holiday season drew near, there were no preparations at our house—no thoughts of a tree with bright packages under it holding wondrous gifts to be revealed Christmas morning, no Daddy to fill the room with laughter. Since our lives had become little more than a daily ritual of survival,

I was hardly aware of Christmas coming. And Sarah didn't seem to care about anything.

One afternoon when Mama was gone Emiline pulled back the front drapes, glanced up and down the street, and picked up her purse.

"I brought somebody to see you, Sarah," she said, and pulled out the Mandy doll. Sarah's eyes brightened more than I'd seen them in months. She took Mandy from Emiline, hugged her to her chest, and walked to the sofa and sat down.

Sarah whispered to Mandy and hugged her close while Emiline watched for Mama out the front window. After ten minutes or so Emiline held out her hand.

"All right, Angel, I think I better put Mandy back in my purse. I'll carry her back home with me and keep her safe for you."

"I love you, Mandy," Sarah said. Then she kissed the doll's smiling face and handed her to Emiline.

Two weeks before Christmas our world nearly came to an end. I remember Mama had on a red satin blouse that night—a long-sleeved one that Daddy had given her for Christmas the year before. The blouse had white mother-of-pearl buttons down the front and on the sleeves, and I thought it was the prettiest one she owned. I think she did too.

No one ever knew for sure how the fire began, but the firemen felt positive it started somewhere near the front of the house. One of Mama's cigarettes may have dropped into the sofa and smoldered until it burst into flames.

Mama had been drinking heavily that evening, and Sarah and I went to bed without telling her goodnight. Before I fell asleep I heard her in the front room, sobbing and crying out: "Reid. Oh, Reid, where are you? I can't make it without you."

We awoke later in the night, and already I could hear the flames crackling near the front of the house. The fire lit up the crack at the side of our bedroom door—a bright orange ribbon that brought panic rising in my throat. I could smell the smoke filtering under the door. I crawled out of bed onto the floor and reached up and touched Sarah; she crawled out and huddled next to me. The two of us crouched low, not knowing what to do.

The wind was blowing from the front of the house to the back, and we heard the flames racing down the outside wall, igniting the dry wood like tinder as they ran. As the heat from the fire grew behind us, I reached up and pushed open the bedroom door. The far wall was ablaze. Flames engulfed the front wall and sofa to our left. Thick smoke rolled into the room, choking us.

Then the front windows blew out. The wind blew in and partially cleared the smoke, creating an eerie, shadowy effect that waxed and waned between us and the flames that danced to our left and lit up the far side of the room.

Sarah and I cowered on our hands and knees in the doorway. The heat scorched our pajama-covered backsides and seared our faces; the flames mesmerized us. We clung to one another, too terrified to move. We'd have remained frozen in that doorway until the fire consumed us.

The wind carried the fire the length of the outside walls, then it shot across the back of the house. The wall behind us burned through. Flames broke out above us. The roof burned, and the attic. Black smoke scorched our throats. Hot sweat ran down our faces.

Suddenly, through the roar of the fire we heard a sharp crash. A shadowy figure charged through the front door, tearing it off its hinges as he came. He ducked his head low to look below the smoke. Finding us crouched in the doorway, he picked up the stuffed chair to our right and threw it into the dining room. It toppled the dining room table. Then he ran toward the opposite wall and disappeared into the smoke.

A faint outline flew through the air and bounced on the dining room floor—the piano bench. Then the piano itself—I saw it begin to move, a dark image moving in front of the flaming wall. He was pushing it.

To our right, a second figure took form in the smoke, moving through the dining room toward the other. A voice, screaming, barely audible above the roar. ". . . OUT OF MY HOUSE, NIGGER!" Both figures moving in the smoke, disappearing, reappearing, converging. A swirl of movement, a muffled scream, a thump.

The piano moved again, a dark mass that seemed to float into the dining room. Then it crashed to the floor. The shadowy figure moved to the left, bent down, pulled the rug from under the flaming sofa, and stomped out the flames at the edge of the rug. With a loud crack the ceiling sagged above his head, a burning mass fell beside him. He whirled and kicked it off the rug.

Flames licked across the floor from the wall behind us; we felt the searing heat on the bottoms of our feet and the backs of our legs as it came. Fire rolled toward us from the front room and dining room walls like something liquid, consuming the floor in its path.

He raced to us, picked us up like matchsticks, and threw us on our sides near the edge of the rug. Leaning close, he reached around our backs and forced us together. We lay face to face with our arms gripped around each other. He grabbed the edge of the big rug and rolled us up inside it. Then he picked it up, his right arm wrapped around the two of us like a vice, the ends of the rolled-up rug draped toward the floor. As we started for the front door, something heavy fell behind us.

The rug partially shielded us from the heat, but the air choked us; my breath came in great gasps. My eyes burned; my throat was on fire. I could hear Sarah coughing, nearly in my ear. We stopped moving, and I felt the flames licking at the rug and heard the roaring and crackling all around. A hard jerk to the left, then to the right. A loud crack. Something fell. Sarah and I were slammed sideways, back and forth, over and over again. Even through the rug the blows bruised our bodies.

Jubal couldn't force himself and the bulging rug through the doorway. He covered his eyes with his left hand and stopped in the middle of the flames. Jouncing his body from side to side like a human hammer, he battered the doorway down. That's when his clothes caught fire, and the rug that we were in.

Sarah dug her fingers into my back and screamed. With

his shirt and pants ablaze and the rug burning against his side, flesh fell from Jubal's fingers as he held us wedged under his arm.

He lunged forward, plunging across the burning porch and off into the yard before he fell, his ruined arm clutching us still. A great moan escaped him that sounded like death.

I heard men yelling, their voices muffled as if in the distance. Then they came closer.

"Pull him back, away from the house!" someone yelled.

The human sounds receded for a moment, then Jubal's voice: "No!" A hand clawed at the rug.

"Hey!" a man shouted. "There's somebody in that rug. Drag it back here!"

Doc Armstead's voice: "Carry him over there to the edge of the grass, boys. Be easy with him."

Hands unrolled us from the rug—the sheriff, the fire chief, others.

"It's Lucas and Sarah," Sheriff Turnbull said.

"My God," the chief muttered.

Doc Armstead was all over us—feeling us, turning us, patting our bodies, touching our faces, looking in our eyes.

"You okay, Son?" he asked, his eyes boring into mine. I nodded. "Does your throat burn? Can you talk? Tell me your name."

"L-Lucas," I said, and went into a coughing spasm. From deep in my throat I coughed up a black wad and spit it on the ground.

"Tell me again," Doc ordered. "What's your name?"

"Lucas," I said.

He turned to Sarah. "Are you all right, Honey?" She

nodded, dazed. "Tell me your name." And they went through the same drill until Sarah said her name clearly.

"Get up on your feet and stand over there with the sheriff," Doc told us. "I've got to see to your savior."

With the red glow of the fire at our backs, Sheriff Turnbull walked us to the edge of the yard. My legs were shaking so badly I thought I might fall. We turned and looked at the blazing house—the house we'd been inside only moments before. The porch began to yaw to one side as we watched; a shower of sparks and flames shot skyward as it collapsed. The sheriff rested a hand on each of our heads.

I could see Jubal lying on his back at the far corner of the yard, Doc Armstead kneeling over him. Others looked down at his charred body and shook their heads. I glanced at Sarah, and realized how I must look. Black soot covered her face, arms, and legs like the camouflage paint of a soldier; her blond hair was mostly black and scattered in tangles, her nightgown streaked and torn.

Lost and confused, Sarah started to walk toward Jubal. Sheriff Turnbull gently pulled her back, squatted down, and put his hands on her shoulders.

"We have to let Doc work on him, Sarah," he told her. "Jubal needs Doc a lot more than he needs us now."

Sarah turned to me, wrapped her arms around my neck, and began to cry.

Clarence Tull, the fire chief, came over and asked if we were all right. Sarah didn't answer, but I nodded my head and told him we were. Then the chief looked at the sheriff quizzically and asked, "What was that you put in your pocket, Anson?"

"My pocket?" the sheriff said. "What are you talking about, Clarence?"

"Up there by the house, right after Dummy carried these kids out of the fire. When we were unrolling them out of the rug I saw you stick something in your pants pocket."

"Oh, that," Sheriff Turnbull said. "It wasn't anything. While I was crawling around on my knees helping these kids up I felt my key ring about to fall out, and I just poked it back down in my pocket."

The sheriff looked back at the house, concentrating on the fire. Chief Tull studied his face for a moment, then walked away.

Grandma Tolliver came charging into the yard, her hair flying straight out behind her. She had on a nightgown, a long robe, and slippers. She had run all the way from her house.

"Where are they?" Grandma screamed. "Where are they?"

Sheriff Turnbull called to her. "Over here, Tessie."

Grandma ran over and knelt down in front of us, her eyes frantic. "Are you kids all right?"

"We're okay, Grandma," I said.

"Where's your mama?" she said, looking around desperately. When I didn't answer she turned her eyes up to the sheriff. "Where's Jessica, Anson?" she asked fearfully. "Where's my daughter?"

Sheriff Turnbull looked at her helplessly and shook his head. Grandma's eyes widened in panic. She leaped up and ran toward the burning house. The sheriff raced after her, and caught her halfway across the yard. Silhouetted against the bright orange flames, she fought desperately to break free from his grasp.

"No! No!" she screamed. "My baby's in that house—my Jessica!"

With the aid of a fireman, the sheriff got Grandma under control, and they pulled her back to where we stood. Doc Armstead left Jubal for a few minutes to come and help calm her down.

About the time the men were beginning to get ahead of the fire, Grandma and Grandpa Dunaway rushed up out of the darkness. They squatted in front of Sarah and me.

"Are either of you hurt?" Grandpa asked.

I shook my head, and Grandma broke into tears.

John Dunaway stood up, cast a questioning glance at Sheriff Turnbull, and said: "Jessica?" The sheriff said nothing, and Grandpa knew.

"How'd the kids get out?" Grandpa asked. Sheriff Turnbull pointed across the yard at Doc Armstead, working over a dark figure lying on the ground.

"Jubal, that Negro they call Dummy. He ran right through the front door and carried them out. Rolled them up inside a big rug. Caught himself on fire doing it. Near burned him up."

Grandpa shook his head in amazement. "Is he alive?"

"I think so," the sheriff said. They both turned their gaze back to the burning house. Sarah released her grip from around my neck and went to Grandpa.

Jubal's heavy shoes had protected his feet, but he suffered second- and third-degree burns over seventy percent of his body, arms, and legs. His neck was badly burned as well as his ears and the underside of his chin. Since he had covered his eyes and nose with his left hand when he stopped to break down the flaming doorway, his face had escaped harm. And miraculously, his lungs survived; he must have held his breath to keep from inhaling the smoke and flames.

Because he had kept his right arm gripped tightly around the rug to protect us, Jubal's hand and forearm had literally been fried. Some of the spectators heard Doc Armstead say he might lose the arm.

Even through the din of the fire and shouting men, we could hear Jubal moaning. Some neighbors brought sheets for Doc to lay him on, then he removed the remnants of Jubal's burned shirt and pants as best he could without tearing more flesh away. He pulled a large roll of cotton bandage material from his bag and wrapped his right hand and arm like a mummy.

When Doc finished working on Jubal, he walked over to where we stood and looked at Grandpa.

"Jubal's in shock now," he said, "but pretty soon he's going to be in more pain than you can imagine. I gave him a shot of morphine, but even that won't help him much."

Doc squatted down to talk to Sarah and me. His face was dirty and his eyes looked weary.

"Jubal saved your lives tonight," he said. "I watched him run up on the porch and through the front door. How he even knew the fire was going on is a mystery to me, but you can thank God that he did."

"Is he going to live?" I asked.

"I don't know, Son," Doc said. "I honestly don't know. I've never seen anyone burned that bad."

Doc studied our faces a moment, then went on.

"I don't know why Jubal did what he did to save you kids, but it was the most heroic act I've ever seen in my life. I'm going to do everything I can to save him."

Doc stood up and looked at Grandpa Dunaway.

"Would you mind watching over Jubal for a few minutes, John?" he asked. "Just keep people from getting too close to him, and try and keep him from moving his right arm. I'm afraid it may have to be amputated. I've got to go home and get my wife; she used to be a nurse, you know. We're going to put Jubal in my car and drive him to the Negro-American Hospital in Yazoo City tonight. She can look after him while I drive. It's the only hospital in Mississippi that will admit a Negro, and the one place where the doctors might have a chance of saving him."

"Yazoo City?" Grandpa said. "That's seventy-five miles from here, Doc. You up to that tonight?"

"I have to be," Doc said. "If I don't get him there he won't make it to morning."

Chapter Twelve

Although sections of the ceiling fell in, the roof of the house didn't collapse. Some of the floor also survived, along with portions of the inner walls.

It was daylight before Chief Tull and his men dared enter the house. Sheriff Turnbull followed closely behind them. They found the dining room heaped with furniture. Some of it had burned and some had not. In order to clear the front room rug, Jubal had thrown everything but the burning sofa into the dining room. The piano had landed on its back near the archway.

They found Mama in the dining room too. She was lying against the right-hand wall, one of the center portions that hadn't burned. Sarah and I weren't told the condition of her body at the time, nor did we feel like asking. We just thought she had burned up in the fire.

Mama's funeral was well attended, though not like Daddy's had been, and her casket remained closed. While Grandma Tolliver was nearly hysterical, Grandpa Burris sat quiet and still, brooding.

If Grandma and Grandpa Dunaway hadn't been there, Sarah and I couldn't have made it through the ordeal. Grandma sat with her arm around me while Sarah clung tightly to Grandpa, her face hidden against his arm. She hadn't said a word since the fire, and I don't think she ever opened her eyes during the service.

Pastor Hogan appeared tired, drained, as he walked past Mama's casket. But he turned and looked out over the crowd, gripped the sides of the pulpit, and pulled himself up to full height. He looked down at Sarah and me, a terrible sadness in his eyes.

"We are here today to mourn the loss of one of our own," the minister said. "Jessica Dunaway, a beautiful young woman, and the mother of two beautiful children. A tragic loss, the second in one family in too short a time.

"Why, we might ask. Why did such a terrible thing happen? And how? How could God allow such an atrocity to occur? What is the use of it all? We may ponder these questions, search our minds, and become angry when we cannot find an answer. I have done so myself on occasion, and still the answer did not come. We can only pray, and believe in our hearts, that God, in His infinite wisdom, has His reasons.

"God often allows things to happen which we don't understand. Sometimes these things seem unimaginably horrible, and other times wonderful beyond belief. Some contain elements of both. Two nights ago, while one life was consumed in a raging fire, the lives of two others, children, were spared. An unlikely savior—a simple Negro man— snatched Lucas and Sarah from the flames. We all know him; we've seen him pulling his wagon around town, delivering clothes for his mother. He seldom talks to anyone, nor does he even look up as he passes by, and because of that he's been called Dummy. His name is not Dummy. His name is Jubal, and I believe that God in His wisdom sent Jubal to save Lucas and Sarah that night.

"I was not personally a witness, but I've heard the story from many lips. With no regard for his own life, Jubal ran into the burning house and carried the children out. He saved them, unharmed, and in doing so was horribly burned himself.

"For whatever reasons the Almighty had, Jessica Dunaway was taken from this earth early in her life. And while we mourn Jessica's passing and pray for her soul, we must also think of the living, and pray for them as well. Lucas and Sarah have long lives ahead of them, lives that will need the stabilizing influence of strong adults. As we pray for Jessica, let us also pray for her children, that God will help them find the love and security they need so badly in their lives. And let us not forget their savior, Jubal, and say a prayer for his recovery as well."

Burris Tolliver straightened abruptly at Pastor Hogan's last line, and uttered a disgusted "Humph."

Only two black people came to Mama's funeral: Emiline and Miss Amanda. I saw them near the edge of the church-yard as we walked out, and I asked Grandma if she would take me to them. She walked me over to where they stood, Grandpa Dunaway following behind with Sarah holding his hand. Emiline had managed to maintain her composure until then; now she dropped to her knees and hugged us to her bosom.

"Lucas," she said," and my Angel." She called our names again and again, tears streaming down her face.

Miss Amanda remained stoic until Emiline stood up. Then she bent down, reached out, and gently caressed our cheeks. Her face looked weary and drawn. Dark veins stood out on her forehead, and the lines in her cheeks seemed deeper than ever. Her eyes held no tears, but behind the steely composure I sensed the same softness I'd seen in Jubal's eyes.

"You fine, fine children," Miss Amanda said. "You precious jewels."

Then she stood up, turned, and walked away.

Grandma and Grandpa Dunaway asked everyone in the family to come to their house after the funeral. They all did; even Grandpa and Grandma Tolliver were there. When Uncle Robert told his kids they could play outside, Aunt Eunice and Aunt Esther sent their children out as well.

Grandpa Dunaway guided Sarah and me to the sofa in the big room, where he sat down in the center and motioned me to sit on one side of him and Sarah on the other. Everyone else sat in chairs that had been gathered from other rooms; somehow they all seemed to be facing the sofa. Grandpa Tolliver took a large stuffed chair that sat in a corner; Grandma Tolliver took a straight-backed one next to him.

After everyone had been seated, Grandma Dunaway served glasses of sweet tea. Hardly a word was spoken as people shuffled in and sat down—only polite nods and thank yous as Grandma handed them their drinks. Occasional sobs and sniffles came from Grandma Tolliver, and guttural sounds as Burris Tolliver cleared his throat.

When Grandma Dunaway finished serving the tea, she took a chair at the end of the sofa next to Sarah. As usual, Sarah was leaning against Grandpa Dunaway. Grandpa took a sip of tea, looked all around the room, and began to speak.

"Pastor Hogan was right; we've got to think of the living. Of course, we'll miss Reid and Jessica every day for as long as we live . . . ."

A painful wail escaped Grandma Tolliver at the mention of Mama's name. Grandpa stopped talking until she regained her composure.

"Lucas and Sarah have got to have a home," he continued, "a place where they can live and find happiness again. And they'll need people to be there for them, to give them strength."

Again Grandpa scanned the room, looking from one person to the next. No one moved, and I didn't see anyone looking directly at him.

"Anybody got any suggestions?" he asked.

Uncle Robert was staring at the floor. He stirred uncomfortably in his chair, then spoke without looking up.

"I guess they could come and stay with us. Our kids seem purty happy, and as many as we got, two more won't make no difference."

Robert's wife, who was holding a baby, their seventh, said nothing.

Neither Aunt Eunice nor Aunt Esther said a word; nor did their husbands look up. Grandma Tolliver blew her nose, wiped her eyes, and straightened herself in her chair.

"The children could certainly come and stay with us," Grandma said. "Our house is there in town where they're used to living, and God knows it's big enough to accommodate two more. Burris and I are the only ones rattling around in it now, and I'm off tending the store a good part of the day. They'd be company for their Grandpa Burris when I wasn't there; it would be good for them and us too."

Grandpa Tolliver sat in the big chair, his hands folded in his lap, his gaze concentrated on his hands. He didn't stir while Grandma was speaking, and he continued to stare at his hands after she stopped.

"What do you think of that idea, Burris?" Grandpa Dunaway asked. Silence hung heavy in the room. No one could have missed the challenge in John Dunaway's voice—certainly not Burris Tolliver. He knew Grandpa Dunaway had him, and everyone else knew it too.

Grandpa Tolliver had to reply. He looked at Grandpa Dunaway for only a moment, but it was long enough for me to see absolute contempt pass between them. "Well, yeah, they could stay with us," Grandpa Tolliver said. "I wouldn't be able to do much for them until Tessie got home in the evenin', but I reckon they could fend for themselves till then."

Grandpa Dunaway let Burris Tolliver's words hang in the air for a long, uncomfortable minute, then he looked down at Sarah. She continued to lean against him, her face devoid of expression. Then he shifted his gaze and spoke to me.

"How do you feel, Lucas? Where would you like to live?"

The question took me by surprise. I fidgeted in my seat, sitting there under the gaze of the entire family, then I looked up and all around at the big room. My world had been turned upside down, everything in my life gone it seemed, yet here was this wonderful room, a place I had always loved.

"Could we stay here?" I asked.

"You mean live here with your grandma and me?" Grandpa asked. "Is that what you'd like to do?"

"Yes," I said. Grandma Dunaway reached over and wrapped an arm around Sarah, and again the room fell silent.

"All right, then," Grandpa Dunaway said. "This will be your home."

Grandma Tolliver went back to sobbing, and Grandpa Tolliver cleared his throat.

A narrow hallway dissected the upper floor of the house, with two bedrooms opening on either side of the hall. Grandma and Grandpa slept in the first room on the left, which was the largest. I took the room next to theirs, and Sarah took the one directly across the hall from them.

That's where Sarah was supposed to sleep anyway, but it didn't work that way for quite some time. She got up five minutes after Grandma tucked her into bed the first night and opened the door to Grandma and Grandpa's room, then just stood there in the doorway.

"What's the matter, Honey?" I heard Grandma say. "Can't you sleep?"

Sarah didn't answer. She still hadn't said a single word since the fire.

"Would you like me to read you a story?" Grandma asked. "Would that help you go to sleep?"

No answer.

"I don't know what you need if you won't tell me, Darlin'," Grandma said. "Are you afraid to sleep alone?"

I heard nothing for another minute or so, then Grandma said, "All right, I guess we can make room for you," and Sarah climbed into bed with them.

I had several nightmares that night, though I couldn't remember them the next morning. I don't think I wanted to.

I stayed out of school until after Christmas; Sarah wouldn't return until the next fall.

Now that Grandpa had sharecroppers working for him, his workday consisted mainly of overseeing the farm. During the weeks before I started back to school, he took me with him everywhere he went, and he introduced me to every man, white or black, who lived in the shacks that dotted his land. They were miserable one- or two-room hovels like all cropper shacks, and few of the coarse women who struggled to raise families in them even showed their faces when we drove up. The men—hard, callused, and maybe toothless—would remove their dusty hats, shake my hand, and call me Mister Lucas. I was only a kid, but my Grandpa was the boss.

Various one-room schools dotted the countryside, and I worried that I'd have to switch to one of those when I started back. The white country schools did look considerably nicer than the dilapidated ones the Negro children attended, but I had enjoyed my school in town, and I dreaded the possibility of changing. That's how I thought of it, my school, and with all the changes I had experienced in the past year

I badly needed whatever small amount of the familiar I could cling to.

One day as I was riding down the road with Grandpa, trundling along in his big truck, he looked over at me and said, "You need to start back to school again after Christmas, Lucas."

"I know," I said.

"Are you looking forward to that?" he asked.

"Yes, Sir," I said. "I like school. I love to read, you know."

I wanted to ask him where I'd be going, but I was afraid to. I guess he knew that.

"Where would you like to go to school?" he asked lightly, acting as if he didn't know it was the biggest thing on my mind.

I hesitated a moment before answering.

"I really like my school in town. Can I go there?"

"Yes, you can," Grandpa said. "I'll drive you into town in the mornings, but when school lets out in the afternoon you'll have to walk back home—at least in nice weather you will."

"Okay," I said quickly, unable to hide my relief. "I can walk home from school, just like Daddy used to do."

"Yes," Grandpa said quietly, his eyes growing distant. "Just like your daddy used to do."

Grandpa brought home a Christmas tree that reached to the ceiling, and set it on a stand in the corner of the big room, a sacred spot where a tree had stood every Christmas of my life, and many more before I was born.

Grandma asked Sarah and me if we'd like to help her decorate it. I said yes, eagerly, and jumped into the job. Grandma and I ended up doing all the decorating while Sarah sat on the sofa holding a doll and watching us. Grandma tried urging her to help us a couple of times, but Sarah didn't move. And though her eyes were open and looking in our direction as we went about our fun, I wondered if she was actually seeing us.

Grandpa took me to the library in town and waited while I picked out several books. And because of what we'd been through they didn't have any of the family over for holiday dinners that year. The house stayed quiet, and I was thankful.

Sarah's dolls had burned up in the fire, so Grandma bought her several more. She carried one with her most of the time, but she didn't play with them or talk to them; she just held them.

The day before Christmas we heard a knock on the door. Grandma wiped her hands on her apron and went to answer it.

"Emiline!" she said. "What brings you way out here?"

Emiline stood at the door, her arms wrapped around herself, shivering, her breath blowing clouds of steam in the crisp air. She had walked the three miles from town.

"Come in this house, Emiline," Grandma said. "You look frozen."

"Thank you, Mrs. Dunaway. It's a right chilly day," Emiline said.

I was upstairs in my room, and I'd never been happier to

hear someone's voice. I flew down the stairs and gave Emiline a hug. Sarah was sitting on the sofa, and hadn't even looked up.

"What you doin' over there, Angel?" Emiline said.

Sarah didn't react.

"Take off your coat and have a seat," said Grandma. Emiline shrugged out of her coat, unwrapped a long scarf from around her neck, and hung them on the rack beside the door. I noticed she was carrying a large purse. She brought the purse with her and sat down on the sofa beside Sarah.

"I'm goin' to hug you, Angel," she said, "whether you wants me to or not."

With that she reached out and wrapped Sarah in her arms. Sarah didn't respond, but Emiline was undaunted. She set the big purse in her lap.

"I brought somethin' for you kids," she said.

All of a sudden I knew what it was. In her first reaction since Emiline had walked through the door, Sarah turned her head and looked at the purse. Emiline opened the top of it, reached inside, and pulled out Mandy and the little iron wagon. She set the wagon in my outstretched hands, then looked over at Sarah. Sarah's eyes were focused on the black doll. Emiline held Mandy out to her, close to her face, and for a moment Sarah didn't move. Then almost in slow motion, she reached up and took Mandy out of Emiline's hands. She pulled the doll to her chest and whispered, "Mandy."

Cradling Mandy in her arms, she began rocking to and fro, gazing into the doll's ever-smiling face as she rocked. I looked at Grandma, and saw tears standing in her eyes.

Grandpa had been out feeding the livestock. We heard him come in the back door and take off his overshoes. He walked into the big room and nodded at Emiline, then looked down at Sarah. His eyes softened when he saw her rocking Mandy, and he looked at Grandma with a faint smile. She reached over and touched his shoulder.

No one had mentioned the fire since it happened. For a while that had been fine; I hadn't felt like talking about it anyway. Now, standing beside Emiline, my mind went back to the bright house we had lived in every day of our lives, and the awful night when it burned.

My thoughts must have shown in my face.

"What's the matter, Lucas?" Grandma asked.

"Nothing," I said.

Emiline wasn't buying that.

"Come on, little man," she said. "Answer your Grandma. What you got on your mind?"

"Jubal," I said. "Is Jubal alive?"

"Yes," Emiline said. "Last I heard, he was still alive. He's laid up in the hospital in Yazoo City, the one that's just for black folks."

"How long is he going to be there?" I asked.

"I don't know that, Lucas," she said. "He got burned somethin' awful, and I hear he's still bad off. He might be in there for some time yet."

While trying to absorb Emiline's news about Jubal, I realized that everyone was looking at Sarah. She had stopped rocking, and though she was still staring directly into Mandy's face, she seemed to be looking through it.

Christmas came and went, and Grandma Dunaway made sure we had plenty of presents under the tree. Grandma Tolliver stopped by with an armload of gifts too, as did both of our aunts. Even Uncle Robert's wife brought some packages—mostly things she had made by hand.

The gifts were nice, and appreciated, but none could compare with the happy return of Mandy and the little iron wagon. I set the wagon on a shelf over my bed, and Sarah held Mandy in her arms day and night.

I returned to school a few days after Christmas, and felt happy to be there. Some of the kids stared at me for the first week or so, and whispered to each other when they saw me coming, but no one mentioned the fire.

In trying to decide whether or not to send Sarah back to school, Grandma and Grandpa had found themselves in a quandary. She ate reasonably well and took baths and changed her clothes when Grandma told her to, but other than that she just carried Mandy around with a blank look on her face and hardly reacted to anything. She didn't even cling to Grandpa as much as she had before. They decided to have Doc Armstead take a look at her.

I was supposed to stay in my room the day Doc came to see Sarah, but I stood in the upstairs hallway and listened to all of the conversation I could hear, which turned out to be most of it. Sarah was on the sofa holding Mandy when Doc knocked on the door, and she didn't look up when Grandma and Grandpa let him in.

"Hello, Sarah," Doc said. "How are you doing these days?"

I didn't hear any answer, just the sofa springs squeaking as Doc sat down beside her.

"You don't know me very well, Sarah," I heard him say, "but I think you know who I am. Is that right? Do you know who I am?"

Sarah didn't answer, but she must have nodded.

"That's right. I thought you knew me," Doc said. "You've been to my office before, and I think you know I'd never hurt you. You haven't been talking much lately, Sarah, but I hear you've said a word or two now and then. Do you feel like talking to me?"

No answer.

"Your Grandma and Grandpa are trying to take care of you, Sarah, and it's almost time for you to start school again. What do you think about going back to school?"

Silence.

"Can you tell me how you feel about that, Sarah? Do you want to go back to school when Lucas does?"

I didn't hear her answer, but I think she told him no.

After a few more minutes of one-sided conversation, Doc retired to the kitchen with Grandma and Grandpa, leaving Sarah alone in the big room. I could hear them even better from the kitchen; their voices drifted directly up the stairs.

"Sarah is depressed," Doc said. "She's suffered a tremendous amount of trauma; everything in her world has come apart. Her parents are gone, both of them, and she went through that fire—an ordeal more terrifying than most of us ever experience in our lives. That's enough to have a lasting effect on a grownup, and Sarah's only seven years old."

"But Lucas seems to be doing so well," Grandma said.

"Yes, Lucas does appear to be doing well," Doc answered. "And that's not altogether surprising—different people react differently to the same things. Sarah's younger than Lucas, and she just isn't dealing with it the same as him, at least not yet."

"How long do you think she'll stay this way?" asked Grandpa.

"I'd wish I could tell you the answer to that, John; but the truth is, I don't know. She could come out of it in a few days, a few weeks, or it could last much longer."

"Do you think we should try to send her back to school?" Grandma asked.

"No, I don't think so," Doc said. "Not yet anyway. It might just make things worse."

Grandpa sounded frustrated. "What can we do for her, Doc? How can we help her?"

"Well, I could have her committed to the state hospital—the mental place—and I'll guarantee you those head doctors up there would tell you that's just what she needs. They'd claim they could treat her and bring her out of it better than anyone else could—they being the experts, of course. I know those doctors mean well, and maybe someday they will figure out how people's heads work, but in my experience I've never seen them do somebody like Sarah any good at all.

"No, I don't think Sarah should go back to school yet, and I don't think she should go anywhere else, either. She'll be better off right here with you two looking after her. You can do more for her than I or any other doctor can."

On the Friday following my first week back in school, Grandpa surprised us with a question. "How would you two like to go see Jubal?"

"Go see Jubal?" I said. "When?"

"Tomorrow," Grandpa said.

"I'd love to see him," I cried, clapping my hands.

"How about you, Sarah?" Grandpa asked. "Do you want to see Jubal?"

Sarah dropped her head and looked at Mandy.

"Sarah?" Grandpa said. "We're talking about going to see Jubal. Can you tell me if you'd like to see him?"

She didn't look up, but we heard a tiny whisper: "Yes."

Early the next morning Grandpa loaded us into the smaller of his two trucks, a stake-bed with a narrow cab. Grandma had packed us a paper sack full of sandwiches and a jar of sweet tea to take along for our lunch. Sarah sat in the middle clutching Mandy as Grandma stood on the step and waved goodbye. We turned down the lane and set off on the seventy-five-mile trip to Yazoo.

Although a few of the roads were paved, most of them were dirt—pot-holed and rough. The trip took us through a number of small towns, all of which looked nearly the same to me: dusty streets with hitching rails and worn watering troughs bordering the sides; colorless store fronts with sagging porches, black men leaning against the walls or sitting on the steps; droopy-headed mules waiting for their owners; freckle-faced kids and suspicious grownups watching us drive by as if they had never seen a stranger before.

The narrow road took us through miles of uncleared forest, zigging and zagging through a foreboding jungle where sunlight penetrated only in spots and patches—a wild place that seemed to engulf us. Grandpa had to dodge several deer that bounded across the road in front of the truck, and once he stopped and pointed off into the woods.

"Look there, kids," he said. "Bears."

A sow bear and a pair of yearling cubs had stopped to watch us go by. The cubs seemed unconcerned when we stopped, perhaps even inquisitive, but the sow's eyes blazed and her lips curled upward in a snarl. She began whipping her head menacingly from side to side and bared gleaming white canines that obviously meant business.

"It looks like Mrs. Bear wasn't expecting company," Grandpa said with a chuckle. He put the truck back in gear and continued on.

It was after noon when we arrived in Yazoo City. The town was at least as big as Linville, possibly bigger. Grandpa told us it was older too, having been founded before the Civil War. And unlike Greenville and some of the other Mississippian cities of similar age, Yazoo had managed to escape the Yankee torches.

Grandpa pulled off the road and parked on the bank of the Yazoo River, a major waterway from which Yankee gunboats had fired regularly on the city—until the good citizens of Yazoo had ambushed one of their boats, sunk it, and killed every Yankee aboard. That spoiled their fun. Sitting in the shade of a tremendous oak that may have borne witness to that historic battle, we ate the lunch that Grandma sent with us.

When we finished eating we set off to find the Negro-American Hospital. A white man lounging in front of a little grocery store looked utterly shocked when Grandpa stopped and asked him for directions.

"Why in hell would you be lookin' for the colored hospital?" he asked, lifting his hat and scratching his head.

"Just tell me how to get there," Grandpa said, impatience edging into his voice, "if you would, please."

The man waved his arm toward the western part of town and said, "It's over there on Webster Street, in niggertown."

We soon found ourselves in the poorest part of town, bumping along a dirty street that hadn't seen maintenance in years. Dilapidated shacks and ramshackle shotgun houses lined the block; black men, women, and children stared at us from worn-out sofas, benches, and car seats that rested on sagging porches, their faces without expression, revealing nothing of the surprise they must have felt at seeing a white man and two children, obviously lost, driving down their street.

I felt very uncomfortable to be on such a street; if Grandpa felt that way he didn't let it show. Suddenly he pointed at a large single-story building.

"There's the hospital," he said.

Sarah hadn't said a word all day, nor had she reacted to anything except to cringe when we stopped to look at the bears. At sight of the hospital she buried her face against Grandpa's arm. Grandpa parked the truck on the street next to the building, then wrapped his arm around Sarah. She lifted Mandy to her face and covered her eyes.

"This is where Jubal is, Sarah," Grandpa said. "They're helping him get well here. Are you ready to go in and see him?"

She didn't answer, so I decided to try and help.

"Come on, Sarah," I said. "Let's go in and see Jubal. I've been looking forward to seeing him. Haven't you?"

I got no response either. Grandpa opened the truck door and nodded to me to get out the other side.

"Come on, Sarah," he said. "I'll hold your hand."

He reached in the truck and took her by the hand. She slid out, albeit rather unwillingly, and we walked to the front door of the hospital.

The Negro-American Hospital was a sprawling structure made of red brick. More functional than pleasing to the eye, the hospital consisted of a long main building located at the back with three wings extending out toward the street at right angles. A hall ran through the center of the main building as well as each wing, separating the rooms and wards on either side. The front door opened on one end of the main building.

The hospital had no lobby, no waiting room. A tidy wooden desk sat facing the door; behind the desk stretched the long hallway, its tile floor spotless, its white walls bare. The long corridor bustled with doctors and nurses hurrying from one room to another, and we were the only white people in sight.

An attractive black woman sat behind the desk, her white uniform and stiff nurse's bonnet contrasting starkly with her dark skin.

"May I help you?" she asked.

"Yes," Grandpa said, as Sarah and I did our best to hide behind him. "We're here to visit Jubal Jefferson."

"Oh, Jubal," the nurse said, "the man who got burned. We've been keeping him isolated. He's not allowed to have visitors."

"My name is John Dunaway," Grandpa said, "and these are my grandchildren, Lucas and Sarah. We drove all the way from Linville today. Lucas and Sarah think a lot of Jubal, and they've been looking forward to seeing him."

"I'm sorry," the nurse said, "but I'm not authorized . . . ."

Out of nowhere, a large black man appeared beside the desk. He was a tall man, stout and full-bodied, and dressed in a suit and tie. Along with his imposing size, the man's stern features commanded a presence that seemed to fill the room. I had never seen such a prominent-looking Negro.

"I am T. J. Huddleston, founder of this hospital," the man said, stepping forward to offer his hand to Grandpa. "And I don't believe I caught your name, sir."

"John Dunaway," said Grandpa, shaking Mr. Huddleston's hand firmly. "I live up near Linville. These are my grandchildren, Lucas and Sarah."

The black man's face lit up in happy surprise. "Oh, these are the children that Jubal saved from the fire?"

"Yes, they are," Grandpa replied. "They owe their lives to Jubal." Then Grandpa turned to us. "Lucas, Sarah, say Hello to Mister Huddleston."

I reached out and shook the man's hand, but Sarah clutched Mandy to her chest and stayed half-hidden behind Grandpa.

"Ever since the fire," Grandpa said, shrugging his shoulders.

"I understand," Mr. Huddleston said. Then he leaned over and touched Sarah's shoulder, his intense eyes suddenly gentle. "Hello, Sarah," he said. "Welcome to my hospital. Would you like to see Jubal?"

"But sir," the nurse behind the desk said. "Jubal is being kept in isolation for fear of infection."

"I know," Mr. Huddleston said, "but he's been despondent lately—depressed, withdrawn. A visit from these children might just do him more good than all of our doctoring can. Please get hold of Doctor Miller and Doctor Fullilove and ask them to come to Jubal's room."

"Yes sir," the nurse said.

"Would you all follow me, please?" Mr. Huddleston said, and we started down the long hall.

Along with the Negro-American Hospital, Thomas Jefferson Huddleston owned more than twenty black funeral homes throughout the Delta. He managed to make himself rich during the 1920s and 30s, and he was the first black person to drive a Cadillac in Yazoo City—a near impossible feat for a Negro, and a testimony to his personal shrewdness.

"This is the first and only hospital in Mississippi built for Negroes," Huddleston said with obvious pride. "I had so much trouble finding qualified staff that I started my own nursing school here; it adjoins the hospital. So far it seems to be working well, but it's still very difficult to find black doctors. And not surprisingly, many of our patients have a hard time paying their bills."

"How about Jubal?" Grandpa asked. "He lives in a little shack with his mother, and they're practically destitute."

"Jubal is a special case," Mr. Huddleston replied. "Jubal is a hero; he saved these children's lives. His stay here is free—on the house."

Grandpa smiled.

"Yes, he certainly is a hero. He saved my grandchildren, and he paid a terrible price for doing it." Then his face turned thoughtful. "Did you know that as a child Jubal wouldn't talk, and that he was taunted and teased and came to be known as Dummy?" Grandpa said.

"No, I was not aware of that," Huddleston replied.

"He still doesn't talk much," Grandpa said, "and some people still call him Dummy. Most folks in Linville think he's feebleminded."

"What about you, Mister Dunaway?" Huddleston said. "Do you think he's feebleminded?"

Grandpa paused, thinking before he spoke.

"I don't know him very well, so I can't be sure. But you asked my personal opinion, so here it is. Jubal appears to be a simple man, in some ways even childlike, but I doubt there's really anything wrong with his mind."

Mr. Huddleston nodded.

"In his present physical condition, we can't be absolutely sure about his mental state either. He's a cooperative patient, quite likable, and heroic."

The doors to most of the rooms and wards were standing open, and a plain brown curtain hung at every window. Jubal's door was closed.

"We'll wait here in the hall for the doctors," Mr. Huddleston said. "As you heard from the nurse, we've been keeping Jubal in isolation. I'm not a physician myself, but I can tell you that our worst fear with burn patients is infection. Infection seems to be the number one killer in these cases. Of course, the fact that he was burned over seventy percent of his body causes a number of problems besides infection, as well as a tremendous amount of pain.

"His bandages have to be changed twice a day, morning and night, and that is by far the most painful part of his treatment. We give him morphine for the pain, a drug which, unfortunately, is addictive. It will be necessary to take him off of it and help him through the withdrawal before he can be released.

"We use sulfa drugs to combat the infection, but they aren't terribly reliable. The doctors tell me he could contract a fatal infection in spite of the sulfa.

"Here come my good doctors," Mr. Huddleston said, his face lighting up in a proud grin. Doctors Miller and Fullilove, both young, black, and intense, came hurrying down the hall.

"This is John Dunaway," Mr. Huddleston said, "and these are his grandchildren, Lucas and Sarah. They're the children that Jubal saved from the fire."

The doctors seemed pleased to meet us, but their faces mirrored concern at Huddleston's next statement.

"The Dunaways came all the way from Linville today in hopes of visiting Jubal. Do you think that might be a possibility, doctors?"

"Oh, Mister Huddleston," Dr. Miller said, furrowing his brow. "You know how concerned we are about infection, and so far we've been lucky."

Dr. Fullilove spoke. "It is wonderful that Jubal saved these children, and a fine gesture that they've come so far to see him. I'm sure he'd love to see them too."

"Jubal has been so despondent lately," said Mr. Huddleston. "I wondered if a visit from Lucas and Sarah might be worth the risk?"

Dr. Fullilove looked thoughtful.

"You're right about the despondency, and seeing the children could brighten him up."

Dr. Miller continued to frown.

"How about just letting them look in from over here by the door?" Dr. Fullilove said. "Jubal is able to turn his head, and that way he could at least get to see them. And they could see him too."

Dr. Miller still looked skeptical, but recognized that he was outvoted. "I believe that would be an acceptable risk," he said.

Mr. Huddleston smiled and moved to the door.

"Step up close, Lucas and Sarah, so you can see Jubal."

I stepped to the door, but Sarah held back, clinging to Grandpa. Mr. Huddleston turned the knob and swung the door inward, opening it wide.

The scene would remain with me for life, every detail as vivid as at that moment. The brown curtains were drawn, the room dimly lit. Jubal lay in a hospital bed on his back, his head to my right. He looked like a mummy. The thick bandages around his body made him look huge beneath the single sheet that covered him. His upper chest and shoulders, which protruded from under the sheet, were wound in white bandages that extended around his neck, across his chin, and upward on the sides of his face, covering his ears and the top of his head. Only his face was exposed.

His left arm was also wound in bandages, though the hand was not. His right arm lay across his middle, both it and the hand encased in thick gauze.

The open door I was standing in allowed more light to

enter the room. Jubal didn't move for a moment, then he slowly rolled his head to the left and caught my eye. A sleepy smile crossed his face, and I heard him whisper, "Lucas."

Sarah held fiercely to Mandy and pushed back against Grandpa, afraid to look at Jubal. Grandpa pushed her forward, gently but firmly, until she stood beside me in the doorway.

"Sarah," Jubal said. He turned his bandaged head further in our direction, and with considerable effort extended his left arm and bare hand. "Come here, Sarah. I loves you, girl."

Sarah lifted her eyes until they met his, then she ran to him, burying her face against his arm. He grimaced with pain, but he made no sound.

Dr. Miller started to protest, then he stopped himself. He shook his head and smiled in resignation. He and Dr. Fullilove exchanged a glance, then Dr. Miller said, "Lucas, you may go in for a few minutes too if you'd like."

I ran to the bed and took Jubal's hand in mine. He smiled.

Sarah also took his hand. She laid her head against it and began to cry. She wept softly at first, but soon she was crying loudly.

"It's all right, Sarah," he said. "I'm all right. Don't you worry 'bout me. Long as you and Lucas is okay, then I's okay."

Sarah continued to cry, long and hard, while Jubal looked down at her and smiled. Grandpa, Mr. Huddleston, and the doctors stood quietly at the door and waited until her sobbing began to wane. Then Grandpa spoke.

"Lucas, it's time for us to go."

I said goodbye to Jubal and walked to the door. Sarah continued to hold his hand, her face lying against it, her tears running across his fingers and onto the bed.

"Sarah," Grandpa said gently, "we have to go."

Slowly she straightened up and wiped her eyes, then turned and began walking toward the door. Jubal called her back.

"Don't forget Mandy," he said, holding the smiling black doll in his hand. "Mandy needs you to take care of her, Sarah."

Sarah turned and took Mandy from his outstretched hand, smiled, and walked to the door to join us.

Jubal looked across the room at Grandpa. "Thanks for bringin' them, Mistuh Dunaway," he said. "Thanks so much."

"It was my pleasure, Jubal," said Grandpa. And we turned and left.

T. J. Huddleston walked us to the truck, where he took Grandpa's hand and said, "John, thank you for bringing these children to visit Jubal." Then he turned to us. "Lucas, Sarah, Jubal loves you more than he loves his own life, and your visit today may have done him more good than you'll ever know."

Mr. Huddleston stood at the curb and waved until we drove out of sight. Sarah and I fell asleep before Grandpa's truck crossed the Yazoo River bridge.

Chapter Thirteen

Our lives went back to normal after our visit with Jubal, or as normal as possible under the circumstances. Grandpa drove me to school each morning, but the afternoons were usually warm enough for walking. I enjoyed the walk, and often thought of my father running the same road when he was in high school.

Although Sarah remained within her shell, somehow she seemed more alert after visiting Jubal, and we caught her whispering to Mandy more often than before.

Grandpa took us to see Jubal a second time, several weeks after the first visit. Before each trip to Yazoo City he drove to Miss Amanda's shack and invited her to ride with us, but both times she declined, explaining that she didn't have the time. When Grandpa returned from inviting her he said she looked like she needed sleep.

Miss Amanda was doing her best to take care of her regular customers, and with Jubal gone she had to make the pickups and deliveries as well as do all the washing and ironing. Several times I saw her pulling the wagon around town loaded with clothes. A terrible weariness gripped her face, but she bent over and pulled the load as relentlessly as Jubal did.

Jubal sat up in a chair during our second visit, and most of his bandages had been removed. His ears were badly scarred, the right one curled and shriveled as if it had been fried in a skillet. His neck was also covered with scars as well as the point of his chin, but the rest of his face still looked like Jubal.

His right arm and hand remained encased in heavy bandages. The arm, which he could only move at the shoulder, was drawn up taut at the elbow and lay stiffly across his waist. The entire limb would remain in this position, forever useless, after the rest of his body recovered.

Jubal was delighted to see us again. He assured us he'd soon be home and back to pulling his wagon around town for his mama. Mr. Huddleston, both doctors, and a crowd of black nurses who had come to meet Sarah and me nodded their agreement. Jubal was clearly the hero of the hospital.

The curtains were open in his room now, and he looked out at the bright sunlight, smiled contentedly, and said, "Sure is a pretty day, ain't it Lucas?"

"Yes, Jubal," I said. "It is a pretty day."

When Jubal came home from the hospital, he stayed at the shack and let Miss Amanda cook for him and fret over him for a couple of weeks; then, just as he had promised, he began pulling his wagon around town once more.

One Saturday morning I asked Grandpa if he would give

us a ride to town so we could walk around the square like we used to. I was hoping to see Jubal, of course. When Grandpa asked Sarah if she'd like to go with me, she nodded her head.

It felt good to be back on the old square; we hadn't seen it since before the fire. Mr. and Mrs. Dinkin made over us endlessly and gave us more sweets than we could possibly eat. We sat on our regular bench, me holding the sack of goodies while Sarah held Mandy in one hand and devoured a huge glazed doughnut with the other.

After a while, just like old times, we looked up and saw Jubal coming down the street toward us. When he drew closer we saw that it wasn't exactly like old times; he was pulling the wagon with his left arm only. His right arm, which rested against his stomach, ended in a blackened claw that protruded from his shirt sleeve like some alien creature peering out of its den. The hand consisted of a gnarled thumb and two spike-like fingers that curled against it like a frozen pincers.

As usual, Jubal bent forward as he walked, watching the street in front of him with a solemn face. When he looked up and saw us he broke into a wide grin. So did we.

I don't know if Jubal had planned to stop and talk with us, but Sarah settled that. She ran out and stopped him. I followed her, figuring it would surely be all right since everyone in town knew he had saved our lives.

We hugged Jubal and he hugged us back with his good arm—a joyous reunion that for the moment seemed to blot out everything we'd been through. Then I became aware that everyone on the square had turned away; not a single person was acting as if they even saw us. They all did, though, and Nap Canfield was among them.

As soon as Jubal picked up the tongue of his wagon and trudged on, Nap came lurching down the sidewalk in our direction. Even at a distance I could tell he was drunk. He waved awkwardly, and called to us in a voice embarrassingly loud: "Hi there, Dunaway kids."

"Hello, Mister Canfield," I said. He stopped in front of us, reeling on his feet.

"There you go with that 'Mister' again," he said. "I like that. I'm gonna tell ya somethin' I don't like, though—I don't like you kids huggin' up on niggers. Even your daddy, God rest 'im, wouldn't have gone for you doin' that."

His words hurt me deeply, and even though he was a grownup I snapped back at him. "Jubal saved our lives, Mister Canfield. You know that. Everybody knows that."

"Yeah, yeah. Everybody knows that," Nap said. "And what about your mama? What happened to her that night?"

Sarah moved behind me. "Our mama died in the fire," I said, my chin quivering, my eyes filling with angry tears.

"Yes, she did," Nap said, leaning toward us in a drunken leer. "But just how did she die? What'd that nigger do to her before he carried you two out?"

"Jubal didn't do anything!" I screamed. "He just saved us."

From the corner of my eye I caught sight of Sheriff Turnbull rushing toward us.

"Nap!" the sheriff hollered. "What do you think you're doing, bothering these kids?"

"I ain't botherin' them," Nap said, reeling in surprise at the sheriff's intrusion.

"What are you doing, then?" Sheriff Turnbull asked, his face inches from Nap's.

"I was just askin' them about their mama," he said. "You know, about how she died in the fire."

"That's none of your business, Nap," the sheriff said. "None at all. These kids have been through enough, and they don't need to be bothered with such gossip. Now you go on. Get outta here!"

Nap turned and started to leave, then whirled back around and stopped, nearly falling down in the process.

"Everybody in town knows about their mama, Sheriff, and about what that Dummy nigger done to her in there. Hell, even Burris Tolliver, their own grandpa, says somethin' wasn't right about all that."

"I said get outta here, Nap, and I mean it." Sheriff Turnbull's eyes looked dangerous. He moved a step in Canfield's direction, raised his arm and pointed down the street. "Now get!"

Nap shook his head, turned, and staggered away.

Sarah and I knew nothing about the condition in which Mama's body had been found after the fire, nor were we aware that people wondered if Jubal might have attacked her that night.

A male Negro could not touch a white woman under any condition; it was as simple as that. If Jubal had done something to Mama that night, even in self defense, it wouldn't matter that he saved us. The town, indeed the entire county, was smoldering over the issue. And Grandpa Tolliver was fanning the flames.

The undercurrent of suspicion didn't escape Jubal. He pulled his wagon around town less and less, then one day he dropped out of sight. Once more Miss Amanda was making the deliveries—to those customers who didn't stop using her services, that is, which many did.

Anson Turnbull instinctively recognized the signs of civil unrest, and he remained resolved that no one would be lynched in Linville while he was sheriff.

To my surprise, and I suppose to Grandpa and Grandma Dunaway's as well, Sheriff Turnbull showed up at the farm one Saturday morning. He and Grandpa stood out in the yard and talked for several minutes while I peeked from behind the curtains and watched. The sheriff appeared to be trying to explain something to Grandpa—something difficult—because Grandpa kept rubbing his chin, shaking his head in protest, and talking back to him. The sheriff persisted, and finally Grandpa nodded his head and reluctantly showed him into the house.

Grandpa nodded gravely at Grandma as they walked through the front door; she took Sarah by the hand and led her outside. Grandpa looked at me and said, "Lucas, Sheriff Turnbull wants to ask you some questions, some things about the fire. He thinks it's important, so I want you to answer him the best you can. Understand?"

I looked up into the sheriff's gray eyes and choked out a reply. "Okay." Grandpa turned and walked out the door, closing it behind him.

The two of us stood in the big room, me staring at the

floor and the sheriff holding his hat in his hands and fingering it awkwardly. Then he looked at me apologetically, stopped his fidgeting, and gestured toward the sofa.

"Let's have a seat, Lucas," he said.

I sat down on one end on the sofa while he settled into the other. He leaned over, laid his hat on the coffee table, and let out a sigh. I realized he wasn't enjoying this any more than I was.

"You're not in any trouble or anything like that, Son," the sheriff said, "but I have to ask you some questions. I have to ask you about the night Jubal carried you and Sarah out of the fire."

"All right," I said, my voice little more than a squeak.

"Did you see Jubal come through the front door that night, Lucas—during the fire?"

"Yes, I did," I said. "I could see him through the smoke."

"Could you hear him when he came in?"

"Yes. I heard a big crash when he hit the door. I think he knocked it off the hinges."

"Where were you and Sarah when he came in?"

"Crouching in the doorway of our bedroom. We were down on our hands and knees, looking out into the front room at the fire."

The sheriff looked at the floor uncomfortably.

"Where was your mama?" he asked.

"I think she was in her room," I said. "I think she was asleep."

"Your mama was still dressed when we found her, Lucas."

"Mama was drunk that night, sir. She probably passed out in her clothes."

He nodded. "Could you see Jubal through the smoke and all, after he came through the door and into the room."

"Sometimes I could see him, just kind of an outline, and other times I couldn't see him at all."

"Could Sarah see any more than you could?"

"I don't know. She was crouched down beside me, real low. I doubt if she could see any more than me, probably not as much."

"What did Jubal do before he wrapped you two up in the rug and carried you out?"

"He started throwing things out of the front room into the dining room, clearing them off the rug. I saw the piano move, and then I heard it crash into the dining room."

"Could you see him when he was doing that?"

"Sometimes. He looked like a shadow."

"Did you ever see your mama during that time, Lucas?"

"No," I said, the word choking in my throat.

"Did you hear anything?"

"Yes. I heard chairs and other things hitting the walls and the floor of the dining room. Most of that was before I heard the piano hit the floor."

"Did you hear any voices?"

I tried to speak, but the words wouldn't come.

"Lucas?" the sheriff persisted.

"Yes," I said. "I heard Mama."

"What did she say?"

"She said," 'Out of my house, nigger.'"

"Is that all?" Sheriff Turnbull asked. "You didn't hear her say anything else?"

"No, sir."

"Did you hear Jubal say anything?"

"No, sir."

"I'm sorry to put you through this, Son—to bring it all up again."

His eyes softened for a moment, then just as quickly turned serious again.

"Did you hear anything else—anything that sounded like a struggle, like people fighting?"

"No, sir."

"Did you hear your mama hit the wall, Lucas? Did you hear her body hit the wall?"

I hesitated, and the sheriff's eyes bored into mine. "No, sir," I said. "I never heard anything like that."

"Has anyone besides me asked you what you saw or heard in the house that night, Lucas?"

"No," I said.

"You haven't talked about it with anybody?"

"No, not with anybody but you."

"I think you should keep it that way, Lucas," the sheriff said. "I mean it. Don't discuss this with anyone except me."

"All right," I said. "I won't."

His eyes softened again, and he seemed to relax.

"You and Sarah are the luckiest kids I know. Even though I saw it myself I can hardly believe that Jubal carried you two out of that fire."

"I know," I said. "I can't either."

Sheriff Turnbull smiled, reached for his hat, and stood up. "Thanks for talking with me, Lucas. You're a brave lad."

The Monday after Sheriff Turnbull talked to me about the fire, an unusual notice appeared on the front page of the *Linville Examiner:*

TOWN MEETING

At the request of Sheriff Anson Turnbull, Mayor Bob Hastings is calling a town meeting. The meeting will be held in the Linville High School Auditorium at 7:00 P.M. this coming Saturday, the evening of March 15, 1935. Every citizen of Linville and Crowden County is urged to attend.

Although I was only ten, I read the newspaper regularly, especially the headlines. The notice about the town meeting caught my attention, and I asked Grandpa why it was being held. "It's got something to do with Jubal," he said.

"Are you going to the meeting?" I asked.

"Yes, and so is your grandma," he said. "And Sheriff Turnbull wants us to bring you and Sarah along too."

Grandpa seemed reluctant to say any more about the meeting, so later that week I tried to press Grandma for information.

"Grandma, do you know what the town meeting is going to be about?" I asked, doing my best to sound very matter-of-fact.

When Grandma looked at me I knew my innocent act hadn't fooled her a bit. She answered my question, though, in much the same vein as Grandpa had. "I think Sheriff Turnbull wants to talk about Jubal."

"The sheriff wants to talk to everybody in the county about Jubal?" I asked. "Why would he want to do that?"

"I don't know. We'll just have to wait and see," she said. "Now go on and play; I've got work to do."

None of this made any sense. I had trouble believing the sheriff would call a special town meeting just to talk about Jubal.

Grandma and Grandpa seemed tense that week, and several times I heard them talking lowly between themselves. I figured they were discussing the upcoming meeting, but since I could only pick up a few words here and there I didn't learn anything worthwhile.

The hours dragged by on Saturday, and since Grandpa seemed to want to work alone I spent most of the day reading. As the afternoon wore on, Grandma told Sarah and me to bathe and wash our hair, then she laid out our best clothes to wear to the meeting. We all dressed before supper, Grandpa in his newest khaki pants and the nicest shirt he owned; me in a pair of brown slacks, white shirt, and tie; Sarah in a yellow satin dress that Grandma had made her; and Grandma in the same white dress she had worn to Mama and Daddy's funerals.

We ate quickly, then Grandma cleaned off the table, straightened my tie, fussed with Grandpa's collar, and retied the bow on Sarah's dress, twice. When Grandma sensed that Grandpa was growing impatient, she stopped her fussing. We all walked out and climbed into the cab of the big truck, the only vehicle that would hold the four of us up front. Normally I'd have ridden in the truck bed, but

Grandma seemed to want us all together that night, even though Sarah had to sit on her lap.

Sarah clung to Mandy and looked worried. I remember noticing that Mandy's head, arms, and legs were beginning to fray at the seams. The old doll had spent a portion of her life on a shelf in some long-forgotten slave cabin, and after that she had managed to remain untarnished for another sixty or seventy years before Jubal gave her to Sarah. Now, in just one year, Mandy had been called upon to shoulder more responsibility than she had in all her previous life. The brilliant sewed-on smile and wide button eyes remained undaunted, however—a face forever happy, forever free.

The old high school was one of those square, three-storied monsters built around the turn of the century. The wide, steep steps, overhung by a massive Greek pediment, led to heavy oak doors that opened onto the second floor.

Dozens of cars, trucks, wagons, and buggies ringed the school that night, and people could be seen walking from every direction, coming from all over town. Grandpa parked the truck a block away and we walked to the school. We mounted the tall stairs, the four of us abreast, and entered the building. I could feel my heart pounding as the doors closed behind us.

The principal's office was just to the left of the entry doors, the same as at my school, and on the right was the administrative office. In the middle of the entry hall stood a life-size statue of Robert E. Lee in full battle dress, its dusty plaster graying with age. A long saber, which had been broken and repaired more than once, hung at his side.

Grandpa and Grandma walked stiffly erect and looked straight ahead. Sarah clung to Grandma with one hand and Mandy with the other. I lagged behind, wishing I could somehow disappear. We turned left down a long hallway, and I caught the musty smell of age and dust that old schools seem to acquire. Halfway down the hall we turned right and passed through a pair of tall doors into the back of the auditorium.

The auditorium was packed. Along with the low murmur of hundreds of voices issuing from the crowd, we could hear the squeaking of wooden folding seats and an occasional raised voice as someone greeted a neighbor, relative, or old friend. And way up front, up on the stage, stood Sheriff Turnbull.

The sheriff was dressed impeccably in starched khakis and shining black boots, his full head of hair neatly combed, his big .45 mounted on his hip. He stood like a post in the center of the stage, his legs parted in a solid stance, his arms folded across his chest. He occasionally nodded at a member of the crowd or raised a hand to wave at someone coming down an aisle.

Four straightback chairs sat across the back of the stage. When Sheriff Turnbull saw us enter the auditorium he raised his hand and motioned us to come forward. The crowd grew quiet as we walked the long aisle to the stage, and every head turned in our direction. The sheriff bent down to give Grandma and Sarah a hand climbing the stairs, and after Grandpa and I walked up them and onto the stage he motioned us to take seats in the chairs behind him.

Grandma and Grandpa sat in the end chairs with Sarah

and me in between, me beside Grandpa and Sarah beside Grandma. Sarah held Mandy in a death grip.

The auditorium seemed huge from our vantage point, and brilliantly lit. A sea of faces stared up at us, most of them familiar. I had never felt so terribly on display.

I recognized several of the town's most prominent citizens seated in the front row: Graydon Hardiman, Doc Armstead, Mayor Hastings, and Harlan Johnson, editor of the *Linville Examiner.* Also in the front row, conspicuously, sat Grandma and Grandpa Tolliver. Grandma tried to smile at us, and appeared quite embarrassed by it all. Burris Tolliver had never been embarrassed in his life. He sat upright, his hands cupped over the handle of his cane, his eyes smoldering. I'd never seen him look so intense since the accident.

Other familiar faces in the crowd: Clarence Tull, the fire chief—tall, prominent, competent; Mr. Tarver, the school principal—grave, concerned; Miss Hawkins, the librarian—proper and quite serious; Mr. and Mrs. Dinkin, who smiled wanly when I caught their eyes; all of the Mercantile employees, including George Holland, the man for whose life our father had given his own.

And near the back of the auditorium, a disheveled bunch consisting of Nap Canfield, Herman Slocum, and twenty or thirty of their ragtag ilk. Nap and Herman sported predatory grins—laughing hyenas on the trail of a wounded prey. When I saw them I knew beyond a doubt that this meeting had something to do with Jubal.

Of course, there were no black people present.

A few minutes after seven, after folks had pretty well

stopped filing in and searching for seats, Sheriff Turnbull looked down at the front row and nodded to Mayor Hastings. The murmuring crowd grew still as the mayor stood up, walked to the stairs, and mounted the stage. The sheriff stepped to one side, giving him the floor.

"Good evening, folks," Mayor Hastings began. "I'd like to thank you all for coming, and also apologize for disrupting your lives, especially on a Saturday night. Of course, at my age Saturday nights don't seem to consist of much revelry anymore anyway."

A chuckle went through the crowd. The mayor was a popular man.

"I can't take credit for this meeting," Mayor Hastings said, "nor am I even sure that I'm in total agreement with its premise. I will say, though, that I've never had any reason to doubt the sincerity and dedication of our good sheriff, Anson Turnbull. And when Anson asked me to call this meeting, despite some arguments of my own against it, he insisted. He believed it to be necessary. So, given Anson's record on the job, and what we all know about the man's integrity, I agreed to call the meeting.

"And now, since this is Anson's meeting, I'll turn it over to him."

The mayor looked to his right, caught the sheriff's eyes, and nodded. "Sheriff Turnbull," he said, then stepped from the stage and again took his seat in the front row.

Anson Turnbull walked to center stage, his jaw clenched, his eyes grave. He turned to face the crowd, and for a long moment said nothing. Then in a voice that dominated the auditorium, he spoke.

"I'd also like to thank you for coming to *my* meeting, as Bob Hastings so clearly pointed out."

A few people chuckled. Mayor Hastings grinned, slightly.

"I know town meetings such as this are unusual," Sheriff Turnbull said. "In fact, they're almost unheard of in this part of the country. I asked for this one because of something that happened in our town a few months ago—a fire, a tragedy that touched all of us in one way or another.

"The fire is long since gone, of course, and as we all know, Lucas and Sarah Dunaway sitting behind me up here (the sheriff gestured toward us) were saved from those flames. A Negro man named Jubal—we all know who he is—saved them. I was there, and I saw Jubal come out of the house with these kids wrapped up in the front room rug. He nearly burned to death doing it, but he got it done."

The crowd sat deathly quiet, every eye trained on the speaker. Sheriff Turnbull paused and scanned the audience, his eyes seeming to meet those of every person there. Then he went on.

"Lucas and Sarah weren't the only ones in the house that night. Their mother, Jessica, was also there. Again, as we're all aware, Jessica did not survive the fire."

A loud sob escaped Grandma Tolliver's lips. She covered her mouth. Grandpa Tolliver remained stoic.

"I helped pull these children out of the rug that Jubal wrapped them in," the sheriff said, "as did several others here tonight. I also helped carry Jubal's burned body away from the fire. And I went into the house with the firemen the next morning, when we found Jessica's body."

Sheriff Turnbull looked down at Grandma Tolliver, who was wiping her eyes.

"I'm sorry to open up old wounds, Tessie," he said, "but I believe this is necessary."

Grandma didn't look up.

The sheriff continued. "Jubal went to the Negro hospital in Yazoo City, and after several months he recovered from his burns. He'll never recover completely, though; his right arm and hand are useless. He can't move them."

Grandpa Tolliver looked up at Sheriff Turnbull with a sneer, his upper lip pulled back in disdain.

"Is this what you wanted us to come here for, Anson— so you could tell us what happened to a colored? What in hell do we care about the condition of a dumb nigger!"

His voice grew as he spoke, until he could be heard throughout the auditorium.

Anson Turnbull glanced down momentarily, his face expressionless, and ignored Grandpa Tolliver's statement.

"After all that," the sheriff said, "after Jubal saved Lucas and Sarah, and took months to recover from his injuries, I'm hearing that people suspect him of something—that somehow he did something wrong while saving the children. That's why I asked you all to come here tonight. That's what I wanted to discuss with you."

Grandpa Tolliver was seething—nobody rebuffed him, especially not in public. "What was that Dummy nigger doing close enough to their house to know what was going on that night?" he demanded to know. "Why wasn't he across the tracks, where he belonged?"

"I don't know the answer to that," the sheriff replied calmly.

Grandpa Dunaway spoke, loudly and clearly, the only words he would say the entire evening.

"Would you rather Jubal hadn't been there, Burris, and not saved our grandchildren?"

Grandpa Tolliver looked stunned. Graydon Hardiman, Doc Armstead, and even Mayor Hastings fought to keep from grinning.

Burris Tolliver wasn't to be stopped so easily. "The nigger threw a man off the levee and killed him," he said. "Everybody knows he can be mean, Anson."

"I recall you beating men up a couple of times, Burris," the sheriff replied, "beating them with you fists, so bad you nearly killed them. Wasn't that mean too?"

"They was niggers," Grandpa said.

"So was the one Jubal threw off the levee."

Fire Chief Tull was an outspoken racist, but also known for speaking honestly. He decided to try and clarify the issue.

"There's been a lot of talk about the condition we found Jessica's body in after the fire, Anson; I think that's what people are concerned about. You were there, and I'm sure you remember it as well as I do."

Chief Tull stood up; he glanced first at Grandma Tolliver, then at Sarah and me.

"I apologize, Tessie, for bringing all this up again, and I'm sorry that the children have to hear these things about their mother."

As he spoke, the chief swiveled his body first one way

and then the other, addressing everyone in the auditorium. "Jessica Tolliver was lying on the floor and leaning up against an inner wall, one that hadn't burned. Her back rested against the wall and her body was leaning to the right. Her head was laying on her right shoulder, because her neck was broken."

Chief Tull paused, cleared his throat, and went on.

"The fire had been moving across the floor toward Jessica. It reached the front of her and her right side before the hoses put it out. She had on a bright red blouse; it was open down the front, unbuttoned, and the fire had burned her feet and legs and the lower part of her skirt. Her right arm lay at an angle from her body; the flames also scorched her right hand and her lower arm, and burned the right sleeve off of her blouse."

Grandma Tolliver sobbed as Chief Tull finished describing the scene and sat down. No one made a sound for a full minute, then a man I didn't recognize addressed Doc Armstead.

"What do you think Jessica Tolliver died from, Doc?"

Doc turned toward the man, who was seated a few rows away.

"I took Jubal to Yazoo City that night," he said, "but Chief Tull and the sheriff left Jessica's body undisturbed until I got back later that morning to examine it. Just like the chief said, the front of her blouse was open. Her slip and brassiere remained intact, covering her, but the buttons had been undone from her neckline to her waist. The limbs that were burned—both of her legs and her right arm—appeared to have remained stationary when the fire reached them; that is, she apparently didn't try to move away from the flames, indicating that she was already dead by the time the fire reached her.

"I can't be positive, of course," Doc said, "but it's my opinion that Jessica Tolliver died from having her neck broken."

The crowd was still, then another man at the far end of a middle row asked: "Did the wall behind her look like her head had hit it? In other words, could she have hit the wall hard enough that that's what broke her neck?"

Chief Tull answered. "Yes, there was a dent in the wall that looked like it had been made when her head hit it. It broke through the plaster. It's possible that somebody threw her against the wall and broke her neck, or broke her neck first and then threw her against it. And it's also possible that she just fell hard against the wall or that something like a piece of ceiling hit her and knocked her against it, and broke her neck that way."

A voice from the back interrupted. "Why are you sidin' with the nigger, Chief?"

Chief Tull, looking thoroughly disgusted, turned toward the back of the room and replied. "Anybody who knows me knows I'm not in the habit of siding with coloreds; in fact, I don't care if the whole nigger race lives or dies. But anybody who knows me also knows I am in the habit of telling the truth. I'm just doing my best to tell you exactly what we found in that house after the fire."

"What about her blouse bein' tore open?" another voice asked from the back.

Again Chief Tull spoke. "Just as I said a few minutes

ago, Jessica's blouse was open down the front, but it was not torn. Her slip was exposed, and it wasn't torn either. Since neither the blouse nor the buttons had been torn, it was impossible to tell if Jessica had unbuttoned it herself or if somebody else did it."

Graydon Hardiman, seated in the front row, had not said a word. Now he spoke.

"Anson," Graydon said, "did you ask the children if they saw anything suspicious in the house that night during the time Jubal was there?"

"Yes, I did," Sheriff Turnbull replied. "I asked Lucas, because Sarah hasn't spoken more than three words since the fire. Lucas assured me he saw nothing that night. He didn't once see his mother while Jubal was in the house."

"Did Lucas hear anything?" Graydon asked.

"No," the sheriff said. "He didn't hear anything."

Grandpa Tolliver jabbed an accusing finger at Sheriff Turnbull. "How about Jubal? Did you ask him about it, Anson?"

"Yes, I did," the sheriff replied. "Jubal told me he didn't see or hear Jessica Tolliver in the house that night."

"Niggers lie," Grandpa Tolliver said. "They lie all the time."

"Then why did you want to know if I asked Jubal about it, Burris?" the sheriff said. "I told you I questioned both Jubal and Lucas, and that neither of them saw or heard Jessica that night."

Looking like a man possessed, Grandpa Tolliver turned his blazing eyes on me. Filled with suspicion, they bored into mine. I looked at the floor.

"Sounds like nobody knows anything for sure," an unknown voice in the crowd said. "Just like the chief said, something could have fell on her and broke her neck for all anybody knows."

"Fat chance," another said. "I'll bet that nigger tried to rape her." This came from the back, and clearly from Nap Canfield, who had stood up. Ugly Herman Slocum, his buddy and admirer, was sitting beside him grinning his approval. Several others seated near Nap also grinned up at him—hard, unshaven men who had never expected to have a spokesman of their own.

Sheriff Turnbull had not spoken for some time, allowing the discussion to proceed on its own. Now, as if on cue, he rose to Nap's accusation.

"Why do you say that, Nap? What makes you think Jubal tried to rape Jessica Tolliver?"

"Why?" Nap cried, his face incredulous. "'Cause he's a nigger. He probably run in there just to try and get to Jessica Tolliver; then, when the fire got so bad, he decided to carry them kids out just to have an excuse—what you might call an alibi."

Nap grinned broadly, proud of himself for having used the word alibi.

"And we all know the nigger was hangin' around their house," Nap continued, "else he wouldn't even have been there in the first place."

Sheriff Turnbull shook his head and allowed a grin to cross his face.

"From what you're saying, Nap, I take it you think Jubal was stupid enough to run into a burning house to try and rape Jessica, yet smart enough to carry the kids out to make himself an alibi?"

"Sure," Nap said. "He's dumb, but he's connivin' too, like all niggers are. They try to make excuses about everything they do; it comes natural to them."

Nap was warming to the debate, feeling the respect of others at last. And though his logic seemed flawed, it didn't appear to matter to him or his admiring cronies.

"Of course he'd come up with an alibi," Nap said. "That don't mean he ain't stupid. Jubal is one dumb nigger, and everybody knows it. He don't talk much, you know, and when he was a kid he wouldn't talk at all. That's when everybody started callin' him Dummy, and lots of folks still call him that. They hung that name on him as a kid, and I still like it. Seems to me like it was true then and it still is."

Nap stood grinning at his cohorts for a moment, then scanned the crowd. He'd gotten too overwhelmed with himself to realize that Sheriff Turnbull was playing hardball.

In a jocular, good-natured tone, the sheriff addressed Nap.

"So you think that name Jubal got as a kid—Dummy— fit him just right, huh?"

Nap was still on his feet, basking in the limelight.

"Yeah," he said, jutting his chin out proudly. "I think the name Dummy suits him just fine."

Anson Turnbull grinned a sardonic grin, then fired the fatal shot.

"Then how about those names everybody used to call you and your buddy there—Pigpen Canfield and Slow Slocum. I guess they're still good too?"

It took a moment for it to sink in. Then Nap seemed to reel on his feet, his eyes registering the shock, and his face fell. For one shining moment he had been someone; then somehow, in an instant, his five minutes of fame had died. He sunk to his seat as the crowd tittered, chuckled, and grinned at his expense.

Sheriff Turnbull kept a straight face, and Burris Tolliver had had all he could stand. His face pulled taut in rage, Grandpa Tolliver hoisted himself to his feet, tottered unsteadily on his cane, and thrust a clenched fist at the sheriff.

"Dammit!" he roared, the curse reverberating throughout the auditorium. "You've forgot our basic values, Anson! You don't seem to care about protecting our womenfolk from them black devils anymore. I am ashamed to call you sheriff."

The sheriff looked him in the eye, but didn't react to the accusation.

"What's going on here, anyhow?" Grandpa Tolliver continued, his voice at high volume. "What's with you, Anson? My daughter was in that house that night, and her clothes was half tore off of her, and she died of a broken neck. To my way of thinking it's time something happened to another neck—a thick black neck, with burn scars all over it."

The sheriff addressed him calmly.

"There's not one scrap of evidence that says Jubal touched your daughter, Burris."

When Sheriff Turnbull made that statement, Chief Tull fixed him with a piercing stare. For a moment their eyes met, then the sheriff turned back to Grandpa Tolliver.

"The only evidence that exists—a hundred eyewitness accounts—shows that he ran into the house and, with no regard for his own life, saved the lives of your grandchildren."

With a loud "Humph!" Grandpa Tolliver reeled on his cane and half sat, half fell into his seat.

"Evidence! Evidence!" a voice in the back yelled. This time it was Herman. "We don't need no evidence. All we need is a good rope and a tall tree."

Surely someone else had thought up such a line and told Herman to use it, but that didn't prevent him grinning at his own eloquence. Nap Canfield remained quiet, but his redneck buddies chuckled and nodded their agreement. The rest of the crowd sat silent.

Now Anson Turnbull roared. "Is that so? All we need is a good rope to take care of this man, huh? This Negro man who ran into a burning house and saved two of our white children?"

Upon hearing the tone of the sheriff's voice, Herman promptly sat down.

Sheriff Turnbull stood with his hands on his hips, scanning the crowd with a ferocious stare. He knew the lowest class always did the lynching, but never without the tacit agreement of the upper and middle classes.

"Is that the way we want it folks?" the sheriff asked, practically shouting. "Is that going to be our answer to a man who risked his life saving our children? Just string him up and be done with it? And go on about our business as if he never existed?"

Sarah had sat with her eyes closed during most of the discussion, now she opened them and looked out on the crowd in a fixed stare. I had no idea that she was even aware of the subject of the heated debate. When she stood up and walked to the front of the stage, my heart nearly stopped. She stood facing the crowd, Mandy dangling from one hand, Sheriff Turnbull looking down at her in dismay. Then she screamed: "No! No! You can't kill Jubal! You can't kill him! He's my friend."

Sarah's face turned red. Tears filled her eyes and burst down her cheeks. Grandma Dunaway leaped from her chair and wrapped her in her arms. She whispered something in Sarah's ear, then took her by the hand and walked her down the stairs and off the stage. The auditorium fell quiet as death as Grandma escorted Sarah to the back; few heads even turned to watch them go. When the doors closed behind them, they all sat in shocked silence.

Then Doc Armstead rose to his feet, turned, and faced the stunned crowd.

"Well," Doc began, "I don't know about the rest of you, but that's enough for me." He paused, and shook his head. "I am sorry to have been a part of this. I am ashamed to think that the good people of Linville found it necessary to debate the life of a simple Negro whose only sin was saving the lives of two innocent children." He shook his head again and repeated, nearly to himself: "I am ashamed."

Doc cast a respectful glance up at Sheriff Turnbull, walked to the aisle, and left the building. Graydon Hardiman was next to leave; he walked out without a word, followed by his employees. Mayor Hastings exchanged a glance with Harlan Johnson, the newspaper editor, then the mayor got up and followed Graydon out.

Harlan Johnson was next to leave, a move that had far more gravity than appeared on the surface. Whenever a potential lynching was condoned by the upper and middle classes, his newspaper always made that fact plain. When he stood up to leave, everyone knew what it meant.

Others began making their exit: Miss Hawkins—stiff, erect, righteous; Mr. and Mrs. Dinkin—straight, serious, noncommittal. Chief Tull stood up and left without a glance at the sheriff. Grandpa Tolliver looked up at Sheriff Turnbull with pure hatred in his eyes, then pulled himself to his feet, tapped Grandma on the shoulder brusquely, turned, and walked down the aisle with all the defiant dignity his wounded frame could muster. Grandma looked at me sadly, then rose and followed him out.

Far in the back, Nap Canfield and his ragged bunch cast spiteful glances at the sheriff, then ducked their heads and slunk away. Then the entire auditorium was in motion— seats squeaking and people talking lowly among themselves as they filled the aisles and filed out the doors.

Sheriff Turnbull turned to Grandpa Dunaway and me, his face at once triumphant and humble, and very, very tired. He knew he had won, and that he had likely saved Jubal's life that night. He also knew he would never win another election.

Part IV
Chapter Fourteen

It seemed like spring came that year before I even noticed it. I had turned eleven, and Sarah was eight. Miss Amanda got most of her customers back—the ones who had deserted her when the talk about Jubal started—and Jubal could again be seen pulling his wagon around town.

We found out he had actually been missing for a while before the town meeting; not even Miss Amanda had known where he was. Now, more than a few people, both black and white, began speaking to him on the street.

Grandpa took Sarah and me to town one Saturday morning and dropped us off at the square. He handed us some money and said, "You two be careful, and head for home when the clock on the bank says four o'clock."

We told him we would, and waved goodbye as he turned the corner and drove out of sight.

Sarah stood up and waved when Jubal came into view, and he stopped and talked with us for several minutes. Although Sarah didn't say anything, she took his hand and leaned against him. I didn't even bother to look around to see if anyone cared. Just before he left he pointed at the blue sky with his good arm and said, "Sure is a pretty day, ain't it, Lucas?" I looked up and smiled. It was a pretty day.

The following weekend I asked Grandma and Grandpa if we could go visit Jubal and Miss Amanda. They said yes. The swimming hole was even closer now than when we had lived in town, so we walked to the creek and then followed the trail to their shack. Miss Amanda looked more rested than when she'd been making the deliveries herself, and Jubal was more than happy to see us.

The little shack still appeared out of kilter, and when we went inside it still felt like I was walking on a tilted surface. Miss Amanda looked at me and smiled, her eyes reading my mind.

"Still the same old crooked house, ain't it, Lucas?"

I just grinned. I don't think Miss Amanda ever realized how much she intimidated me in those days.

Something else puzzled me. The curtain that separated Jubal's bedroom from the rest of the shack was open, providing a view of the tree-jammed back door, Jubal's narrow bed, and the orange-crate bedside stand on which his father's books were stacked. I had seen his little bedroom before, but this time one of the books lay open, face down on the stand. When Jubal caught me looking at the book he reached over and closed it, muttering something about books having a habit of falling open that way.

Sarah didn't say anything when we arrived, but she sat down on the bed next to Jubal and took hold of his stiff arm with both hands. She leaned her head against his shoulder and stayed right there until we left.

When it came time to leave, Sarah surprised us all. She wrapped Jubal's ruined right hand in both of hers and kissed it. Then she looked up into his face and said, "Good-bye, Jubal."

A quizzical grin crossed his face. "Good-bye, Sarah," he said.

Later that evening, at supper, Sarah said, "Pass the potatoes."

Grandma looked over at Grandpa, then back at Sarah. "Can you say, please?" Grandma said.

"Please pass the potatoes," Sarah said, looking at Grandma with an impish grin. And that was the end of it. Sarah joined the world again. She had missed too much school to start that year, but she went back in the fall, reluctantly, and she finally stopped sleeping with Grandma and Grandpa.

I went on loving school, Sarah went on tolerating it, and Mandy got a well-earned rest. Although Sarah still hugged her close in her sleep, during the day when Sarah was at school Mandy sat leaning against her pillows, smiling and awaiting her return.

During the past year I had often found myself dreaming of the day when things got back to normal. They never did, of course; too much had changed for our world to ever be the same again. Our lives did settle down to a pleasant routine, however, and Grandma and Grandpa did more than most grandparents are ever asked to do. They fed us, clothed us, and loved us, and eventually we found a new normal.

The country entered World War II when I was a sophomore, and a few days after I graduated I joined the Army. It was 1943. I left Linville for basic training on one of those

gray mornings when a blanket of clouds covered the Delta—
a vast ceiling that stretched from horizon to horizon.

Grandma, Grandpa, Sarah, and Uncle Robert waited
with me at the train station. Strange how the mind works
at such times; for the first time, I noticed that Grandma
and Grandpa were getting old. And also for the first time,
I remember thinking what a handsome man Grandpa was.

Sarah was a sophomore in high school now, and to the
astonishment of everyone she was finally getting decent
grades. Her body had begun to blossom, and her long
blonde hair shimmered a different shade with every move
she made. People predicted she'd grow up to be at least as
beautiful a woman as Mama had been.

I had only one small bag to carry; the recruiting sergeant
had told me not to take more than one change of clothes
because Uncle Sam would be giving me all new ones. The
sergeant also told me I wouldn't be coming home after
basic; I would be shipped overseas immediately. I wasn't
overly excited about the new wardrobe or the prospect of
going to war, but most of the young men I knew had
already gone, and I felt it was my turn.

Grandma and Sarah were sniffling, and Grandpa's eyes
looked distant, pained. I knew he hated to see me go. But
although Grandpa could probably have gotten me a mili-
tary deferment to help him run the farm, he hadn't offered
to try. I'm not sure I'd have stayed anyway; I had a duty to
fulfill, and it seemed like something that Daddy would
have wanted me to do.

While we stood waiting for the train, trying to make

conversation and doing a poor job of it, I saw Jubal round the corner of the station with his wagon. "Jubal!" I said, "what are you doing here?"

"You only goes off to war once in your life, Lucas, and I wanted to see you and tell you goodbye."

I had told him I'd be leaving for the army, and now I felt guilty for having neglected to tell him when. I was happy he'd found out on his own.

"Oh, Jubal, I'm so glad you came," I said. "Please wait with us till my train comes."

Jubal looked at Grandma, Grandpa, Sarah, and Robert, and they all smiled and nodded.

"Okay," he said. "I'll help you wait for your train."

With that he parked his wagon against the side of the station, a distance twenty-five or thirty feet away, and leaned up against the wall beside it. He stood there, politely separate, until the train came.

As I was struggling to say my goodbyes to the family, Jubal walked over. He looked into my eyes, reached up with his good hand, and touched my shoulder.

"You be careful over there in that war, Lucas," he said. "I'll say a prayer for you every day, and I'll be waitin' right here to meet you when you comes back home."

Then he turned quickly and headed back toward his wagon. I stood and watched him go.

Before he reached his wagon, Jubal stopped and turned toward me again. Tears were running down his cheeks. His chin quivered as he raised his arm and stammered, "Lucas, I . . . ."

I ran to him, and hugged him as if he had been my own father. I wept on his big shoulder, and I didn't care if every cracker in Mississippi was watching.

Just as the recruiting sergeant had promised, as soon as I finished basic I boarded a troop ship and started across the Atlantic, bound for the European Theater of war. I found myself anxious to join the fray and get it over with—that is, if our convoy managed to dodge the U-boats that patrolled those waters day and night, seeking to put us on the bottom before we ever got the chance to fight.

Grandpa had taught me about guns during my teen years, and though I hadn't been as intensely interested in hunting and shooting as many of the boys I grew up with, I did become a good shot. I had never dreamed I might be going to war, but marksmanship turned out to be a valuable skill for an infantryman.

It's been said that war brings out the best and the worst in us. During the first firefight I ever experienced, I discovered something within myself that I hadn't known existed, something I would never have known if the war hadn't come along, and maybe something I'd just as soon not have known. When the guns started, when the rumble of battle filled the air and shells began exploding all around, a strange thing came over me. I preferred to think of it as a heightened awareness—a focused concentration that allowed me to rely totally on instinct and reflexes. The men in my company described it differently; they said I went crazy.

The other men often described my own actions better than I could, because when the battle was over I sometimes had difficulty recalling details. I made sergeant and was decorated for bravery three times, and though my memory of the battles may have been fuzzy, the number of enemy soldiers I took down attested to what I became during those sieges.

One memory—the final shot of my final battle—remains clear. Five German soldiers had my entire company pinned down. Manning a machinegun nest on the side of a hill, the enemy occupied a well-camouflaged foxhole from which the chattering barrel spewed death down upon us. We could neither advance nor retreat, and every time someone moved we lost another man. I have no idea what went through my head at the time, but the men closest to me said I screamed, then charged up the hill alone. I must have thought I was invincible, or maybe I was just in a hurry to end the war and get back to the Delta.

Evidently my unexpected move unnerved the machine-gun crew; they must have shot five hundred rounds at me on the way up that hill, and they missed me every time. My men provided all the cover they could, but because I kept bobbing and weaving back and forth in their line of fire, most of them were afraid to shoot for fear of hitting me.

Somehow I got close enough to drop to my knees and lob a hand grenade into the foxhole. I remember falling prone, and the ground shaking under me when the grenade exploded. The machinegun fell silent, and I did a dumb thing: I ran to the edge of the foxhole and looked down into it.

None of the enemy soldiers were moving; their bodies lay twisted and still. I released my breath, relieved that it was over; but it wasn't. When I turned my head to look back down at my men, one of the soldiers in the foxhole raised a pistol. Mustering the last strength in his dying body, he shot me through the chest.

The bullet missed my heart, but clipped the lower lobe of my left lung. I remember lying on my back and hearing somebody say the most ominous words a wounded soldier can hear: "sucking chest wound." I figured that was the end, and it was the last cogent thought I had for several days.

I spent those days back in the Delta. I swam in the old swimming hole with Daddy and Sarah; I held the little wagon that Jubal gave me and rolled its iron wheels with my fingers; I went to the square with Sarah and ate doughnuts from Mr. and Mrs. Dinkin's shop; I saw Mandy's smiling black face; and I watched Sheriff Turnbull thwart a lynch mob. The sheriff ran the hostile crowd off at gunpoint, walked under a big tree, and removed a noose from around Jubal's scarred neck. Jubal was crying and shaking, more terrified than any man I'd ever seen, even in battle.

I woke up in a makeshift hospital somewhere in France, and at first I thought the army nurse standing over me was Sarah. When I saw she wasn't Sarah, I thought she must be an angel. And, of course, she was.

While recuperating in the hospital, I received letters from Grandma Dunaway, Grandma Tolliver, Sarah, and even Grandpa Dunaway. To read his letters one would have thought the war was over. He seemed to believe I had wiped out Hitler's entire army before I went down.

One day after I'd gained enough strength to walk around the hospital a bit, I heard my name at mail call. I slowly made my way down to the far end of the ward, where a young soldier we called The Postman handed me an envelope.

"Glad to see you up and around, Sergeant Dunaway," he said with a grin. "You must have a new fan. I don't recognize the handwriting on this envelope."

I didn't recognize the handwriting either. It appeared juvenile, like it might have been written by a child. I puzzled over the letter as I shuffled back to my bed, and was glad I decided to walk back and sit down before I opened it. I think I'd have fallen off my feet if I'd tried reading it standing up.

Dear Lucas,

I heard you got shot, and I was worried to death over you. I walked out to your farm and asked your grandma. She told me you was still alive. She must have been embarrassed, because I set down on her step and cried when she told me you wasn't dead. She set down and cried with me.

You know my secret now, and your grandma does too, cause she mailed this letter for me. I know how to read and write. I have known how to for a long time, but I never let anybody know about it. I never told it before, but when I heard you was alive I had to write to you. It makes me feel like I'm talking to you. I'm so glad you are alive.

I still pull my wagon around town. Its getting old and I have to fix it sometimes. I know how to fix it though, so I'm doing good.

I'll see you at the train station when you come back Lucas. I love you.

Jubal

I leaned back against the head of my bed, stunned. I remembered those books on Jubal's bedside stand, and the one I found open when Sarah and I visited him and Miss Amanda after the fire. Jubal had been embarrassed when I discovered the book lying open, but I figured he'd just been looking at the pictures. I never dreamed he knew how to read. And now that I did know, I couldn't imagine why he had been so determined to keep it a secret.

The army gave me another medal, along with a Purple Heart, and sent me home. Grandma, Grandpa, and Sarah met me at the station, accompanied by a smiling crowd that appeared to comprise half the town. And back behind the crowd, in the very spot where I'd left him two and a half years before, stood Jubal.

After shaking a hundred hands and hugging every family member I'd ever known and some I didn't know, I made my way back to Jubal. He grinned, wrapped his good arm around my neck, and said, "Welcome back, Lucas. You's a sight for sore eyes."

"You are too, Jubal," I replied. Then without thinking I said, "What a surprise your letter was!"

His grin faded, and his eyes grew wary in an instant. He glanced at the people behind me to see if they had heard me mention the letter. I bit my lip and silently cursed myself.

Jubal picked up the tongue of his wagon, smiled wanly, and walked away. I prayed that no one had heard what I said. Fortunately, no one had.

I went to town the next afternoon and looked for him until I found him, walking down a side street delivering clothes. His face lit up when he saw me, and we sat down on a curb and had a long talk. I didn't mention the letter, and neither did he.

A few days later Sarah and I walked to the shack to visit Jubal and Miss Amanda. Miss Amanda opened the door as we were coming through the yard.

"What'd you stand in the way of that bullet for, Lucas?" she said with a fond grin. "You give us a terrible scare."

"I know, Miss Amanda," I said. "I gave myself one too."

Miss Amanda was still lean and wiry, but the years of hard work had begun to take their toll. Her thin face was more heavily lined and her hair was nearly white. She gave me a long hug, then looked at Sarah.

"My Lord, girl," she exclaimed. "It ought to be a sin to be as pretty as you are."

Sarah blushed. My sister was the same shy girl she'd always been.

We sat in the shack visiting much longer than we had planned. It was nearly dark when Sarah and I made our way back down the creek bed to the swimming hole and walked out the little road we had traveled so often as kids.

My curiosity about Jubal's ability to read and write wouldn't rest, and one day when I knew he was in town making deliveries I went to see Miss Amanda by myself.

"Lucas," she exclaimed as I walked into the yard. "What a surprise. But you missed Jubal. He's in town makin' deliveries for me."

"Why, I just came to see you, Miss Amanda," I said facetiously.

"Sure you did," she said, nodding her head with a wry

grin. "You walked clean out here to see a skinny ol' washer-woman like me. Go ahead, tell me another one, Lucas Dunaway."

Miss Amanda held the door open for me, then poured me a glass of water and sat down on the edge of her bed. I pulled one of the chairs over near the front window and sat facing her.

"All right, Mistuh Lucas," she said. "What you got on your mind?"

I had to smile. I'd been overseas, in a shooting war, and she could still intimidate me.

"What you grinnin' at, soldier boy?" she asked.

"Just you, Miss Amanda. Just you," I replied.

"I've been wanting to ask you something," I said. "It's about Jubal. It may sound like I'm prying into something that's none of my business, but my curiosity is killing me."

"I never knew you to be the pryin' sort, Lucas," Miss Amanda said. "You and Jubal goes back a long ways, so go on ahead and ask me."

"When I was overseas recovering from my wound in a hospital, Jubal wrote me a letter. Getting a letter from him was almost as big a shock as getting shot. I'd known him since I was a kid, and he even saved my life, yet I never had any idea that Jubal knew how to read and write."

For a while Miss Amanda sat silent, then she nodded her head.

"I didn't know about Jubal writin' you the letter," she said. "It's surprisin' he let you find that out. He never lets anybody know he can read and write. He don't even like to talk to me about it, even when he's layin' right there in his bed readin' a book."

"Why, Miss Amanda?" I asked. "Why would Jubal want to keep such a thing secret? I'd think he'd be proud of knowing how to read and write."

For a long, uncomfortable minute I felt as if she were looking through me.

"All right," she said. "Since Jubal chose to tell you about his readin' and writin', you already know more'n anybody else ever did. I'll tell you why he always kept it a secret.

"He kept it a secret 'cause he was afraid. He was afraid for people to know."

"Afraid?" I said.

"Yes, afraid—the same reason he acted simple around other folks, 'specially in town, ever since he was a little boy. He was afraid people would find out he wasn't dumb."

Miss Amanda paused, collecting her thoughts, then went on.

"His daddy, Rufus, knew how to read and write, and it all goes back to him. Rufus was a big man like Jubal, and oh, he was a corker. Rufus was always laughin' and jokin' and carryin' on with folks, and he was smart. He knew how to read and write, and he knew his arithmetic—even the multiplication tables. He was the first black man I ever knew that learned how to multiply. Most of them didn't know what the word meant; most of them still don't. Jubal does, though. He even knows how to do long division. He learned it by himself, out of his daddy's books.

"Rufus started teachin' Jubal how to read and write

when he was just four years old. I never thought it'd work with him bein' so young, but it did. He started showin' him to count and teachin' him about arithmetic too. Jubal was smart, like Rufus. The boy listened to everything his daddy told him, and he'd even sit and practice it on his own. He loved learnin', whether he got it from his daddy or out of a book."

It didn't seem possible. I had never known much about Jubal's childhood—only that he had been reluctant to talk and because of that he'd been called Dummy. Listening to Miss Amanda describe his early years, I felt like I was dreaming.

She stopped talking and sat staring past me, out the window, her eyes far away. I couldn't stand the suspense.

"What happened, Miss Amanda? What changed it all?"

Miss Amanda dropped her eyes to the floor and began kneading her forehead with the fingers of one hand. Then she looked up, cleared her throat, and continued.

"Rufus knew he was smart, and he was a hotshot— walked with a cocky swing, like he didn't have a care in the world, so sure of himself it hurt. He had a wonderful outlook on life; he was always sayin', 'Sure is a pretty day, ain't it?' I loved that about him, and so did Jubal.

"Rufus spent a lot of time with Jubal—playin' with him, teachin' him things—and Jubal worshipped the ground his daddy walked on. He loved everything about Rufus, and I did too. There wasn't nothin' not to love.

"Rufus couldn't never hold down a job very long, but that didn't seem to bother him. He made friends easy, and everybody liked him—everybody that lived across the tracks, that is. He had a problem with folks on the other side of the tracks, the white folks. They didn't think Rufus was quite as cute as he thought he was. And the worst part was that Rufus didn't care what they thought. At least he didn't care as much as he should of.

"The white people got to thinkin' of Rufus as an 'uppity nigger.' He wouldn't stay in his proper place—wouldn't quite act like a black man was supposed to act toward whites. He walked that cocky walk and bragged about bein' able to read and write. He made sure everybody knew that, 'specially white folks.

"My ol' daddy, Jubal's grandpa, used to say a cocky nigger would eventually get his comeuppance. He said it to Rufus too, but Rufus wouldn't listen to him any more'n he'd listen to anybody else. He just went on walkin' that walk and braggin' about readin' and writin'.

"Well, one day there come an accusin'; I suppose it was bound to happen. Somebody said Rufus had been pesterin' a white girl. They said the white girl accused him of makin' eyes at her, of flirtin' with her, tryin' to make a date with her."

"Who was the white girl?" I asked.

"I don't know who she was," Miss Amanda replied. "Nobody ever said. I don't know if she even existed. Rufus said she didn't."

She paused, drew a long breath, and went on. "It all happened so fast nobody had time to know anything for sure. I guess somebody had it in for him good.

"Rufus come runnin' in the house one evenin'; it was late, after dark, and he was in a sweat and out of breath. He looked more scared than I'd ever seen him. Jubal and me was sittin' here in the shack when he come runnin' in the front door. "'They's after me, Mandy!' Rufus said. 'They's after me!'

"'Who?' I asked. 'Who's after you, Rufus?'

"'White men—a bunch of them's after me,' he said.

"'What you done?' I asked.

"'I ain't done nothin', Mandy,' Rufus hollered. 'I ain't done nothin'. They sayin' I pestered a white girl, but I didn't. I swear I didn't.'

"Then Rufus hollered at Jubal. 'Gather up all the books, son, and hide them under the bed. Hurry now. Mandy, help me grab some clothes so I can get outta here before they catches up with me.'

"While I was rushin' to get Rufus some clothes to take with him, I heard the dogs howlin', and then it was too late. The men come up in the yard, lanterns burnin' and dogs barkin' right at our front door. They had a wagon with a team of horses hitched to it. Rufus blew the lamp out, grabbed Jubal and me, and pulled us down on the floor. Of course, that didn't do no good by then.

"One of the men hollered: 'Come out here, Rufus. We know you're in there, nigger.'

"Rufus whispered, 'Be quiet, and stay down,' and he held his arms tight around Jubal and me. I was shakin' and Jubal was cryin', kinda low like.

"The man in the yard hollered again. 'You better come out here, Rufus, and be quick about it. If we have to come in there after you, we'll get you all. We'll bring your woman and your boy out here with you, and we'll make you watch what we do to them.'

"Rufus started cryin'; I could feel his tears runnin' on my face. He pulled Jubal close and said, 'Son, you take care of your mama. You're gonna be the man of the house now.'

"Then Jubal started cryin' and carryin' on, loud. He was holdin' onto Rufus and screamin', 'No! No, Daddy. No!' It was the awfulest thing I ever heard."

She stopped and covered her eyes with her hand.

"You don't have to go on, Miss Amanda," I said. "You don't have to tell me the rest."

"No," she said, raising her head and wiping her eyes. "I want to tell you. I want you to know." And she went on.

"The men built a bonfire out in the yard, close to the big cottonwood. It lit up the whole place. The one doin' the talkin' said, 'This is the last time I'm sayin' it, Rufus. Come out or we're comin' in to get you, all of you.'

"Rufus kissed me and whispered in my ear, 'I didn't do nothin' to no white girl, Mandy. I loves you.' I held onto Jubal, and he got up and walked out into the light of that fire.

"I crawled up to the window on my hands and knees, that low one there behind you, and peeked up over the sill. Jubal was standin' beside me, lookin' out the same window. He wasn't cryin' no more; he wasn't makin' a sound, just lookin' out the window.

"The men grabbed Rufus, real rough like, and tied his hands behind his back. Most of them was grinnin' and laughin'. One of them got up in the wagon and drove the horses under that big limb on the right-hand side of the cottonwood, the one that's about ten feet high. He stopped the wagon right under that limb."

"Who were the men, Miss Amanda?" I asked. "Did you recognize any of them?"

"No," she said, her eyes darkening. "They didn't have faces; they didn't have names.

"After they tied Rufus's hands behind his back, they stood him out in the middle and circled around him. The one that had told him to come outside had a bullwhip in his hand, curlin' out on the ground behind him like a great long snake. That one started talkin' again, started chidin' Rufus.

"'Well, Rufus,' he said, 'Mister Uppity Nigger, Mister I Know How To Read and Write. How smart you feel now?' Rufus didn't say nothin'.

"'You know why we're doin' this, don't you, Rufus?' the man with the whip said.

"'No,' Rufus told him. 'No, suh, I don't know why you's doin' this to me.'

"'Aw, come on,' the man said, grinnin' like the devil himself. 'You know what you done to that white girl, don't you nigger?'

"'No,' Rufus told him again. 'I ain't done nothin'.' The man laughed at him, and snaked that long whip out through the air. It snapped across Rufus's back like a rifle shot, and tore his shirt half in two. Blood started runnin' down his back.

"'Give it to him again!' one of the others hollered, and the man did. The whip popped and cut Rufus's back from one side to the other, and near took his shirt clean off of him.

"'How's that feel, nigger?' the whip man hollered. 'How's that feel, Mister Book Learnin'?'

"Rufus didn't answer, and the man hit him again. 'Now you remember what you done to that white girl?'

"'No,' Rufus said, and he was cryin' when he said it. The man cut him with the whip again, and again, and again. Rufus was staggerin' around in the middle of them, and I could hear him cryin', but he kept on sayin', 'No, I ain't done it.'

"They laughed and cheered the whip man on, and he whipped Rufus till blood run all down him. He was cut all over—his back, his chest, his arms, his legs—everywhere. His shirt was gone, tore to pieces and layin' on the ground. The whip popped around his head several times, and when he turned toward us I saw that one of his eyes was out—a big streak of blood was runnin' down from it, runnin' down his face and drippin' on the ground.

"One of the men got up in the wagon and tied a noose around the big limb. Then they grabbed Rufus and tried to hoist him up into the wagon. He started fightin' them. He went crazy, and Rufus was a strong man. Even with his hands tied behind him he gave that bunch quite a battle. They got blood all over them just tryin' to get him up in the wagon.

"I was still down on my hands and knees. About that time I looked up and noticed Jubal. He was just standin' there beside me, lookin' out the window. God help me, I had got caught up in all that was goin' on and forgot the boy. I got up off my hands and knees and sat down on the floor beside him. That way I could still see out the window, and I reached over and took hold of his hand. His hand just laid limp in mine, like he didn't even know I was holdin' it.

"The men finally got Rufus hoisted up into the wagon,

and one of them put the noose around his neck. Several of them was a bloody mess by the time they got him up there, and they cussed him for messin' their clothes up. One of them got right up in his face and said, 'How uppity you feelin' now, Rufus? How much good's all that fancy readin' and writin' doin' you now, nigger?'

"Rufus spit in the man's face, and then he hollered at me, 'I ain't done it, Mandy. I ain't pestered no white girl—ever.' That's the last thing he said to me.

"Rufus begun threshin' around and cussin' the men, even though he was standin' there with his neck in the noose and his hands tied behind his back. One of them said, 'I know how to put a stop to this,' and pulled out a long gun, a rifle. 'Stand back, boys,' he said, and when they cleared out of the wagon he shot Rufus, twice, once in each leg.

"When his shot legs went out from under him, the rope started chokin' him, and Rufus tried to stand up again. His legs wouldn't hold him, though, and he was still chokin'. Finally one of the men took hold of the horses and led them away, pullin' the wagon out from under him. He kicked and shook on the end of the rope for a long time. The men just stood around and grinned, like they was watchin' some kind of show or something. When Rufus stopped shakin', they took the horses and wagon and left, and left him hangin' there in the tree. The bonfire was still burnin', lightin' up the yard.

"I started cryin' and screamin' like a crazy woman. I run out the door, out to Rufus. I took hold of his legs and tried to lift him up to take the pressure off his neck. He was too heavy for me to lift, and he was dead anyway, of course. I stood there and hung onto him, hung onto my man, and cried like I never cried before. I cried till I was so weak I barely could stand. I was wet all down the front of me, from my tears and Rufus's blood. I held onto his legs just to keep from fallin' down.

"And then, God help me again, I looked over by the edge of the light, nearly in the dark, and saw Jubal. The boy had watched it all, and now he was just standin' there.

"'Jubal, Honey,' I said. I let go of Rufus's legs and started to walk over to him, holdin' my arms out in front of me. Jubal stood there till I got almost to him, then he turned around and run off into the night.

"I stood at the edge of the light and called and called to him—till I was too hoarse to call anymore—but Jubal never come back. After a while I walked back over to where Rufus was hangin'. I stood there lookin' at him till the fire-light begun to die, then I sat down and leaned up against the trunk of the tree. I sat there all the rest of the night.

"The news of such things travels fast among black folks. The next mornin', a little while after the sun come up, some of Rufus's friends come over and cut him down out of the tree. They had a mule hitched to a wagon, and in the wagon they had a wooden box. I don't where they come up with such a big box in so short of a time, but it was big enough to hold Rufus.

"I was still sittin' under the tree when they got there, and I didn't even get up when they lowered Rufus down off the limb. After they got him in the box, one of the men, a kind ol' black gentleman I'd known forever, come over and told me they was takin' him to the graveyard behind Ebeneezer Holiness Church to bury him. He said he thought maybe I'd want to go with them. The old man held out his hand, and helped me up onto my feet.

"I was a mess, all dirty and bloody and everything, and I'd cried till my face was a sight, but I climbed up in the wagon and rode beside Rufus to the graveyard. "Some men there at the church had just finished diggin' the grave. They stood off a ways from it, sweat soakin' through their shirts, and leanin' on their shovels. They took their hats off when we drove up with Rufus in the wagon. I saw tears in some of their eyes, and they couldn't bear to look at me. The preacher was there too, holdin' a Bible in his hand. I don't recall what all he said over Rufus, but I remember it had to do with heaven, and his immortal soul. The preacher didn't say a word about how Rufus died. Instead, he talked about hope, salvation, and the perfect knowledge that we'd see him again one day in Paradise.

"I didn't cry when they buried him; I guess I didn't have no more tears in me."

Miss Amanda cleared her throat, then continued.

"The preacher and another man took me back home in the wagon after they buried Rufus. I looked all around the shack and down in the creek, but Jubal wasn't nowhere to be found. He didn't come back that night either. In fact, he didn't come back for three days.

"I was heartsick, and had about give him up, when I looked out one mornin' and seen him sittin' on the porch, leanin' against the front of the shack. I walked out and sat down on the step, afraid if I tried to touch him he might run off again. I just sat there awhile lookin' out in the yard, then I turned my head and looked over at him.

"The boy was a sight. He was filthy, all covered with dirt and dried mud, even in his hair, and when he looked up at me his eyes were all red and hollow-lookin'. I could've cried just lookin' at him, but I didn't. I took him by the hand and led him into the house.

"I didn't know where Jubal had spent those three days; I still don't. The boy was so thirsty I thought he'd make himself sick drinkin' water, and he was hungry too. I set him down and cooked him a big meal before I even cleaned him up. He just sat and waited for the food, and when I put it on the table he ate it without sayin' a word. In fact, he didn't say a word for more'n two weeks. He stayed right around close to me—wouldn't let me out of his sight—but he wouldn't talk at all.

"I didn't try to push him. I talked to him, not about anything in particular, and never about what happened to his daddy, but I talked to him every day, and I told him I loved him. He just stayed near me and didn't say a thing.

"One evenin' I went out and sat down on the edge of the porch, and Jubal come out and sat down beside me. He leaned over against my arm and stared at the ground awhile. Then he lifted up his eyes and looked at the big limb on the cottonwood, the one they hung Rufus from. He begun to cry. I put my arm around him and held him. He cried for the longest time, maybe an hour or two. When he finally stopped cryin' he fell asleep leanin' there against me. It was dark by then, and I carried him in and laid him in his bed.

"After that, he begun to talk a little, but just to me. He'd been a friendly boy before it happened—kinda like his daddy—but afterwards he didn't even want to see other folks, let alone talk to them.

"Jubal had put all the books under his bed when the men come that night, like his daddy told him to, and that's where they stayed for two or three months. Every now and then I'd mention the books, and suggest that maybe he'd want to get one out and look at it, but he wouldn't do it. Then one day I'd been outside choppin' wood, and when I come in he was sittin' on the bed with one of them open in his lap. After that, he went back to readin' and studyin' on his own.

"I got the notion that goin' to school might help him get more comfortable around people, so I put him in a Negro school in town. That ended up bein' a mistake. Jubal wouldn't say a word to nobody, not to the teacher nor any of the kids. And he never forgot those men chidin' Rufus about his readin' and writin' the night they hung him—he wouldn't look at a book nor make a mark on a paper.

"So, Jubal just sat at his desk, not sayin' a word, and that's when the other kids started callin' him Dummy. It didn't seem to matter to him, though; he didn't care what they called him. I guess if everybody thought he was a dummy it made him feel safe. I thought about takin' him out of the school sooner'n I did, but I kept hopin' he'd take an interest in learnin' there like he did at home. He never did, and finally I just quit takin' him.

"Jubal had been a loving, affectionate child before the lynchin'. Watchin' his daddy get killed the way he did changed him. It made him shy, and afraid folks would find out he was smart. I worried it might make him mean when he got older, which it could have, but it didn't. I thanked the Lord for that.

"Jubal was happy just stayin' home readin' and studyin' his daddy's books, and he didn't mind helpin' with chores like choppin' wood and bringin' in water, but I begun to need help with my deliveries. I used to pick up all the clothes and take them back myself after I washed and ironed them, but that took up a lot of my time. I needed time to take care of more customers or we was goin' to lose this old shack.

"After Jubal got big enough, I insisted he start goin' to town for me. He balked at it at first, and worried that he didn't know what to say to people. I made him go anyway, and he got to sayin' what a pretty day it was, just like his daddy used to."

Miss Amanda stopped talking, and for a moment I just stared at the floor, so mesmerized I'd forgotten where I was. Then I looked up and grinned at myself.

"Go on, Miss Amanda, tell me the rest."

"There's not much more to tell," she said. "Jubal got to noticin' you and Sarah when he was in town makin' deliveries for me, and he just fell in love with you."

"I'm glad he did," I said, "or we wouldn't be here today."

Chapter Fifteen

Grandpa Tolliver died in bed, swearing to the end that Jubal had killed Mama. But his bite had lost its venom, and he could never again muster enough support for his cause. His bitterness—fueled by physical weakness and his inability to do a day's work—remained intact. Neither Sarah nor I ever spoke with him again after the town meeting.

Grandma Tolliver outlived Grandpa by several years. Happily, we were able to reestablish ties with Grandma after he died.

A year or so after Grandpa Tolliver died, Grandma came face to face with Jubal on a downtown street. To his surprise and that of everyone in sight, she stopped and thanked him for saving our lives. Witnesses said she couldn't stop looking at his scarred neck, his shriveled ears, or his gnarled hand, and that she broke down while she was talking to him.

Jubal stood and listened quietly. When she finally finished thanking him and stammered to a stop, her face soaked with tears, he said, "You's welcome, Miz Tolliver. It was my pleasure."

Sarah stayed in Linville after she finished school, and she remained a beautiful person inside and out. She also remained shy, and fearful of emotional bonds. She didn't marry until she passed thirty, an age bordering on spinsterhood in those days, and although she loved children she never had any of her own.

Sarah's grades continued to improve through high school, and she even made the honor roll in her senior year. In a strange twist of fate for a girl who never liked school, she took a job as assistant to Miss Hawkins at the library. She took to the job readily; I think the rigor and the organization appealed to her. When Miss Hawkins retired, Sarah became head librarian.

Sarah continued to live with Grandma and Grandpa Dunaway until she married, and she watched over them until they passed on. It felt like losing our parents all over again when we lost them, but we thanked God that they had been there when we needed them the most.

With the help of the G.I. Bill, I enrolled at Ole Miss, majoring in English literature, of course, and loved it so much I didn't stop until I had earned a doctorate. I was then fortunate enough to be offered a professorship at a small university in Georgia, where I spent thirty-five years teaching and writing. Early in my teaching career I fell in love with a lady who loved words as much as I, and she agreed to share her life with me. We raised two sons and a daughter.

Emiline and Miss Amanda died in the same year, 1970, and I went home for both funerals. I never knew Emiline's exact age, but Miss Amanda made it to seventy-three, a long life considering the work she'd done. Each time I made the trip I brought Jubal a stack of books. By then, most everybody in Linville knew he could read, and he had finally grown comfortable with their knowing. He read constantly, and between Sarah and me we kept him supplied with books.

They laid Miss Amanda beside Rufus in the little country graveyard behind Ebeneezer Holiness Church. After the funeral I drove Jubal back to the shack. It was a bright, cloudless day, a warm breeze filtering through the trees as we sat down on the edge of the porch to talk. As soon as we got comfortable, an old cat started rubbing on Jubal's good arm. He picked the cat up and set it in his lap, where it immediately lay down and began to purr.

"I'm gonna miss Mama," he said. "Gonna miss that lady bad. But it sure is a pretty day, ain't it, Lucas?"

"Yes, it is, Jubal," I replied, then I brought up a question I'd been pondering for some time. "Have you ever thought about living anywhere else, Jubal? I mean, somewhere besides out here?"

The question caught him by surprise.

"Oh, I don't know," he said. "Never thought much about it."

"Besides my salary at the college, I've published a couple of books, you know. And Grandma and Grandpa Dunaway left me part of their savings when they died, plus an interest in the farm. You're beginning to get some years on you, Jubal; I'd be glad to help you get a house in town. It might be easier for you to live there when you get older."

He looked around the yard and beyond, out into the

field that butted up against the grove of trees the little shack was nestled in. He shook his head.

"No, I'm used to it out here, and I own this old shack now. I thank you, Lucas, but I wouldn't feel at home anywhere else. I only did two things in my life that I feel proud about. One was helpin' Mama pay off this shack and this little piece of land, and the other was savin' you and Sarah from that fire."

Then he looked up at the big limb on the cottonwood. In his entire life I had never once heard Jubal mention his father.

"They killed my daddy on that tree, you know, and when they did that it like to killed me too. I went away, in my mind, for a long time. You and Sarah saved me; you brung me back."

"I guess we all saved each other," I said.

So Jubal stayed on in the little shack on the bank of Sorghum Creek. He still walked to town to get his groceries, but instead of bringing them home in his wagon he carried them in a sack. The old wagon he'd pulled so many miles sat at the end of the porch, sprouting gardenias that Sarah had planted in it.

His hair grew snowy, and although he still chopped his own wood, swept out the shack, and cooked for himself, Jubal failed rapidly in his mid-seventies. Sarah started finding excuses to look in on him more often. At least every other day she'd drive out to the shack about nine o'clock in the morning, before she went to work at the library, and bring him breakfast and a cup of coffee. He'd be up and dressed by then. He always protested that she shouldn't have done all that, but she knew he loved it.

One morning Sarah tapped on his door and got no answer. She pushed the door open, and found him in bed. He was lying on his back, his stiff right arm resting across his middle, his old cat stretched out beside him. Sarah said he looked like he had gone in peace.

I was close to retirement by then. Returning to Linville to bury my old friend and savior was a journey back in time, and it turned out to be a revelation as well.

Sarah had worshipped Jubal all her life, and I expected her to have a difficult time with the funeral. She smiled when I picked her and her husband up at their house that morning, however, and she seemed in good spirits on the way to the church.

When she caught me looking at her with a question in my eyes, she said, "I've shed my tears, Lucas. The morning I found Jubal I sat down beside his bed and wept for two hours, and after that I held his hand for two more. The crying is done, and now we can bury the man who saved our lives."

A planter who lived in town now owned Grandpa's land, and cotton farming had become an automated operation. Human hands no longer chopped the cotton and picked it; huge machines lumbered across the fields on tires as tall as a man. Most of the sharecropper's shacks were either gone or abandoned. Some landmarks had not changed, however; Ebeneezer Holiness Church was one of them.

Ebeneezer Holiness stood a few miles beyond Grandpa's old farm, and cotton still grew right up to the churchyard and along both sides of the little dirt road leading to it. A pair of giant oaks framed the front of the building, and several more shaded the graves behind it. Although some of the graves had modern headstones, many were marked by crude wooden crosses, hand-carved angels, and rocks on which names had been scratched by hand.

The little church and graveyard together occupied less than half an acre of land—a spot that black congregations had considered holy ground since 1893, the year it was built. The faded white building reminded me of a country schoolhouse to which an undersized bell tower had been attached at the front of its steep-sided roof. An ancient iron cross, rusty and canted several degrees to one side, clung to the top of the little tower. Hand-painted pictures of Jesus adorned the windows. The swayed roofline looked like it might collapse at any time, but it had looked that way as long as I could remember.

Inside, the little church felt confining, its closely-spaced pews only adding to the feeling. The pulpit sat on a platform that rose a foot or so above the level of the pews. To the right of the pulpit stood an upright piano, its ivory keys chipped, its finish scarred and worn. At the piano sat an austere black woman dressed in white. The choir, also in white, stood on either side of the piano and behind it.

On a bench to the left of the pulpit lay a wooden casket, sprays of bright flowers surrounding it. In the casket lay Jubal.

The Reverend Franklin Reams, a small, intense man whose skin was nearly as black as his suit, met us at the back of the church. He welcomed us warmly and swept an arm toward the pews, inviting us to take a seat wherever we chose. Only a few white people were seated in the church, and I didn't recognize any of them at first. I had been gone from Linville for a long time, of course, and from where we stood I could see only the backs of their heads.

Then the broad shoulders of an elderly white man caught my attention. His full head of white hair was neatly combed, and he sat up as straight as the back of the pew. The man was seated halfway down on the left side of the church, and something about him stirred my memory.

Sarah saw me looking at the back of the old man's head. She leaned over and whispered, "That's Mister Turnbull."

"Turnbull?" I said, louder than I realized. "Sheriff Turnbull?"

"Yes," Sarah said, shaking my arm to shush me.

I hurried to the row where he sat, and stopped in the aisle beside him. He slowly turned his white head and looked up at me, assessing me instantly, a lifelong habit. I'd have known those eyes anywhere, and he knew me too. Sheriff Turnbull smiled, scooted over, and motioned us to sit down. I slid in beside him and shook his big hand; it was rough and work-worn, the skin loose with age, but the grip remained firm. He reached behind me to pat Sarah on the shoulder.

I hadn't seen Anson Turnbull in more years than I could remember, but Sarah had kept me apprised of his life. After the town meeting ended his career as sheriff, he followed in his father's footsteps. He went back to the cotton fields and worked among the blacks as a foreman until advancing age and the big machines shut him down. And though he still appeared vigorous, I knew he had to be at least eighty-five.

Black people know how to worship. I was caught up in the service from the moment it began. The lady at the piano, closing her eyes and swaying sublimely, played from her soul. The choir held hands and sang and rocked with the rhythm of the music they made. The little building vibrated with the power of their belief—a faith that had sustained them through a history that might have destroyed a lesser race.

Reverend Reams held the pulpit in a death grip as he spoke of Jubal's life—the lynching of his father, his fear that people might learn of his ability to read and write, the injustice of being called Dummy, his heroism in saving Sarah and me from the fire, the burns he suffered and the loss of the use of his arm. Sweat stood out on the preacher's face, and at every pause the congregation punctuated his speech with nods and amens—a tangible affirmation of his moving words.

The Civil Rights Movement had changed the social atmosphere considerably, and given blacks the courage to speak their minds more freely than they had ever dared before. Reverend Reams leaned over the pulpit and apologized to Sarah and me for bringing up a painful subject, then he went on to describe how Jubal had been wrongly accused of attacking our mother during the fire, and how Sheriff Turnbull had foiled Jubal's accusers by publicly humiliating them at a town meeting. When the minister finished, the congregation did something I never dreamed I would see at a funeral. They rose from their seats and applauded the sheriff.

The old man looked embarrassed, but I know it pleased him.

When the service ended we watched them lower Jubal into the soft Delta earth. He and Rufus and Miss Amanda were reunited at last. As we turned to leave, Sheriff Turnbull reached out and touched my arm.

"Lucas, would you have time to stop by my house for a while this afternoon?" he asked. "I've got something I'd like to show you."

"I'd love to, Sheriff," I said, both surprised and curious at the invitation.

"I still live in the same house on Ewell Street, the one I've lived in for about a hundred years," he said. "I'll see you in an hour or so."

Sheriff Turnbull's house reminded me of the one we had lived in as kids, the one that burned. His wife had died a few years before, but the black maid they had employed for most of her life remained with him. She'd always been a large woman; now she was immense, and bent with age.

When she answered the door I said, "Hello, Isabel. I'll bet you don't remember who I am."

Her old eyes lit up.

"Oh, go on with you, Lucas Dunaway—Mister College Professor," she said with a huge grin. "How could a body ever forget the likes of you? Go on back to the sittin' room; the sheriff's waitin' for you." Sarah had told me that some white people still referred to him as the sheriff, and all of the blacks did.

Sheriff Turnbull's sitting room was located in a back corner of the house, where tall windows let in light from two sides. A worn rolltop desk, standing open and stacked high with books and papers, dominated one end of the room, The old man sat at the other end, the afternoon sun pouring in behind him. His wingback chair looked like it had weathered nearly as many years as he, as did a small table that sat beside him. On the table lay a faded manila envelope that looked as old as anything in the room.

"Have a seat, Lucas," he said, pointing to a second over-stuffed chair that faced his. "Thanks for coming."

"My pleasure, Sheriff," I said. "I'm enjoying seeing you again."

Isabel brought us glasses of tea and disappeared as quickly as she had come.

"I'm glad to see you too, Lucas," the old sheriff said. Then he paused, picked up his glass, and took a long sip of tea. He seemed preoccupied, and took his time setting the glass back down on the table. I picked up mine and took a drink too, beginning to feel uncomfortable with the silence.

"Oh, hell," he said, "I've never been very good at small talk, nor at beating around the bush when I've got something on my mind."

With that he picked up the aged envelope and handed it to me. I could feel something soft inside it, and I saw that the top was sealed.

"Open it up, Lucas," he said. "I've been saving it for you, for a long time."

"For me?" I asked.

He nodded and handed me a letter opener. I couldn't imagine what it was, and I began to feel uneasy, afraid of what I might find. Maybe I didn't want to know what was in the envelope.

"Go ahead," he said. "It won't hurt you."

I carefully slit open the top of the envelope, then turned it up and poured the contents into my hand. A piece of red fabric fell out. It was satin, and it looked old. I picked it up between my thumb and forefinger and slowly turned it around, studying it from all sides. One end of the fabric was torn, as if it had been ripped from some sort of garment. Then it dawned on me what it was—the torn end of a sleeve. And attached to the sleeve was a white mother-of-pearl button. Suddenly I felt lightheaded, and thought I might faint.

Sheriff Turnbull watched me closely as I turned the sleeve over and over in my hands. My mind raced back in time—back to a night of terror in a burning house, shadowy figures moving in the smoke.

I began to smile, and the old man smiled too.

"I could never let anybody know until Jubal was gone," he said.

"How did you get this, Sheriff?" I asked. "Where did you get it?"

"That piece of sleeve was rolled up in the rug that night—the rug that Jubal carried you and Sarah out of the fire in. I spotted it when we unrolled you from the rug, and I grabbed it up and stuck it in my pocket. Chief Tull almost caught me in the act, but he didn't see what it was. He asked me about it that same night, but I passed it off. I was never sure he believed me, though. I think he stayed suspicious about it all his life, but he never asked me again.

"You told me you heard your mama holler, 'Out of my house, nigger.' Jubal and your mama clashed that night, Lucas. They probably came face to face about the time you heard her say that."

"How do you know that?" I asked.

"Jubal told me," he said. "I asked him about it after he got back from the hospital."

"But at the town meeting you told everyone that Jubal had denied seeing or hearing Mama in the house that night."

"I know," he said. "And I told them you didn't hear anything either. Remember?"

I nodded. I had always wondered why he told the entire town I hadn't heard anything.

"Evidently your mama came out of her bedroom while Jubal was throwing the furniture into the dining room, and she saw him through the smoke. She ran at him and hollered, 'Out of my house, nigger.' At the same time she raised her right arm and swung at him. Jubal reached up and caught her arm in his left hand and grabbed her around the body with his right.

"She fought him like a demon, and during the fight she whirled around to the left, trying to break loose from his grip, and Jubal's hand raked across the front of her blouse. That must have pulled all the buttons loose and opened up the blouse, but it didn't tear any of the buttons off. Jubal still had hold of her right arm with his left hand, so your mama started slugging him with her left.

"That's when Jubal pushed her away, into the dining room. He pushed her with his right hand, and that piece of sleeve must have ripped off in his left hand when he did it. The sleeve fell down on the rug. He didn't even know he had torn it off. He just rolled it up in the rug along with you and Sarah.

"She probably did break her neck when she hit the wall, but Jubal told me he never meant to harm your mama. She just wouldn't stop fighting him, and he only had a minute to save you and Sarah. He told me he'd have saved her too if he could have, and I believed him. Nobody else would have, though.

"Jubal was scared something awful when he told me that—shaking so bad he could hardly talk. He said, 'They's gonna kill me for touchin' that woman, Sheriff. They'll come and get me and hang me.' He was right too; they would have.

"I'm sure Jubal thought I wouldn't believe him either," Sheriff Turnbull said. "I tried to calm him down, and told him the same thing I told you—not to talk to anyone else about what happened that night. I told him never to mention it to a soul as long as he lived. And I guess he never did."

The sheriff was right; Jubal had never even told me. I sat and stared at him until finally I found my voice.

"If even one of those buttons on Mama's blouse had torn loose, or if the rest of this sleeve hadn't burned so that nobody could tell it had been ripped off, everybody would have known. And they'd have known anyway if you hadn't found it and put it in your pocket."

Sheriff Turnbull nodded. He alone had known it all. I thought back to the town meeting so long ago, the night he had given up his badge and relegated himself to the cotton fields for the rest of his life.

He looked out the window, smiled, and said, "Sure is a pretty day, ain't it, Lucas?"